The Whispers of Nemesis

Anne Zouroudi

BLOOMSBURY

LONDON · BERLIN · NEW YORK · SYDNEY

First published in Great Britain 2011
This paperback edition published 2012

Copyright © 2011 by Anne Zouroudi
Map on p.vi © John Gilkes 2011

The moral right of the author has been asserted

Bloomsbury Publishing, London, Berlin, New York and Sydney

50 Bedford Square, London WC1B 3DP

A CIP catalogue record for this book is available from the British Library

ISBN 978 1 4088 2191 6
10 9 8 7 6 5 4 3 2 1

Typeset by Hewer Text UK Ltd, Edinburgh

Printed in the UK by Clays Ltd, St Ives plc

www.bloomsbury.com/annezouroudi

DRAMATIS PERSONAE

Hermes Diaktoros – an investigator
Santos Volakis – a poet
Leda – the poet's daughter
Frona Kalaki – the poet's sister
Maria – the poet's housekeeper
Roula – Maria's mother
Attis Danas – the poet's literary agent
Yorgas Sarris – a publisher, owner of
Bellerophon Editions
Papa Tomas – a priest
Katerina – a widow
Myles Antonakos – an alcoholic
Eustis – a café proprietor
Hassan – a taxi driver
Nufris – a crewman on the ferry
Poseidon

GLOSSARY

Kali mera (sas)	Good morning, good day (*sas* – polite/plural form)
Kali spera (sas)	Good evening
Yassou (Yassas)	Hello or Goodbye (lit: 'Your health')
Chairo poli	Formal greeting
Kalos tou	Informal greeting
Kalo risiko	Congratulations offered on a new purchase or acquisition
Panayia mou	By the Virgin
Kamari mou	My son (lit: my pride)
Agori mou	My boy
Pedi mou	My child
Kori mou	My daughter
Agapi mou	My love
Glika mou	My sweet
Mori, kalé	Familiar terms of address
Oriste?	May I help you?
Embros?	Polite greeting when answering a telephone
Amessos	Right away, immediately
Kyrie	Sir, Mr

Kyria	Madam, Mrs
Despina	Miss
Pappou	Grandpa
Thea	Aunt
Poustis	Homosexual (slang)
Malaka	Term of abuse
Kafebriko	Small, long-handled pot for brewing coffee
Stifado	Meat stewed with onions
Mezedes	Appetisers, a variety of small dishes

His end was recorded somewhere and then lost;
Or perhaps History passed it by,
And with good reason, a thing as trivial
as that she didn't deign to record.

C. P. Cavafy, 'Orophernes'

Exhumation

The rite of exhumation . . . is the last important rite that must be performed individually for a particular dead person by his surviving kin. The relationship between the deceased and his relatives is for the most part ended at the exhumation. After this the obligations of the living to the deceased are carried out collectively on occasions that serve to honour all the dead.

Loring M. Danforth, *The Death Rituals of Rural Greece*

One

All uniformed in worn, black coats, all their lined and bitter faces bound in black headscarves, the old women gathered at the graveside. Under the broad-spreading branches of the oak which shaded the plot, the components of the grave's furniture had been dismantled. The headstone's front face leaned against the cemetery wall, hiding the inscription and the glassed-in photograph of the poet as a smiling young man; the candle-lamps (which had not often been lit) and the flower-vase (which had, in the main, held artificial flowers) lay discarded on a neighbouring tomb. In the years following the burial, the once-white marble kerbstones had rarely been scrubbed, and were discoloured with algae and yellow lichens. The old women took in the stone's neglected state, and cast their offended eyes up to the heavens.

The bell of Vrisi's village church began to toll. In these northerly mountains, there was no hope yet of spring, and the wind which flapped the men's trouser-legs and stirred the evergreen branches was raw; the sky was an ashen veil, cast over the day's end.

'There was a woman over in Loutro they buried too close to a tree,' muttered one crone into the cold-reddened ear of another, inclining her head towards the oak, and to the bare and stony ground where the coffin had been laid, four years before. On that occasion, the earth – freshly dug and mounded up for the interment – was the lively brown of spring sowing; now that same earth, settled and sunk, was cracked and pale. 'Its roots were poking through the poor soul's eyes! Bound by that tree, she was, until they cut her free. And this tree will have claimed him, just the same!'

The sexton leaned on his spade, impatient for his cue to break the ground, but the old women were still busy with their preparations, checking the necessities for the ritual: holy basil for blessing, and red wine to wash the bones; white kerchiefs to wrap them, and a metal box to hold them in their final place of rest.

A little apart, in fashionable black jackets and court shoes, two younger women stood, one of an age to be parent to the other. Ready to proceed at last, the old women hustled them closer to the graveside.

'Come forward, *kalé*, come forward,' they insisted. 'It's the faces of his close kin he'll want to see, as he comes back to us.'

The poet's sister and his daughter complied reluctantly, his sister encouraging her niece with an arm around her shoulder.

'Courage, *glika mou*,' said Frona. She hugged Leda close, and placed a kiss of comfort on her temple. 'Courage, and it'll soon be done.'

Leda wiped her nose on a cotton handkerchief, and turned her miserable face from her father's grave. Behind the eager old women, Attis Danas drew on a slender cigar, and tried in vain to catch Frona's eye. The widow Katerina – whose deceased husband had once been mayor and still bestowed on her some status, even years after his death – gave a signal to the sexton, who raised his spade, and brought down the blade

4

with all his strength to break the grave's hard earth. As he threw aside the first shovelful of stony soil, Katerina raised her voice in a lament, and the old women gathered around her began to wail. They moaned and shrieked to break all hearts, and the widow's tears ran freely as she sang: of their grief at the poet's final sight of daylight, and of their loss of him to the darkness once again; though the weight of the earth would be removed at last from his chest, his time with them was gone, and soon he would be lost to them for ever.

The sexton dug down deeper into the grave, where he was hindered, as anticipated, by roots of oak. The old women nudged each other, and made flamboyant crosses over their breasts. Frona put her hand up to her mouth, and bit a knuckle. Leda looked towards the cemetery gates. Attis wandered away along the paths between the tombs, struggling against the wind to relight the stub of his cigar.

'That woman in Loutro,' muttered the crone into the ear of the other. 'She was the widow of a jealous man, whose tormented spirit possessed the tree to keep her bones out of the ossuary. Her being in there, with everyone else, was more than he could bear.'

'Why did he object to that?' asked the other. 'If his own bones were in the ossuary, why didn't he want her in there, with him?'

Her companion tapped her nose, and glanced around as if it mattered who was listening.

'They said she'd had a lover, in her youth,' she confided. 'The spirit feared she might be put to rest near him, so it had the tree bind her bones, to keep them in the ground. *Mori!* It took an age to get her out. The roots were tough as rope, and woven all together, like a net. They had to fetch a hacksaw, and they cut for hours and hours. But the bones were white, I remember that. The bones were white, so she was blameless.'

'I doubt his bones'll be white,' replied the other, pointing at the hole where the sexton worked. 'We'll know for certain the man he was, when he comes back to the light.'

A gust of wind blew cold. Under Frona's arm, Leda shivered.

'She feels her father's spirit,' whispered the women. 'Her father knows we're here.'

The sexton dug down, and down; the work was heavy, and sweat beaded his face, until he pulled off his dirty jacket and threw it on to the dismantled kerbstones. Katerina's lamenting rose, fell and died away, rose, fell and died away; the women's tears dried, and flowed.

When Attis returned to the gathering, the earth the sexton was shovelling was showing changes of colour, a vein of black within the paler soil.

The sexton stabbed his spade into the ground, and wiped the last sweat from his face.

'Katerina!' he called out. 'Katerina, come down here, kalé! Come and take your turn!'

Katerina pulled on a pair of rubber gloves; the old women gave her a trowel, and handed her down into the hole as the sexton climbed out. They crowded round the grave, elbowing each other to get closer, their mourning role forgotten in their enthusiasm.

'Find the skull first, mori!' called one. 'Make sure you bring out the skull first!'

'Don't break it!' called another. 'Fetch it out in one piece if you can!'

Frona raised her face to the sky, and closed her eyes; Leda covered her mouth, as if she might be sick.

'I can't watch this,' she said, shaking her head. 'Please, aunt. Don't make me.'

'We must,' said Frona, though her own doubt was clear. 'A

few minutes of courage, and all will be done. Hold my hand, and be strong.'

The widow squatted in the dirt, and scraped at the loosened earth with the edge of her trowel until the soil gave way to the first fragments of rotting wood.

'I've got him,' she said quietly, and made a cross over her breast. 'Santos, *kamari mou*, come home!'

Under her hands, and with the leverage of the trowel, the softened remnants of the coffin lid were soon removed. Beneath, there was no hollow space, but the outline of the casket filled with dirt, which gave off an intense smell of organic matter, natural as the essence of earth distilled, without putridity, but heavy with fungal decay.

As the widow sifted through this darker, richer soil, the old women squabbled over where the head would be – *Higher up, kalé, away from you, up here towards the wall* – until the trowel rang out as it struck the first hard bone. Dropping the trowel, the widow covered her left hand with a white kerchief, and with her gloved right delved down into the pit.

'I've got it!' she said, at last.

'She's got it, she's got it!' they murmured.

'It's stuck,' she said, a moment later.

'The roots have him,' they muttered. 'The roots have him trapped!'

'Wait!'

Holding on his priest's hat against the wind, an anorak zipped over his robes, Papa Tomas hurried along the path towards the gathering, limping from his bad hip. As he pushed his way through, he greeted those he passed closest to by name, and marked those of whom he was especially fond with a touch, until – panting from his speedy walk up to the cemetery – he reached Frona and Leda.

'Forgive me, forgive me,' he said to Frona, pressing her free hand between his own. 'That old clock of mine has stopped again! It's unreliable, and I should throw it out, but we grow attached to things, don't we, we grow attached. Leda, *kori mou*, have courage. We shall honour your father, and carry his bones to their final rest. How are we getting on?' He released Frona's hand, and looking down on the widow, wished her *kali spera*.

'You're just in time, Papa,' said Katerina. 'He's here, beneath my fingers.'

A scrawny hand gripped Leda's shoulder.

'Don't you worry, *kalé*,' said an old woman, speaking low in Leda's ear. 'Your father was a good man, and his bones will be white, and clean.'

'I have him!' cried Katerina. 'I have the skull!'

She pulled from the earth an object black with soil, and held it before her.

'Pass it up,' called one of the gathering, impatiently. 'Pass it to his daughter, so she can wash him.'

But no one joined her in her demand. All were staring at the object in Katerina's hand.

Bewildered, Frona turned to Papa Tomas.

'*Panayia mou*,' said Papa Tomas, and made several urgent crosses in the air.

Leda ran, and no one moved to stop her; she ran the path between the tombs, as far as the cemetery gates, where she kicked off her shoes, picked them up and ran on faster, down the lane between the snow-banks which still lay at the verges. The cement was cold and hard, and sharp stones pricked her feet; but in the exhilaration of running barefoot, her stricken face relaxed, and as she slowed down to a walk, the redness of exertion brightened her pale cheeks.

The lane led her to Vrisi's village square. Breathless, she brushed the dirt from her feet; the small cuts on their soles were seeping blood, and the nylon of her stockings was in shreds. She slipped her shoes back on her feet, and glanced behind. No one, as yet, was following. Out of habit learned from her father, she looked up above the foothills, searching for airborne eagles, but the skies were empty; on the road which wound in hairpins through the pine-forests, nothing moved.

She walked slowly towards the heart of the square, where a statue stood on a plinth engraved with her father's name – *Santos Volakis, Poet* – and the dates of his birth and death. The granite figure was a bland-faced man, undistinguished, and dressed in a style of suit her father had worn only at his own wedding; it held one finger to its cheek, in an effeminate gesture her father had never made, mocking in its vacuous contemplation of a wordless book the incisiveness she had so admired in him. Bright scraps of litter lay in the hardy weeds around the statue's base; pigeon-droppings fouled her father's shoulders and the toe-caps of his shoes.

Along the cemetery lane, voices high with the excitement of a drama were growing close. Leda drew her coat tight round her, and lowered her head; and, trusting in this attitude to defend her against unwanted enquiry into her welfare, she set off uphill on the familiar road, in the direction of the house she had once called home.

Four Years Previously

Fence your own vineyards, and covet not those of others.
Greek proverb

Two

The audience was alive with anticipation. Most of its members had arrived early, and checked the slowly passing minutes on their watches, flicking through well-read volumes brought for signing as they exchanged pleasantries with strangers. As the hands of the wall-clock moved close to the hour, a man – somewhat overweight, and rather taller than most – took a seat amongst them, tucking a leather holdall between his feet and unbuttoning his raincoat before settling into his chair.

On the platform of the draughty hall, the Dean in all his pomposity at last rose from his seat, and spreading his arms wide as a circus ringmaster, exhorted the warmest of welcomes for the visiting speaker.

'It is an unsurpassed honour for the university, and for the Department of Hellenic Studies in particular, to present to you our most distinguished guest. Santos Volakis has been called the finest poet of his generation, but I suggest that the innovative nature of his work, his mastery of contemporary poetic form and the beauty that he weaves from the words of our noble language might easily earn him a place amongst the greatest of *all* generations. Ladies and gentlemen, it is my absolute pleasure to introduce him to you now – Santos Volakis!'

Clapping his fleshy hands together, red-faced and beaming, the Dean led the light (though enthusiastic) applause from the forty-two people before him, and sat down on his carved-backed chair before a bust of an ageing Homer.

Through the hall's high windows, rain dribbled from broken guttering to the lintels, and splashed into pools spreading across the car park. Behind the platform's long, oak table, Santos Volakis stood, opened up a slim volume at a page marked with a strip of yellow paper, and slipped his hands in the pockets of his gabardine trousers, stooping as though his back carried some burden, his head low, as if he bore some grief. Too young by at least a decade for grey-haired gravitas, he cultivated that quality through an older man's style of dress – a brushed-cotton shirt, a waistcoat lined with silk, a jacket with the elbows patched in ovals of green leather – and as a mark of his creativity, wore his hair down to his shoulders. With languorous abstraction, he brushed stray strands from his eyes.

'Thank you,' he said. 'I shall read, if I may, from *Songs from Silence*, my latest collection. And aiding me with a dramatic interpretation of my work, my lovely daughter, Leda.'

Leda stepped from behind a stage curtain of faded velvet, slender in a gown of powder-blue chiffon, satin ballet shoes tied with ribbons on her feet, her hair pinned up in an elaborate arrangement of ringlets. She brought with her to the stage two masks, mounted on silver rods: sinister, porcelain faces drawn from the dramas of ancient Greece, one showing the despair of Tragedy, the other – which she held up to conceal her own face – Comedy's ridiculing grin.

The clock on the wall ticked away the expectant seconds. At first, the poet seemed to have no intention of beginning. He looked down at his audience, regarding them as if they were curios on display, until his eyes fell on a young girl in the front row, at whom he smiled. Then, with only a glance at the pages of the open book, he began his recitation. In unhurried, seductive tones as dark as chocolate, his mesmerising verses span webs of erotic craving and love, of loss, grief and regret, of fierce patriotism and stirring longings to be carried home. And as he spoke, Leda gracefully mimed the poem's sentiments, illustrating through artful movements the subtle nuances of her father's words, from time to time switching masks, always whilst her back was to the audience, so her own face was always hidden by a false smile, or a bogus frown.

At the end of each poem, there was a pause, which seemed to wake the poet's listeners from the dreams he had inspired and prompt them to eager applause. As he turned the page to each fresh poem, he surveyed his audience with arrogance, assessing their ability to grasp the finer shades of meaning in his verses; and wherever he had doubts, he turned the page again.

For forty minutes, he went on in this way – reciting, captivating, judging, moving on – until he finished the last poem in the volume. Sighing, he closed the book, said 'Thank you,' and sat down, as Leda slipped away behind the curtain.

In a light sweat of excitement, the Dean tugged at his bow-tie to loosen it, and rose once more from his seat.

'Marvellous!' he said. 'Breathtaking, absolutely! Such a privilege for all of us to hear that *astonishing* work read by the man who created it. And *Kyrie* Volakis has very kindly agreed to stay with us a while, to answer your questions and sign copies of his books, which are on sale at the back of the hall. Now, will you please join me in thanking him once again in the accustomed manner? Ladies and gentlemen, Mr Santos Volakis!'

The Dean ushered the poet off the platform and through the hall. The people who had been his audience stood back, and watched the poet curiously as he passed, as if surprised to find him merely human.

A short queue had already formed before the desk where the poet was to sign copies of his books; behind a table stacked with Santos's three published anthologies, a young man waited with an open cash-box.

The man with the leather holdall rose from his seat. Beneath his raincoat, he wore a charcoal-grey suit, whose excellent cut disguised his corpulence, to a degree, though the quality of his tailoring was blighted by the old-fashioned, white canvas tennis shoes on his feet. He made his way to the bookseller's table, where he picked up a copy of *Songs from Silence*, and read a few lines before turning it over to examine the stiffly posed black-and-white photograph of the poet on the back cover.

The fat man smiled at the bookseller.

'The photograph does him no justice,' he said, in the clear, accentless Greek of TV newscasters. 'The man, in life, has the charisma of an artist, which the camera cannot capture. I'll take the book.'

As the bookseller counted out change, the fat man glanced across at the signing-desk, where the short queue had grown longer.

'A pity I don't have time to wait to have my copy signed,' he said, pocketing coins. 'I am a great admirer of *Kyrie* Volakis's talent. Still, life's twists and turns are unpredictable. Perhaps he and I shall meet some other time. Thank you.'

As the fat man left the hall, the Dean saw that the poet was comfortably seated, and snapped his fingers at a faculty secretary, who rushed up with a carafe of water and a glass of acidic wine. The poet held her eyes as he thanked her, and the secretary – a woman close to forty, and no longer used to flirtation – dipped her head to hide the blush spreading up her neck, and hurried away.

Santos removed the cap from a black fountain pen, brushed his long hair abstractedly from his eyes and looked up at a girl whose own tight-plaited hair reached down to the small of her back.

Nervously, she smiled at him, and handed him a copy of the slender, hard-backed book from which he'd read – a handsome edition whose pale-blue jacket carried the poet's name and the title, *Songs from Silence*, in graceful, white script, and on whose spine, below the publisher's name – Bellerophon Editions – a spread-winged Pegasus carried a sword-wielding warrior.

'I'm such a fan of yours,' she said.

'Who is it for?' asked the poet, his pen ready over the title page.

'Marianna,' she said. 'And could you please write a line from the *Songs*, too?'

As the queue dwindled, the Dean came to Santos's side.

'Is your daughter not with us?' asked the Dean.

'Leda had a train to catch,' said the poet. 'She wanted to be home by this evening. She has an examination tomorrow, and she's conscientious in her studies. She hopes to go into higher education, later this year.' The poet's speech was pedantic, and not like other people's; he chose his words like a poor man at a market, as if they must offer best value, and once the words were chosen, they were carefully fitted together, so his sentences emerged perfect both in structure and in meaning, each one a puzzle already completed. There were no corrections, no hesitations or reversals, none of the verbal tics of common conversation. The poet was a master of his language: his most casual communication declared it.

'How admirable, then, that she took the trouble to be here,' remarked the Dean.

The poet took a volume from the man before him, and having asked his name, began to write.

17

'She's a devoted daughter, and I, for my part, appreciate that devotion,' he said. 'She has, in the past, covered hundreds of miles to be with me at my readings. Happily, the journey today was not such a long one.'

'Speaking of journeys, what time will your driver be here?' asked the Dean.

The poet finished an elaborate signature, and handed the autographed book back to its purchaser. He looked up at the Dean.

'My driver?' he asked. 'They don't supply me with a driver. I shall no doubt find a taxi, when I'm done. Please.' He beckoned to the last customer in his queue.

'No driver?' asked the Dean. 'But surely . . .'

Again, the poet looked up.

'There was a time,' he said, 'when poets were venerated, when the rewards for the work were just.' He pointed with the end of his pen towards the bust of Homer on the platform. 'Those days, sadly, are gone, and I shall end my days, like some Van Gogh, in penury, yet with the small hope that my work will live on, when I am gone.'

The candour of his statement drew sympathy, whilst the pathos of his stated situation shocked his listeners – the customer waiting for his signed book, the Dean, the faculty secretary counting the proceeds from the book sales.

'But there must be no question of public transport!' said the flustered Dean. 'We shall arrange something for you, of course! If you will give me a few minutes . . .'

'Might I offer?' asked the secretary, looking up shyly from the coins she was stacking in careful piles. 'Wherever you're going, it would be an honour for me to drive you.'

Three

Responding to discomfort – the rhythmic and persistent stabbing of an object in his lower back – the man unwillingly came to, and waved his hand weakly towards the prodding, which stopped, but too late to avoid the return of consciousness; and consciousness brought awareness of urgent nausea (which he swallowed down as best he might), of severe headache and of a mouth so dry, his tongue stuck to his mouth-roof, and produced a strange, crackling sensation as he peeled it free. There was a bad smell around him, a reminder of his grandfather in his incontinent dotage.

Nausea, and headache: he closed his eyes against them, but as soon as he did so, the stabbing came again.

He opened one eye on a familiar vista – the rose-patterned fabric of his daughter's sofa. He could make out the roses clearly, and so concluded it must be day. Blinking both eyes open, he winced at the mid-morning light that filled the room, and turned his head from the sofa-back to find the source of his tormenting.

His young grandson stood beside him, earnest in his concern. '*Pappou.*'

The man's nausea threatened eruption. The only cure was sleep.

'Go away, God damn it!' he shouted at the boy. 'Leave a man to sleep, why can't you?'

Through the pounding of his head, the man heard small feet pad across the room, as far as the doorway. From there, the boy called out, *Mama, Mama*, and from the yard outside, his mother responded.

'What is it, Myles? I'm busy.'

'Mama, *Pappou*'s wet his trousers!'

The man opened his eyes, and sniffed. The bad smell, the old people's smell – was that him? In consternation, he put his hand under the blanket and touched his groin. The cloth of his trousers was damp.

He heard his daughter hurrying through the kitchen, and her instructions to the boy to go outside. The man pressed his face to the sofa-back. There were quick footsteps, and the blanket was ripped away.

'Papa! Papa! Get up!' She shook his shoulder. 'For God's sake, look at the state of you! Get up, get up now, and get out!'

Even through the haze of his hangover, the heat of her anger was disturbing. His headache was immediately worse.

'Hush your noise, woman, and leave me be!' he demanded. 'Let a man sleep!'

'Leave you be! To stink up my house, lying there in your own *piss*, like an animal! Get up, and get yourself cleaned up, whilst I see what I can do with this mess! And when you've cleaned yourself up, pack a bag. Enough, now! You can't stay here any more.'

He opened his eyes, and saw the roses on the sofa-back with fresh clarity.

'What do you mean?' He turned his head to look at her. She stood over him, hands on hips just like her mother, a tired, run-down woman, getting old before her time.

'You have to go,' she said. 'I can't cope with you any more. And Yiorgos won't allow you in the house, not after last night. You can't blame him, Papa. Not after what you did. And this . . .' She wafted a hand over the sofa, over him. 'You have to stop the drinking, Papa. Take yourself to a doctor, please! You're killing yourself! You must see that, surely?'

He pulled himself up to a sit and put his head in his hands, pitying himself his misery.

'What do you care?' he said. 'A daughter who puts her own father on the street!'

'What can I do?' In exasperation, she spread her hands. 'How many chances have I given you? I love you, Papa, but you have to leave here, for a while. For everyone's sake – for Myles's sake. You frighten him when you get like that.'

'Like what?'

He looked up at her, blinking.

'Like last night. When you get violent.'

'Violent! I'm never violent!'

Tears grew in her eyes.

'How can you *say* that, Papa? You hit Yiorgos! He's gone to work with a black eye!'

'That faggot you married? He should stand up for himself! He's not much of a man to let an old man like me land one on him!'

'Papa, you woke the neighbours again, you woke Myles. You terrified him so badly, he was screaming! And when Yiorgos asked you to stop singing, you hit him in the face!'

The man laughed.

'Did I, by God?' He examined his knuckles, where there were grazes and the blue of bruises. 'Looks like I got him good!'

'It isn't funny, Papa. I'm sorry, but you have to go.'

The man shook his head.

'My own daughter,' he said. 'It's a dark day, when it comes to this.'

He put only necessities in his bag: clean underwear and socks, a change of shirts, what money was left under the mattress, a half-bottle of ouzo she hadn't managed to find. As he left the house, she cried, and tried to hug him.

He pushed her away.

'You take care of yourself,' she said. 'Please, get some help. There are places where . . .'

'Where what?'

She didn't go on, but pressed something into his hand: a piece of paper, folded over coins.

'Take this, and look after it. It's our phone number. I wrote it down. I know what your memory's like, these days. Call me when you get settled. And keep that money by; don't spend it. It's for the phone, for emergencies. And you'll let me know where you are, won't you? Papa?'

'As if you cared,' he said, slamming the door.

The boy banged on the window, and waved goodbye.

His grandfather blew him a kiss, and walked away.

He caught a bus as far as the port town, and found himself a bar where they bought him drinks, as long as he amused them with his ramblings. But when his ramblings turned to ranting, they threw him out; so he staggered along the waterfront, singing for his own amusement, and shouting to anyone who passed to come and drink with him.

At the last berth on the quay, a ferry was preparing to sail, the crewmen ready to cast off the heavy ropes which bound the vessel to the shore; and struck by a fancy to journey who-knew-where, alive with the thrill of adventure, he called out.

'Wait for me!' he said, 'I'm coming with you!'

'Come on, then, friend!' The crewmen laughed behind their hands, winking at each other. '*To malaka!* Come on, you'll make us late!'

He staggered up the ramp, and fell down amongst the cargo. The crew left him alone, and at the ports they called at through the night, still didn't wake him, but let him sleep, unconscious, until the first rays of a red sun lit the sky.

As the same dawn broke over the university, the faculty secretary left the poet's hotel room. Hair dishevelled, her make-up left behind on the pillowcases, she made her way downstairs to the lobby with a new lilt to her hips, which the yawning night-porter appreciated, as he unlocked the front door to let her go.

By the time Hassan reached home, that first light had touched the chicken coops and set the backyard roosters crowing.

He slipped off his down jacket, and laid his car keys on the table alongside the night's takings. In the children's room, the baby and his young son were both sleeping. Hassan stood a few moments over the cot, and leaned down to touch the soft, black curls on the baby's head.

But in the neighbouring bedroom, his wife was wide awake. Fully clothed, she lay rigid on the bed, her arms wrapped round herself against the chill.

'What's wrong?' he asked. 'Are you all right?'

She turned to face him. Her usual smile of welcome wasn't there.

'Hassan,' she said. 'You and I need to talk.'

Another night, and far from the city and the university, cold rain was falling on the village of Vrisi. In the study of the old house, Santos Volakis sat alone in the candlelight, his chair drawn up close to the dying fire. The last glass from a bottle of indifferent wine stood beside him on the hearth; on his lap was a typewritten letter, signed in blue ink. He laid back his head and stared up at the lime-washed ceiling, where the oak beams were solid and straight, but the plaster was swollen with water damage and yellowed by smoke, and strands of broken cobwebs wafted in the draught from the hallway. The rugs on the stone-flagged floor were worn and faded; the shelves Santos's grandfather had made – where old calfskin-bound volumes of mythology, philosophy and biography stood beside modern works of poetry and fiction – were riddled with woodworm.

The poet's eyes stang with weariness and wine, and he rubbed at their lids as if his knuckles might soothe their redness. The candles had burned low, and he switched on a lamp to brighten the room. Taking up a ram's-head poker, he knocked a shroud of ash from the hot embers, and placed several small pine logs on the fire. New flames grew from the fresh fuel; when the blaze was at its height, he dropped the letter on to the fire, and watched the paper's centre char in a round of black, before flames caught its edges and consumed it.

He stood, and crossed to the window. Hands in pockets, for some minutes he looked out; but the lamplight and candle-light together showed him nothing but the sheen of wetness on the yard, and rain falling in silver needles from a sky where the stars were hidden by clouds.

The phone rang. The caller was persistent, but the poet seemed indifferent as the phone rang on, and on. When it at last fell silent, he returned to his chair, and drank down in two swallows the wine left in his glass. He held up the empty glass, twisting it to catch the firelight in the crystal's facets, until he held out his open hand and let the glass fall to the rug, where, dribbling its dregs, it rolled beneath his chair.

The phone rang again. From his chair, the poet watched it, until seeming to find resolve, he stood, and picked up the receiver; but before the caller could speak, the poet depressed the cradle and broke the connection. He lifted his fingers, and the dial tone buzzed in the earpiece.

He laid the receiver alongside the telephone.

As the small hours approached, the wind's force increased; sharp squalls bent the pine trees and smattered dead needles on the window, where rainwater held them fast. Troubled by his dreams, the poet drowsed uneasily in his chair, called back to wakefulness by the wraith's touch of a draught on his neck, or the rattle of a loose latch somewhere in the closed and sleeping house. One by one, the candles all went out.

In the hour before dawn, the headlamps of a car shone through the window. Outside, the driver cut his engine.

The poet blinked away sleep, and rose from his chair. In the chill of the hallway, he switched on no lights.

His suitcase was ready at the stair-foot. When he left, he closed the door behind him with no noise.

Four

Sirens were wailing across the city; the cold wind carried smoke and fragile fragments of charred ash. On the roof terrace, summer's chairs were piled up and bound together with rope; all but one of the folded tables were stacked and secured in chains. As Attis Danas climbed the stone steps to the terrace, his view was of the city's geography painted in lights: an arc of streetlamps marking the curving shoreline, with the sea black behind; drifts of house-lights making bright the eastern and western suburbs; and to the north, amongst the foothills, scattered lights reaching up to the famed church of Ayia Triander, high on its floodlit rock. At the head of the stairs, the savour of seared meat from the taverna's charcoal grill was displaced by the smell of burning, and the diners' chatter below gave way to tourist music, piped through speakers strung from the spindly cordons of a winter-naked vine.

At the terrace corner, overlooking the intersection, a single table held a wine bottle and a flickering candle burning in an amber tumbler. Leaning on the terrace wall, looking down on to the street below, a man swilled burgundy wine in his glass and sniffed at its bouquet.

'*Kyrie* Yorgas Sarris, if I'm not mistaken,' said Attis, with mock formality.

The man turned, and gave him the warmest of smiles.

'Attis! How are you, *pedi mou*, how are you?'

With clasped hands and back-slapping, the men embraced; as they broke away from each other, Yorgas ran his amused eyes over Attis, and raised his eyebrows in exaggerated admiration of Attis's clothes.

'Look at you,' he said, 'the man-about-town. And what have you done to your hair? You dog! Have you been dyeing it?'

'Don't be ridiculous,' said Attis. 'I make an effort, at least.'

Yorgas laughed, and looked down at himself: at the overcoat he'd had for years that no longer fitted him, at the suit in need of pressing, at the white shirt missing a button at the chest. More than a day had passed since he'd shaved, and several weeks at least since he'd seen a barber.

'Well, I'm an old dog, so expect no new tricks from me,' he said. 'As my good wife says, I'm beyond help.'

On the streets below, tail lights flared as traffic slowed for a red signal.

'What are you doing up here, out in the cold?' asked Attis. 'They're holding our table downstairs. I'm sorry I'm so late. The taxi driver took a short cut, and cost us twenty minutes. Half the roads across town are closed.'

'Have an aperitif, first.' Yorgas picked up an empty glass from the terrace wall and filled it from the bottle on the table. He gave the glass to Attis, and raised his own in a toast – *Yammas* – before he drank. 'They say all access to the campus area is closed. I've come up here to watch the sorry sight.' He looked out to the horizon, where the glow of fire was orange against the sky. 'Our students are burning their books. That's enough to make a publisher's blood run cold, and a literary agent's too, wouldn't you say? No doubt they're infiltrated by anarchists. They should round the bastards up and hose them down with water one degree above freezing.'

27

'Your publisher's soul overrides your nose for business, Yorgas,' said Attis. 'Forget the offence in your handiwork being burned. The books they're burning tonight will have to be replaced, come the morning. No books, no studying; no studying, no degree and no fat doctor's pay cheques. Why not just look forward to an increase in sales?'

'That's what I admire about you, Attis. You always see the opportunity.'

'In my experience, most problems have a solution that'll take you forward.' Attis drank more of his wine. 'This is very palatable. Is it French?'

'Pah!' A flake of ash settled on Yorgas's hair. 'The French are amateurs at the wine-making game, compared to us Greeks! This nectar comes from Kefalonia. You know, I wish I had more of your positive view of the world. Sometimes, I feel disaster waits to ambush me round every corner.'

A look of wariness crossed Attis's face. Down on the street, a nightclub's gaudy sign flashed across the windscreen of a waiting taxi.

'When you say disaster, do you mean disaster in business?' asked Attis.

'Where else? I inherited a noble publishing house and a raft of liabilities.'

From the speakers, the over-familiar melody of 'Zorba's Dance' began. In the taverna below, a plate smashed on the floor tiles, to cheers and applause.

'You're not thinking of Santos as a liability?' asked Attis, uncertainly. 'I know sales could be better, but he brings you a certain cachet, surely?'

Yorgas shook his head.

'Not Santos. He's a jewel in both our crowns. My problem is, Bellerophon has several such jewels, all breaking even or making losses. The market's skewed, and it's never talent that makes money. Sales come from popular appeal, and popular appeal is not Bellerophon's long suit. It's the same for you, of course. Let me ask you: who is it who makes you your money?'

'Such money as it is, those you'd expect. A couple of my novelists do well – romance, if there's sex in it, thrillers, if there's violence. And the cookery writers. I secured a TV deal for one girl, and now she's selling in the thousands. Santos is disgusted. He doesn't understand why a woman who shows the nation how to make soup should be better rewarded than a man who holds up a mirror to the nation's soul. He says he's under-appreciated, and he's right. I feel sorry for him, but what can I do? I've tried to tell him there's no money in poetry, but he thinks he can change the world with his words. I'm afraid he's destined to go through life disappointed; but he would be very grieved indeed to think he had disappointed you.'

The glow at the horizon was growing brighter, lighting ever more of the sky.

'Looks to me as if they've set the buildings on fire,' said Yorgas. 'And speaking of fire – how's it going with Santos's sister? What's her name?'

'Frona.'

'So, have you asked her for a date yet? No? So ask her. Pick up the phone. She won't bite.'

'Don't be ridiculous. I'm an old man, in her eyes.'

'You're too hard on yourself. Look at you. Hardly a grey hair in sight.'

'Go to hell.'

'Well, don't wait too long, friend. Maybe she'll get snapped up. Shall we eat? I'm freezing my balls off here, and there's *kleftiko* in the kitchen, if we're quick.'

He drained his glass, and picked up the half-full bottle from the table.

Attis put a hand on Yorgas's arm.

'If you had a problem with Santos, you would tell me?'

'Of course I would,' said Yorgas, heading down the stairs. 'His fortunes tie you and me together.'

Two nights later, in the hour before dawn broke over Vrisi, the tyres of a fast-moving police car scattered the loose stones in the yard, and cracked the ice which had covered the pooled rainwater. The car's headlamps, on full beam, lit up the house façade; the dark rooms were filled with white light, like the arrival of celestial hordes.

The uniformed officer at the wheel turned the headlamps down to side-lights and killed the engine. His companion stubbed out the last inch of his cigarette in the dashboard ashtray, and exhaled a smooth stream of smoke.

'Let's go,' said the policeman.

'Pray God there are no hysterics,' said his companion. 'Wailing and weeping get on my nerves.'

'If you don't like hysterics, you shouldn't have begged the favour,' said the policeman. 'Now come. And treat them with respect.'

They climbed from the car. As they crossed the yard, the policeman buttoned his blouson jacket against the cold, and pulling his beret from under his shoulder-tab, positioned it on his head to cover what he could of his baldness. His companion turned up the collar of his sheepskin jacket, and pulled his slacks up higher on his waist.

In the village below, a dog barked.

Darkness hid the old place's many flaws – the walls cracked by invading tree roots, the sagging gutters, the young borage and thistles choking the pots of narcissi – leaving the house a half-seen grandeur. The men stood on either side of the doorway, the policeman taking up an official's stance: feet apart, hands clasped over the groin.

From inside his jacket, his companion produced a spiral-bound notebook.

'You can put that away,' said the policeman. 'You keep quiet, and hang back, like you said you would.'

His companion raised a conciliatory hand.

'It's all the same to me,' he said, putting away his notebook. 'My memory's infallible when it comes to what people say, and what I can't remember, I make up. But if I need corroboration, I'll come to you. I like to get good value for my money.'

He gave a smile; the policeman turned from him, and spat on the ground.

'Just leave all the talking to me,' said the policeman. 'Don't be upsetting them with questions.'

'Whatever you say, friend. Whatever you say.'

The policeman cleared his throat, and banged on the door, hammering with a force which rattled the frame. His companion licked the pad of his thumb and ran it over his modest moustache.

They waited. Behind the door, there was silence.

The policeman hammered again. His companion stepped away from the doorway, and craned up to the first-floor windows. All remained dark.

'Louder, friend,' he said to the policeman. 'It's a big house; they can't hear you.'

'What do you mean, louder?' asked the policeman. '*Malaka*. My hand's bruised black already, banging on this door. If you can bang louder, take a turn.'

His companion shook his head.

'Banging on doors is official business,' he said, 'and official business isn't my place. Seems to me there's no one here. I'll take a quick look round, and we'll be off.'

'They're here,' said the policeman. 'Where else would they be at this time, except here at home, in their beds?'

'Maybe in someone else's bed?' suggested his companion. 'There might be a story there. What d'you think?'

But before the policeman could answer him, light showed at the door-foot and behind the keyhole, and through the door a female voice asked, 'Who is it?'

'Police!'

A bolt slid; a key turned in the lock.

A woman opened the door. Wrapped in a candlewick robe, a man's leather slippers on her feet, she looked at the policeman through light-blind eyes, and tried to smooth the mess of her tangled hair.

'What is it?' she asked. 'What time is it?'

'Police,' said the policeman, again, as his companion looked with interest at the woman. 'Are you *Kyria* Volakis?'

The woman shook her head.

'No,' she said. 'No, I'm not.'

The policeman frowned.

'This is the house of Santos Volakis, is it not?'

'Yes,' said the woman. 'Yes, Santos lives here.'

'May we come in, then, *kyria*?' asked the policeman, and not waiting for a reply, he passed through the doorway and stood at the centre of the hall. His companion followed, and took up a position behind the policeman's shoulder.

The woman closed the door.

'Is this about Santos?' she asked. 'Is he all right?'

'Are you a relative, *kyria*?' asked the policeman.

'Of Santos's? Yes, of course I am. I'm his sister.'

'And your name?'

'Frona. Frona Kalaki. What's going on?'

The policeman hesitated. His companion stared round at the hall's ornaments and artefacts – watercolours and sepia photographs hung in old frames, a chess set carved from olive wood laid out on a dowry chest, the tusked head of a boar glowering from the wall – taking in as he did so the house's dilapidation.

'There's bad news, about your brother,' said the policeman.

Frona's face fell. Feeling behind herself with her hand, she touched the corner of the dowry chest and lowered herself to sit down on its edge. The belt of her dressing-gown caught the chessboard; pawns, knights, monarchs rattled as they went down.

From above them, over the banister rail, Leda called out.

'Frona? Frona, what are you doing? Is Papa back?'

'It's not your father, no. Go back to bed. I'll deal with this.'

But Leda had reached the head of the stairs, and crouched down to see who was in the hall. The policeman met her eyes, then looked away.

'Papa!' cried Leda, and sank down on the staircase, burying her face in the long nightdress which covered her naked legs.

The women's distress troubled the policeman, making him reluctant to say more, to provide unwelcome details. His visit had conveyed the painful message; was it not now better to depart and leave the questions that would inevitably come – how, when, why? – to another man, by daylight? He removed his beret, and holding it across his chest, looked up at Leda, whose face was still hidden in folds of pink cotton, and at Frona, and in preparation for departure, said, 'I'm sorry for your loss.'

He gave his companion a nod of dismissal, and the companion took a step towards the door.

Then Frona spoke.

'Tell me what happened,' she said to the policeman.

'Do you want anyone with you?' he asked. 'I can call a relative. Is there someone in the village who would come?'

'Please,' said Frona. 'I want to know.'

'We had a call from our fellow officers in Nafplio. They say your brother died by choking. On an olive, they believe. He

33

was alone in his room, and there was no one there to help him. Your brother's body has been passed into an undertaker's care, to be sent here, to you. He's on his way already. You should expect him tomorrow, or, at the latest, the day after.'

Frona fell back into silence.

'So is there anyone?' asked the policeman. 'I can fetch them in the car, if you'd like.'

'Maria, our housekeeper,' she said. 'She must be told. She must come and be with us.'

She gave the officer directions to Maria's house. Nothing remained, then, but for the men to leave. The policeman's companion offered Frona his hand; she did not take it, and the companion let it drop back to his side.

'May your brother's memory be eternal,' he said. 'I don't doubt it will be so. He's a great loss to us all. Not just to you, as his family, or to the people of your village, but to all of Greece. The nation mourns him. Perhaps when you've had a little time, we might talk. Maybe as his next of kin, you'd make a statement?'

He took out a business card featuring a newspaper's logo, and, ignoring the policeman's glare, laid it on the dowry chest.

'A statement?' She seemed bewildered. 'It's Attis you should go to, for a statement.'

'Attis?'

'Attis Danas, Santos's agent. He handles Santos's publicity. He handles everything.'

'Do you have a number for him?'

'I'll call him. I'll call him myself, and give him your number.'

The policeman ushered the journalist out of the door, and the women were left alone.

As Attis Danas unlocked the apartment door, the phone on the hallstand was ringing. The fabric of his jacket stank of cigar smoke, his breath of stale brandy; his silk tie was rolled up in his pocket. As he picked up the phone, he glanced in the mirror, and rubbed a smear of lipstick from his cheek.

'*Embros?*'

'Attis, for God's sake, is that you? Where have you been?'

'Frona! This is a surprise! So early!'

'Attis, I've been calling you for hours! Where have you been?'

'Celebrating. A client of mine – that woman who writes the cookery books – made this week's Top Ten. Frona, are you all right?'

'Attis, you must come. You have to come, come now. Something terrible has happened. I still can't believe it! I still can't believe he's gone!'

'Who's gone? Frona, what are you talking about?'

'You must come, Attis, and help us. The police have been here. They came to tell us poor Santos is dead!'

For a moment, Attis didn't speak, but looked out through the window at the hall's end, where grey clouds drizzled over city rooftops.

'That's not possible,' he said. 'How can he be dead? I spoke to him myself, only . . . When? When are they saying he died?'

'I don't know, Attis, I don't know! You must come now, and help us. There's only me and Leda, and Maria, and I don't know what to do! The press were here, too. You need to speak to them.'

'Of course I'll come,' said Attis. 'Don't worry. Trust me. You know you can leave everything to me. Just let me make some calls, and I'll be leaving. So just stay calm, Frona, and I'll be there with you in a few hours.'

35

Five

Anxious to get out of the rain, Father Tomas hurried through the final words and cast a fistful of wet earth into the grave, where soil and stones thudded dismally on the coffin lid. The mourners in their turn picked up handfuls of the freshly dug ground, and tossed them after the priest's.

They left the graveside slowly, under the shelter of umbrellas: bright parachutes of colour which hid the stricken faces of the bereaved.

As they made their way towards the cemetery gates, Attis Danas held a blue umbrella over his own head and that of Yorgas Sarris. Rain pattered on the nylon fabric; wind gnawed easily through their urban clothes. Amongst the tombs, under the dripping portico of a small chapel, the journalist in his sheepskin jacket sheltered from the rain. Seeing Attis and Yorgas, he dropped a half-smoked cigarette to the ground and hurried along the path to join them.

'Gentlemen, *kali mera sas*,' said the journalist, stepping in front of them, shrugging up the collar of his jacket. 'Forgive my intrusion on this sad occasion; but I am told you, *kyrie*' – he looked at Yorgas – 'are Santos Volakis's publisher. Is that right?'

Yorgas held out his hand from under the umbrella, as if he thought the rain might have stopped. In only moments, his palm was wet.

'I'm his publisher, yes,' he said, wiping his hand on his raincoat. 'Who wants to know?'

'Might you have a few words for the press?'

The journalist held up a reporter's notebook, poked a blunt pencil out of its spiral binding and flipped through many pages of untidy shorthand.

He readied his pencil over a blank page.

'It's up to you, Yorgas,' said Attis, 'but I've sent out a press release already.'

'A personal statement always gives a better story,' said the journalist. 'If you wouldn't mind?'

Yorgas shrugged his agreement.

'Your name?'

'Yorgas Sarris. I'm the proprietor of Bellerophon Editions, and we have the privilege of publishing all of Santos's work.'

The reporter made notes; despite its untidiness, the speed of his shorthand was slow, and the marks of his pencil were faint on the damp paper.

'And how have you been affected by his death?' he asked.

Out of respect for the dead man, neither Attis nor Yorgas had shaved. Overhanging the collar of his shirt, Yorgas's jowls were rough with stubble. He brushed away the watery beginnings of tears.

'I myself have lost a friend, and that's a personal tragedy,' he said, pacing his words to the speed of the reporter's slow pencil. 'But this is a tragedy of epic proportions, which will have its effect on us all. The fact is simple: Santos was one of the brightest stars Greek poetry has ever seen. He was a genius, the Seferis of his generation, a man of extraordinary talent.

And to leave us so young, when he had still so very much to give! It was an honour to publish him, a true honour. His loss leaves a vacuum that may never be filled.'

'You describe his death as a tragedy,' said the reporter, writing down Yorgas's last sentence. 'But would you say it's true that his life was as tragic as his death?' He looked up from his notebook, watching the publisher for his reaction; but though Attis frowned, the publisher's face did not change. 'I've heard he was a lonely man. Divorced.'

'A divorced man needn't be lonely,' said Attis. 'What are you suggesting?'

The reporter gave the same pleasant smile, and made a gesture which invited Attis to make a suggestion of his own; but before Attis could speak, the publisher interrupted.

'What you have to understand, friend,' he said, 'is that Santos was an artist in the true sense, and the artistic temperament tends from time to time towards melancholia. It's in the nature of the artist to reflect on the human condition, and the human condition has many aspects. Of course Santos was low on occasions; of course he had his moods, as we all do. But he had family he loved deeply, and he was wholly committed to his work. His career was going from strength to strength; his new collection of poems came out very recently, and we were looking forward to excellent sales. Santos's life was no tragedy. It was a celebration of language, and of the literary arts. Excuse us.'

'A moment more, please,' said the reporter, turning to a clean page to complete his record of Yorgas's remarks. Attis loosened the knot of his black tie. At the graveside, a gathering of women remained. Frona, Leda and Maria, the housekeeper, were weeping; others entreated them to leave.

'Local people say he never recovered from losing his wife,' said the reporter, his attention still, apparently, on the page.

'She left him, didn't she? Is it true she ran off with another man? Is she here, today?'

He looked back towards the grave, searching amongst the women for one who might be the poet's wife. A trickle of water ran down his forehead from his wet hair, and he brushed it away with his cuff.

'She's not here, no,' said Attis. '*Kyria* Volakis lives abroad now, in the United States. She couldn't possibly have got to Vrisi in time for the funeral.'

'But there's a daughter, isn't there? What's her name?' He scanned the earlier pages of his notes. 'Leda. I had the pleasure, the other night; a pretty girl, and unmarried, I believe. Who'll be taking care of her, now she's an orphan? Deserted by her mother, and now her father dead in his prime – her future'll be uncertain, I suppose.'

'She'll be well cared for by the family, as she's always been,' said Attis. 'And what do you mean, you had the pleasure?'

The reporter looked at him.

'May I ask your name, *kyrie*?' he asked, his pencil ready at the start of a new line.

'My name is on the press release I'm sure you've already received,' said Attis. 'I knew Santos for many years. They call me Attis Danas, and I am – I was – his literary agent. I built Santos's career; I nurtured him and guided him in his work. Above all else, I like to think that he and I were friends.'

The reporter looked from Attis to Yorgas, and again at Attis.

'That's very interesting,' he said. 'So we have here two men who have lost both a dear friend and a valuable source of income. Truly, it's a sad day for you both.'

On the path behind them, a babble of women's voices was growing closer, as Frona, Leda and Maria were guided from the grave under an assembly of umbrellas. The reporter's eyes brightened.

'Gentlemen, I thank you for your time,' he said. 'May I offer you my card? I'd welcome a call, if you've anything that might be of interest.'

'Scum,' said Attis, when he was certain the reporter was out of earshot. He reached into his raincoat, and producing two small cigars, gave one to Yorgas, and lit both with a petrol lighter. 'Time for a drink, I think.'

They moved on, keeping ahead of the women, whom the reporter was delaying. Rain drummed on the umbrella, and dripped from its spokes.

'Poor Santos,' said Yorgas, as they reached the cemetery gates. 'It's a sobering thought that any one of us might be gone, just like that.' He snapped his fingers.

'And yet,' said Attis, thoughtfully, 'as I was saying to you the other night, even what seems black may bring opportunity. We must look for the good in this disaster.' He pointed to his temple. 'We have to use our brains, and take care of our own interests. And of Frona's and Leda's, of course.'

'The truth is, we've had more orders for Santos's books in the last two days than we've had in his whole career,' said Yorgas. 'I've been thinking we might do another print run. Another five thousand maybe, see how they go.'

'Poor Santos,' said Attis. He glanced at the tip of his cigar, which had gone out. 'Man has many projects, and God cuts them short. To hear that he was selling well would have been balm to his very soul. You might let me have the figures, when you get back to the office. In the meantime, let me buy you that drink.'

Maria found no comfort in her tea; there was no soothing in the floweriness of the camomile, nor any sweetening for her bitterness in the melting honey. She untwisted her damp hand-kerchief, and dabbed again at her eyes.

'Such a loss I never thought to feel,' she said. 'And the casket closed and sealed, so I never even kissed his face goodbye! *Kamari mou, kamari mou!* Like a son he was to me; he was the son I never had!'

'He was, *kalé*, he was,' said the next-door neighbour, squeezing Maria's hand before taking another biscuit from the plate. 'You were a mother to him, all those years.'

Roula, Maria's own mother, was preparing vegetables for pickling. On newspaper spread over the good table, she pared the earth-darkened skins of carrots pulled from the garden; the acid smell of vinegar hung in the air.

'It must have made him ugly, for it to be closed casket,' she said, making a triple cross over her heart. 'They say with a choking, the face is blue. It makes them goggle-eyed, and swells the tongue. And you doted on him too much, *kori mou*. You spoiled him, you and that sister of his. Writing poetry was never honest work, for a man.'

Maria was about to object, but the neighbour spoke first.

'What about the will, *kalé*?' she asked; the pap of chewed biscuits stuck in the gums of the new teeth she was so proud of. 'Tell us what you know about the will.'

'He left a little to me,' said Maria, tearfully. 'He left me a little token, as I expected.'

'I hope it isn't books,' said Roula, dropping carrot slices into a preserving jar. 'It's cash you want. Is it cash?'

'He left me a few drachmas,' said Maria. 'It's not a great deal, but it's something.'

'Not a great deal, for all your years of service?' asked her mother. 'Don't let them insult you. If it's not enough, you give it back.'

'I don't think he was wealthy,' said the neighbour. 'If he

41

was wealthy, he hid it very well. And they say no one left the will-reading with a smile.'

'Why should anyone be smiling at a will-reading?' asked Maria. 'They were doling out a dead man's effects. Who would be smiling at that?'

'They might be smiling more in four years' time,' said the neighbour darkly, as she chose another biscuit.

'Four years? What do you mean?' Roula brushed carrot parings from her apron lap. 'Pass me those biscuits, Maria; let me have one whilst there's still one to have, and tell me what she means.'

Maria pushed the plate towards her mother.

'That's what he said in the will. It's how he wanted it. There's nothing for anyone for four years.'

'Four years!' said her mother, a biscuit only halfway to her mouth. 'What was he thinking of? Had he lost his mind? Does he want his family to starve?'

'He didn't *say* four years, exactly,' said Maria. 'The lawyer read out his words, so we could hear them for ourselves. Santos put it very poetically. *When my bones finally see daylight.* Something like that.'

'I suppose he meant, then,' said the neighbour, chewing thoughtfully, 'until his exhumation.'

'Yes,' said Maria, nodding slowly. 'Yes, I suppose he did.'

Roula gave a hard, barking laugh.

'I'd have paid money to see their faces, when that was read out!' she said. 'How did they take it, *kori mou*? All credit to the poet, after all! He had a sense of humour I never saw.'

'He was never a humorous man, in truth,' said Maria. 'He was always very earnest, from being a boy.'

'Sounds to me as if he earnestly doesn't want them to have his money,' laughed her mother. 'Well, they won't be liking that, I shouldn't think. And I don't suppose you like it either,

42

kori mou. Four years till you get your little legacy! Maybe I'll take a leaf out of his book, and keep you waiting the same way!'

'There's no point in that when you've nothing to leave,' said Maria, sourly. 'What legacy are you going to will to me?'

'Only wisdom and memories,' said Roula. 'Wisdom and memories, *kori mou*. For which you should be grateful. Mine's a legacy you won't wait years for; and what better gifts could a mother possibly leave?'

Pre-exhumation

Six

The island of Seftos was no siren, no draw for crowds of visitors. Long, flat and featureless, its unremarkable landscape had an undistinguished history, with no mention in the myths of ancient times nor any references in the guidebooks of today. Set on a wide and sweeping bay which gave no shelter, its town was ranged like a battalion, with tradesmen's premises and stores all at the centre, and commonplace houses on either flank. Behind the town grew acres of medlar orchards, whose old trees blossomed, at the appropriate season, into an attractive pink; but the market for medlars was never better than slow, and despite the growers' co-operative's ardent efforts at promotion, the fame of the Isle of Medlars had never spread beyond the boundaries of its own prefecture.

A few days before the poet's exhumation, the weekly boat to Athens – a vast vessel, whose long-serving captain was always apprehensive of Seftos's shallow waters – docked hours late alongside the island's own small ferry, which had no sailing scheduled for that day. Anxious to make up time and press on to the next port on their route, the crew handled the offloading with efficiency, lowering the ramp as the ship-to-shore lines were being secured, ushering off the disembarking foot passengers as they beckoned forward those waiting to board.

The arriving passengers were hurried away by relatives complaining of the delay, or disappeared down alleyways to back-street homes. But a figure watching from the ramp-head – an overweight man in an overcoat, with white tennis shoes on his feet – seemed undecided whether to leave the boat or not: he stepped on to the ramp, then back on to the deck; he checked his watch, and bit his lip, and stepped forward and back again.

The freight was light, and soon claimed and carted off, in trucks, on motorbikes, by hand. The ferry's hefty ropes were already cast off, and a crewman's hand was on the lever to raise the ramp, when the watching man called out to him to wait and stepped forward a third time.

The engines were powering up, and the crewman shouted over the water's churning.

'Run, friend!'

The fat man ran down the ramp, a hand raised in thanks to the crewman. The ferry moved away from the quay, whilst on the harbour-side, the fat man seemed to be doubting his decision. But as the foghorn gave a short blast of farewell, and the boat disappeared round the northern headland, he shrugged, picked up his bag and walked away from the dock towards the town's heart.

Along the quayside, boats hauled from the sea in autumn were still waiting for spring painting. Pigeons sheltered beside a chimney stack on the bakery roof; the tattered flag at the war memorial fluttered on its pole. An old man limped slowly by, a seaman's cap pulled down over his ears; as he passed the fat man, he gave a nod of greeting, and muttered, *Krio* – cold.

Over the doorway of the general store, the stems of last year's May Day flowers hung, long dead, as good luck, with a carbon cross from an Easter candle's smoke marked on the lintel. Tied with old rope to a trestle table lay a long-legged black hound, too dejected to raise his head as the fat man passed. With rain threatening, one of the narrow double doors remained bolted shut, so the fat man was forced to enter the store sideways. Hessian sacks of dried goods – lentils and chickpeas, rice and chicken-feed – obstructed his passage, and he edged between them to reach the counter.

The shop was lit only by a single bulb, and the daylight was blocked by boxes of stock – biscuits and pasta, canned fruit and shampoo – stacked up in front of the window. There were smells of garlic and onions, of salt anchovies, soap powder and oranges, and of cheese from the humming fridge, above which a caged linnet chirped once, and was silent.

The shopkeeper had tried to make himself comfortable: an empty coffee cup was at his elbow, a tumbler of spirit was on the till-top, the remains of a ham sandwich lay on a plate. He was past his prime, and had let himself go; his cheeks had four days' worth of stubble, and his fingers were stained ochre with nicotine. On the shelf behind him, a radio was tuned to a talk show, where two men argued about a basketball team's performance.

'They played like spastics, as usual,' said the shopkeeper to the radio, and switched it off. Rubbing his hands to restore their warmth, he turned to the fat man.

'*Yassas*,' he said. '*Kalos tou, kalos tou!* A winter visitor! You're a very rare bird, if I may say.' He looked the fat man up and down, admiring his cashmere overcoat in midnight blue, his grey suit with its subtle stripe, his waistcoat buttoned over a pale shirt. The fat man's owlish glasses gave him an air of academia, and his greying hair, though in need of cutting, was thick with curls; he placed his bag – a holdall of the type favoured by athletes, not new, but of some vintage, in well cared for navy leather – between his feet, drawing the

49

shopkeeper's attention, as he did so, to his white shoes. 'But visitors are a rarity at any time, in this backwater, and I don't ever recall one turned out like you. No offence, friend, but are you sure you're in the right place?'

The fat man smiled, and held out his hand.

'Hermes Diaktoros, of Athens,' he said. 'And I must admit, Seftos wasn't my intended destination. I disembarked on something of a whim. Many years have gone by since I was on the Isle of Medlars.'

The shopkeeper laughed as he shook the fat man's hand.

'It's a strange thing to be known for, wouldn't you say? A fruit too sour to eat until it's rotten? But if you want medlars, you must come back in the autumn. We're buried in the damn things, then.'

'It's medlars I've come for now, if I can get some,' said the fat man. 'I know it's not the season, but I'm hoping to find some spoon sweets, or other preserves. I'm intending to pay a visit to an old friend, and when I heard Seftos announced on the ferry tannoy, I was reminded of her partiality to the fruit. I shall be late, now, where I was going, but that business must wait. Medlars are such a rarity, these days, I thought I should take the opportunity when it presented itself. Did you know medlars were regarded, centuries ago, as an aid to chastity? Men made their women eat them, to stop them straying.'

'I can shoot holes in that remedy, in a second,' said the shopkeeper. 'The women here are medlar-eaters from birth, so by that logic, you'd expect them all to be virtuous as St Agnes, and that, they most certainly are not. I've got medlar jam, if you think it would suit.'

'Since it's not in my power to change the season, it will,' said the fat man. He looked around the shop, and his eyes fell on the fridge's display of cold meats and cheeses. 'I wonder if you would cut me a few slices of salami? And is the cheese I see there by any chance *kopanisti*?'

'It is,' said the shopkeeper, climbing off his stool, blowing on his hands as he went behind his fridge. Reaching into the display, he placed a fat sausage of salami in the crook of the steel blades of the electric slicer, and cut the first slices on to a piece of waxed paper.

'So you've been in Seftos before? Forgive me, friend, but I don't remember your face.'

'I was a younger man, then,' said the fat man. 'My family and I used to visit a little islet, just around the coast. My memories of those times are very happy. Maybe I should make the journey over there, for old times' sake.'

'You might not be very welcome, if you did,' said the shopkeeper, as more salami dropped on to the paper. 'The islet's occupied, these days, by a man not always keen on company. Our hermit, as we call him. Though he's not there, now. You've no doubt come in on the big boat, so maybe you saw him at the dock. He's just taken that boat himself, and gone away. He's left me to care for his dog, that beast outside. I don't like dogs, and I mistrust that one especially, but his master's a good customer, so I said I'd do him the favour.'

'The dog seems placid enough, at the moment,' said the fat man. 'When you say his owner's a hermit, do you mean he's religious?'

The shopkeeper smiled a wry smile at some private knowledge. He wrapped the paper around the salami, and secured the packet with an elastic band.

'He's a man who likes the ladies too much to be religious,' he said, reaching into the fridge for the *kopanisti*. 'Though they're not over-fond of him. Women like a man to smell sweet, and there's more of goats than roses about our hermit. Which isn't his fault; the man lives pretty rough. Folks used to say he was a fugitive from the law, but folks here'll say anything to shine up a dull story. Witless and slow as the law may be, if they were after him, even they'd have tracked him down by now. If you ask me, he's just a fellow who prefers his own company, and there's no married man alive who doesn't have some sympathy with that.'

He cut a wedge of the soft cheese.

'But what does your hermit live on?' asked the fat man. 'I remember that place as barren, just olive trees and scrub.'

'He does all right for himself,' said the shopkeeper, wrapping the cheese. 'He has his goats, and a few chickens. He grows a few vegetables, and catches a fish or two. And he's been enterprising.' Moving back behind the counter, he reached down to a shelf and held up an unlabelled bottle of *tsipouro*, a potent spirit distilled from grape skins and stalks. 'He makes this stuff. There's a glass here, if you'd like to try it.'

The fat man nodded agreement; the shopkeeper poured a measure into a fingermarked glass, and handed it to the fat man, taking his own glass from the till-top.

'*Yammas.*'

The men drank, and the fat man smiled.

'Quite a kick,' he said. 'Where does a man learn to distil *tsipouro* like this?'

'Our hermit bought a still from old Mikey, and Mikey was happy to teach him the tricks of the trade. And he's been a good student, wouldn't you say?'

'I would indeed. But a man living alone needs to take care. It's all too easy, under those circumstances, to make the bottle too close a friend.'

'You're right there,' said the shopkeeper. 'And the fishermen who go over there have found him red-eyed and ranting, more than once. But he's never too drunk to find the exact change when he's selling a bottle, and he's never been known to hand over a bottle for free.'

'I suppose it's no crime to enjoy the product of your own still,' said the fat man.

'And knowing the value of money doesn't make him unique. I'll find you that jam.'

The shopkeeper turned to the shelves behind him, and taking down a jar, rubbed dust from its lid with his sleeve.

'So where does a hermit go travelling?' asked the fat man, as the shopkeeper listed the prices of his purchases with a pencil, and began to tot them up. 'What tempts a solitary man back into the world?'

'He didn't say,' said the shopkeeper. 'He never says much. One thousand six. One thousand five, for cash.'

'Now I'm here, I need a place to sleep,' said the fat man, as he handed over his payment. 'Where would you recommend?'

'I'd recommend the only place you'll find a bed, at the taverna at the back of the square.' The shopkeeper slipped his money into the till. 'You'll do fine there, and they'll give you a decent dinner. But if you're not planning a long stay, you'd better drink no more *tsipouro*. The ferry out sails at six tomorrow morning.'

'Can I help you, *kyria*?'

At the city police station, the early shift was coming to an end. The officer on duty had plans for his free afternoon, and no intention of being late leaving the building.

The woman held tight to the boy's hand; the boy looked up in awe at the man in uniform.

'I want to report a missing person,' said the woman.

The officer made no comment, but opened a drawer in a filing cabinet, and found the correct form.

He made a note of her details: her name, her address, her date of birth.

'And the missing person?' he asked.

'It's my father,' she said. 'His name is Myles Antonakos.'

The name was familiar to the officer.

'You've been in here before,' he said.

'Six months ago. And six months ago before that. I'm hoping this time you might help me, instead of sending me away.'

The officer gave her a condescending smile.

'Is your father over the age of eighteen?' he asked.

'He's forty-five, next birthday.'

The officer put the form aside.

'Then, once again, I must tell you there's nothing we can do. Unless you have evidence of foul play?'

'I have no evidence of anything,' said the woman. 'But he's been missing such a very long time. We've had no contact from him at all since he left – not a letter, not a phone call, not even a postcard for my son.'

'That's your father's choice, *kyria*. In the eyes of the law, he's a free man.'

'But he has – problems. He likes a drink. Sometimes, he drinks too much, and it gets him into trouble. Or he might be ill. His health was never good, because of his drinking.'

'You might try the hospitals, then.'

'All those locally, I've tried.'

'Try other towns. Try other prefectures.'

'Which towns? Which prefectures?'

The officer shrugged.

'That, *kyria*, I don't know.'

'Please, listen. In a week, it's my son's name-day. My father's, too; the boy is named for him. I promised Myles I'd do everything I can to find his grandpa by then, so they might at least speak on the phone. He misses his *Pappou*, don't you, Myles?' Sadly, the boy nodded. 'And I miss him, too. But how to find him – I don't know where to begin.'

54

'With respect, *kyria*, neither do we,' said the officer. 'And, since you're not aware of any crime having been committed, either by him or against him, I'm sorry, but he doesn't fall under our remit.'

There were tears in the woman's eyes.

'But I keep telling you, he's missing!' she said. 'He'd have come home to us by now, if he could.'

'We've only your word for that,' said the officer. 'If you're determined to track him down, my advice is to hire someone privately. But maybe he doesn't want to be found. That's often how it is, in these cases.'

With tragic eyes, the boy looked up at him. The woman squeezed the boy's hand.

'Come on, Myles,' she said. 'We're wasting our time, in this place. There's no one here who'll help us find *Pappou*.'

The drunk's companions were long gone; he had no memory of them leaving, only an awareness that for some time, he'd been alone. Maybe there had been no companions this evening; maybe he was thinking of yesterday, or of last week. He craved sleep, but who would help him home? There was no home; and so he must stay here, upright and suffering in a bar-room chair, when only lying down would ease the pain of his swollen belly.

A drink would help.

'Ouzo!'

He reached out his shaking hand for his empty glass, and knocked it over. Addled, detached, he watched it roll to the table-edge, and fall.

The glass shattered on the tiled floor.

The barman was restocking the fridge with Dutch beer. He slammed the fridge door and pulled himself up from a crouch.

'OK, that's it,' he said. 'We're closing.'

At the end of the counter, he threw a switch. The back-lighting on the bottle shelves went out; the alluring, mirrored images of vodkas, schnapps and brandies all went dark.

Head lolling, the drunk peered down at his feet.

'An accident,' he said, as his eyelids – against his volition – half-shut. He lifted his chin, to see better through the remaining slits. 'Bring me an ouzo, friend. And have one yourself.'

The barman fetched a broom, and found a dust-pan beneath the unwashed cloths he used to wipe the bar. As he swept shattered glass from around the drunk's feet, the drunk looked around himself in confusion.

'Who broke that glass?' he asked. 'Why is there no service? An ouzo, friend, an ouzo!'

'You don't need an ouzo, you need a doctor,' said the barman, walking back to the counter. 'And we're closed.'

The drunk fumbled for his trouser pocket.

'Doctors be damned!' he said. 'And damn you too! Don't think I can't pay. I'll pay you, and you'll bring me another drink.' He dropped what money he found in his trousers on to the table along with a bottle of pills, and squinted down uncertainly at the two small banknotes. 'I've enough there, see. There's enough there, isn't there?'

'I've told you, I'm closing,' said the barman. 'Out.'

'May I buy you a drink, friend?'

From the shadows at the back of the bar-room, a man stepped up to the drunk's table. The drunk peered up at him with unfocused eyes. Whether the man was known to him, or not, he couldn't say.

The man looked down at him, appraising. The dim light accentuated the yellow cast to the drunk's skin; it showed his face, wretched and sunken, and his shoulders emaciated to bone, and his limbs softly plumped with the same oedema which distended his stomach.

'There's a place down the street where they open late,' said the man. 'We'll have a drink or two there.' He turned to the barman, who was watching, arms folded. 'And I'll settle this gentleman's bill. What does he owe?'

'Nothing,' said the barman. 'There's nothing to pay.'

The man scooped up the drunk's cash, and the pill bottle.

'Let me look after these,' he said, and slipped both money and medication into his pocket.

He stretched out a hand, and the drunk gladly accepted the help to stand. He cursed at the pain, but managed to sling an arm about his new friend's neck, and was ready to stumble from the bar.

But the barman stepped forward and blocked their way.

'Whatever you do, don't buy him a drink,' he warned the stranger. 'A single glass'll finish him.'

The stranger was bowed under the drunk's weight.

'Seems to me he's had a few drinks already,' he said.

The barman shook his head.

'Not from me. His liver's shot, and packing up. Makes them act like they'd downed a barrel of brandy. Just ply him with water, like I've been doing. He's too far gone to know the difference.'

The stranger looked at him, and smiled.

'Thanks for the tip, friend,' he said, and led the drunk away, into the night.

Post-exhumation

Seven

By running from the exhumation, Leda had left the others far behind, and reached the poet's house well ahead of those following. At the gate, she stopped, and looked back down the road. No one was in view. The house door was closed; no one was there to welcome her in.

She passed the gate, and went on along the uphill road.

The road ran through pine forest, overhung by the branches of lofty trees, each almost identical to the next and with no path between them. The forest was dense and dismal, without light for growth and greenery; instead, around the tree trunks spread a mat of rotting pine needles, whose russet softness absorbed and muffled Leda's footsteps as the heels of her shoes struck the concrete road.

Melting snow released the clean scent of the pine needles. The first drops of a threatening rain shower touched her face, but came to nothing. She walked on, around a bend in the road, and on, until ahead of her was the chapel of St Fanourios and its shrine.

The shrine was a wooden cabinet, mounted on a pole. An unlit lamp stood on its roof; a glass door covered its front, and locked within, piled one on another, were seven jaundiced skulls, with stained teeth set in gaping grins. From childhood, the women around Leda had encouraged her to fear them: *Don't look them in the eyes*, they said. *One of them was a bad man, and will curse you.*

The chapel was squat and ugly, with a round roof too flat to be conical, and its tiles covered with moss; its windows were of tiny proportions to save on glazier's bills, or – as people said – because its builders feared a tax on daylight. People said many things about the chapel. They said the family that built it was afraid of hellfire, but had no corresponding love of God; that they'd tried to buy their places in heaven on the cheap, and built the chapel shoddily and meanly, thinking God wouldn't notice their disrespect. But God, they said, had noticed, and wouldn't grant his blessing to the place. They spoke of spooks and spirits seen by twilight, and of strangers at the shrine, there and then gone, in the same instant.

The family's descendants had moved away, except for an ill-natured bachelor who had no more care for God's house than his relatives, and refused to fund its maintenance. On the saint's day, in August, a few of the pious came to pay their respects, but there was no celebratory music, or dancing, no wine, or feast. St Fanourios's visitors were few; only those who needed his special kind of help crossed the threshold. Those passing on the road made their crosses and went by quickly, avoiding the fourteen eyes which watched them from the shrine.

Yet as Leda drew close to the chapel, a man was there. He had opened the shrine's glass door, and was holding one of the skulls in the palm of his hand. The old stories of vanishing strangers came immediately to her mind, and believing herself unnoticed in the gloom of approaching dusk, she intended to retrace her steps and make her escape; but the man at the shrine seemed to sense she was there, and looking up from the skull he was examining, turned towards her.

Knowing she was seen, she felt obliged to continue on, towards the chapel. Drawing closer, she saw the man was tall, and overweight to the point of fatness, with glasses which gave him an air of academia, and a peculiar choice of footwear: old-fashioned, canvas tennis shoes, which – in spite of the muddiness of the road – were perfectly white. Between his feet was a holdall of the type favoured by athletes, not new, but of some vintage, in well cared for navy leather.

As she noticed his shoes, he seemed also to take an interest in her feet and the ladders which ran from the soles of her torn stockings up her heels and ankles.

He held out the skull on the palm of his hand. Fearing both the skull and the stranger, Leda slowed her walk.

But then the stranger smiled.

'*Kali spera sas*,' he said, politely, in a voice clearly of this world, and she wished him the same, moving, eyes averted, to pass by him.

'Don't be concerned that I take an interest in this skull,' he said, to her back. His words were beautifully enunciated, his speech clear and accentless as the Greek of TV newscasters. 'I was having a close look through the glass, and saw something about it which intrigued me. I admit to some mischief in picking the lock, but it's a poor one, and a few seconds' work even to a child, and I shall lock it again, when I go. I wanted a better look at this gentleman, for laudable reasons. Here, take a look for yourself.'

He offered the skull for her to see, and, curious, she glanced back.

'There's a crack, here on the parietal bone,' he said. On the back of the skull, he ran a finger along a narrow line. 'I'm afraid this man didn't die of natural causes. Too late now, of course, to discover if his death was accidental, or not; but this poor fellow died from a blow to the head. It might have been a fall, or a branch dropping from a tree; or it might have been an attack from some enemy. It's too late, now, ever to know; so I shall assume a broken branch, and return him to his companions.' With care, he replaced the skull with the other six, and closed the shrine's glass door. 'I should take some photographs,' he said. 'My father would find this collection most interesting.'

'You should be careful,' said Leda. 'Local legend has it one of them is cursed. And this place is rumoured to be haunted. It's not somewhere you should be alone.'

'Yet you have come alone,' said the fat man. 'I don't suppose you were expecting my company.'

'Excuse me,' said Leda. 'I have something I must do, and it's growing dark. I shall take care to be gone before nightfall.'

She followed the path to the chapel, and opened its arched door. The stranger had lit no lamps or candles, and inside, all was dark. Leaving the door open to let in what daylight remained, she placed a few coins on the offertory plate and took a candle from the box; but amongst the charcoal discs for the censer and the little boxes of wicks and incense, there were no matches.

'Allow me.'

The fat man was suddenly by her shoulder, and startled, Leda jumped. In his hand was a gold lighter, which he struck, holding out its blue flame to her candle's wick, and as the candle's own flame grew, its reflection showed his eyes as pools of disturbing depths. Leda took a step back.

'Forgive me,' he said, with a smile, slipping the lighter into his overcoat pocket. 'It was not my intention to frighten you. Sometimes, I move too silently in these shoes, and people think I'm sneaking up on them. Sometimes, of course, I am, though that was not my plan in your case. Please, don't let me interrupt your devotions.'

'I came to light a candle, that's all,' said Leda. 'And now I've done so, I'll leave.'

'But you haven't paid your proper respects to the saint,' said the fat man, obstructing the door, perhaps unintentionally. 'Who is the idol here? St Fanourios, it would seem. Please, I truly don't wish to disturb you. I shall wait outside until you're done, before I undertake my little tour. As the place is so small, I shall be done in half a minute, unless I find something of particular note. My interest is not in the present structure but in its foundations, and whether this chapel usurps an earlier building, an ancient temple. There have been rumours, down the years, of a temple to Demeter in this area. Whether this is the chapel that covers it, would be interesting to find out.'

He left her. Leda carried the burning candle to all the icons, and twisted it into the candle-box sand.

Outside, the fat man was standing once again before the shrine, smoking a cigarette whose tip glowed red in the twilight.

'The Orthodox habit of digging up the dead has always seemed peculiar to me,' he said, waving his hand towards the skulls as she appeared. 'Why not leave them in the ground where they are comfortable? And these fellows here have it worse than most, displayed like goods in some shop window. They may be useful as a reminder of mortality, but these men have been left no dignity. Even as I made my way up here, they were exhuming some other poor soul at the cemetery. Perhaps you know who it was?'

The evening shadows seemed to diminish his stature, and his affable expression encouraged confidences.

'It was my father,' she said.

The fat man raised both his hands in apology.

'How tactless of me!' he said. 'Please, forgive me. Your

father, then . . . May your God forgive his sins. But – forgive me again, it is my unalterable nature to be inquisitive – on such an important occasion, why are you spending your time here with St Fanourios and not at home with your family?'

'You're right,' she said. 'I should go back to them.'

'Before you go, will you permit me a question?' He dropped what remained of his cigarette to the ground and crushed it under the sole of his white shoe; then he bent to pick up the butt, and placed it on top of the shrine. 'I shall dispose of that properly, in a moment. Now, please advise me: St Fanourios, the Revealer, your patron saint of lost things. I have misplaced a ring, which perhaps he may help me find. It's gold, and an antiquity, but its value to me is more sentimental than mone-tary. It was a gift to me from my mother, and she will be most upset to think I've lost it. If you would confirm that my under-standing of the ritual is correct, I might invoke Fanourios's help myself. I must offer to say a prayer for the soul of his mother, is that right?'

'You must offer to bake him a cake,' said Leda, 'a *fanouro-pita* for the soul of his mother. Then you must take the cake to seven different houses, and before your neighbours eat, they must pray for St Fanourios's mother, too. All the cake must be eaten; none must be thrown away.'

The fat man looked doubtful.

'How can I undertake this ritual?' he asked. 'I don't know the recipe for *fanouropita*, and if I did, I have no kitchen to bake cakes.' He considered. 'Do you think we might econo-mise, and join my request with yours? When you bake your cake, will you ask for the return of my ring, as well as what you have lost?'

'I shan't be baking any cake,' said Leda. 'I'm sorry. I can't help you.'

66

She turned her back on him, and set off down the road, in the direction of the poet's house, and the village.

The evening was growing dark; the nearest trees were still visible, but in the deeper forest, night had already fallen. Leda walked as quickly as she dared, wary of irregularities in the road which would trip her. A kicked stone bounced away from her feet, and a second, much larger, hurt her toe. Then, her foot caught something else, a small, light object, which rolled tinkling over the ground.

She stopped, and peered down at the road. At first, she could see nothing; then her eye caught the glint of metal close to her shoe. She crouched, and picked up a ring. Clearly antique, the plain band was set with an unusual coin, stamped with a rising sun on one side, and a young man in profile on the other; and, even in the shades of evening, the ring shone with the glow of old gold.

Thinking of the fat man, she looked back along the road, but the chapel was round the bend, and out of sight. She considered going back, and giving him the ring, but night was closing in, and she was cold. She tried the ring on her middle finger. Made for a man, it was too big; so she slipped it in her pocket, and carried on along the darkening road.

Eight

Frona, Attis, Papa Tomas and Maria made their way in silence back to the house. Papa Tomas carried the metal box which held the remains from the poet's grave. Attis kept a guiding hand on Frona's back, by way of comfort.

The room where Santos had worked was never used. His papers and pens had long been cleared away, but on the old kitchen table which he had used as his desk, his typewriter still held the last sheet he had typed between its rollers, with the opening lines of an unfinished poem at its head.

The food which was to have welcomed the guests after the exhumation – sweet biscuits and Turkish delight, pine nuts and peanuts, crackers spread with fish-roe, brandy and wine – lay untouched on the starched, white cloths. Maria had prepared a dish of *kolyva*, food for the dead – boiled wheat flavoured with rose water and cinnamon, mixed with pomegranate seeds and raisins, and blanketed in icing sugar – which she had decorated with a cross in blanched almonds and silver dragées.

At the fireplace, Frona held her cold hands to the ash-choked fire. She had put on make-up for the ritual, but, no expert in the art, had chosen shades of rouge and lipstick which bled the bloom from her skin. Attis sensed in her the weariness of the careworn; her mouth was developing a downturn he hadn't seen before. He poured himself a Metaxa, and passed a glass to the priest, who sat on an ornate horse-hair sofa which belonged to another age, his anorak still zipped over his robes, the box holding the bones from Santos's grave between his feet.

'I think before we go any further, we should take another look at what we've got here,' said Attis. 'Papa, would you mind?'

'Not at all, not at all,' said Papa Tomas. 'Not if you think it will help.'

'I don't want to see,' said Frona, closing her eyes against the images from the graveside.

'There's no need for you to look,' said Attis. 'Not if it distresses you. Papa?'

Papa Tomas lifted the lid of the box. On a lining of white cotton, the many unwashed bones from Santos's grave were caked in earth, but the covering was too light to hide their form. The skull was elongated, and wide at the jaws; the teeth remained, with a set of almost human molars in the rear jaw, but at the front – at the snout – a dozen more protruded oddly, and two – curling upwards – were obviously tusks. There were bones clearly from a leg, but the creature they came from was not human; the leg was too short to be a man's, and ended not in the intricate bones of feet and toes, but in a point which could only be a hoof.

Papa Tomas crossed himself.

'I'm afraid these are definitely from a pig,' he said to Frona, gently. 'I don't think there can be any doubt of that.'

Attis peered into the box, and shuddered.

'I'm afraid Papa Tomas is right,' he said. 'Unthinkable as it is, somehow poor Santos has been . . . changed.'

He drank down his Metaxa.

'Don't be absurd,' said Frona. 'There's surely been some trick, some malicious prank.'

She looked towards Attis for reassurance.

'Of course you're right, Frona,' he said. 'Papa, you might close the box. The question is, what do we do now?' He put on his reading glasses, and from an envelope in his pocket, withdrew several papers held together with a legal seal. 'Because, following today's events, the wording Santos used in his will takes on new meaning.'

'What new meaning?' asked Frona. 'What do you mean? Four years, he said, and four years have gone.'

Her face was troubled. Attis looked down at the papers; in the twilight, they were impossible to read. He switched on the lamp, snatching his hand from the sting of an electric shock. At the room's corners, the shadows deepened in the lamp's sallow light.

Attis scanned the pages.

'I don't think he said four years, exactly,' he said, as he read. 'That's what we assumed he meant. Here it is, here's the paragraph: the monies are to be distributed, *when my bones finally see daylight*. So I suppose everything rests on whether we can reasonably assume his bones have seen daylight today.'

The priest looked dubiously at the metal box at his feet.

'But to declare those – whatever they are – are Santos's remains would make us look idiots,' said Frona. 'They're not human; we can see that.'

Maria carried in a stack of plates, and laid them on the table.

'Eat, all of you, please; come, eat,' she said, gesturing at the food. 'What can I do with all this, if you don't eat? And where's Leda? She should eat something. She's had nothing since breakfast this morning.'

'She isn't here,' said Frona. 'I don't know where she is. She's had a great shock. How must the poor girl be feeling? Attis, will you go and look for her?'

'I will,' said Attis, 'when we've decided what to do. Papa Tomas will be wanting to get away.' He replaced the papers in their envelope. 'Maria, tell me something. What are they saying in the village about this business?'

'Business? What business? Papa, let me fill you a plate.'

'Thank you,' said the priest. 'That's very kind.'

'This business.' Attis pointed at the metal box. 'What are they saying about this?'

'I haven't been to the village to find out,' said Maria, choosing from the best of the food for Papa Tomas. 'But if I had to guess, I'd guess they'd be saying the poor boy's bones have been transformed.' She touched the corner of her eye, where tears were gathering. 'Someone put the evil eye on him, is what I'd be saying. What else could they say, if it's the truth?'

In exasperation, Frona threw up her hands.

'See! They'll have us in horns and hoods in no time, dancing on his grave at midnight. Their stupidity and superstition is beyond bearing.'

Papa Tomas blinked; Maria turned her back, and busied herself with the Turkish delight.

'They have faith in powers beyond the earthly,' said the priest, 'as should we all.'

'So what do you say, Papa?' asked Attis. 'In your professional opinion, are what we have here Santos's bones? Are you happy to inter them as such?'

The priest cleared his throat, and took his time in taking a drink which emptied his glass. He wiped a small dribble from his mouth.

'Well,' he said, holding out his glass so Attis might refill it, 'if they are – and I'm not saying they are – then clearly there's been some kind of – let's say something's been at work. So

71

that would prevent me from interring them. They might be – well, tainted. If something has – interfered with them.'

'You're saying,' said Frona, as Attis poured more brandy for Papa Tomas, 'if there's been witchcraft or the devil's work, it might infect the other remains in the ossiary. Maybe they'll turn into pigs, too. Or sheep, or chickens.'

'Well,' said the priest. 'The bones in the ossuary are sacred remains. They await their resurrection in their blessed natural form.'

'People wouldn't want to see their grandmother resurrected as a goat,' said Frona. 'Is that what you're saying? What claptrap.'

'Frona, please,' said Attis. 'Papa, please go on.'

'To continue,' said the priest, accepting a plate from Maria. 'If there has been no unusual intervention, then we must assume this is the work of human hands. Of malicious hands, in fact. In which case, plainly these are not Santos's remains. So I couldn't inter them as such, no.'

Attis sighed, and poured more brandy for himself. Maria lifted a silver dragée from the cross marked on the *kolyva*, and replaced it exactly straight.

'But if they're not Santos's bones,' asked Frona, 'where is he? Who would have done such a cruel thing?'

'People,' said Maria, darkly, prodding the blanched almonds with her fingertip. 'Bad people.'

A longcase clock ticked away the moments of a silence.

'You'll be wanting to know,' said Attis, at last, as he removed his glasses, 'how much is in the account.'

Frona, Maria and the priest all looked at him.

'How much?' asked Frona.

'A substantial amount.'

'How substantial?'

'Exactly, I couldn't say. Substantial.'

'And who knows this?'

'Myself. All of you, now. The bank where the account is held, of course. And Yorgas Sarris, as the publisher, of course; they have paid the royalties over the last four years.'

'So there might be,' suggested Frona, 'more money than he made in all his life.'

'After his death, sales grew to an impressive level, as you know,' said Attis. 'It's a sad fact that Death may bring rewards for a talent which brought little success for the artist in his lifetime. Santos often compared himself to Van Gogh, who lived in poverty and became wealthy as he lay in his grave. And the comparison was fair. Now he's gone, Santos's beautiful poems are set texts in schools and universities, even internationally; I'm told he's under consideration by the Sorbonne. Santos would have been very gratified, there's no doubt of it, even though he was no businessman. His life was his art.'

Frona laughed, bitterly.

'If you believe that, you didn't know him at all. He worried constantly about money, about bills and debts. This house has had nothing spent on it since our grandmother's time. It's cold, and it's draughty, and it's inconvenient. The wiring's unreliable at best, and when it rains, it's dangerous. The roof leaks and the window frames are rotten; it's overrun by mice, and riddled with damp. Santos loved this house, but he couldn't afford its upkeep, and he hated to watch it fall down around his ears. And his wife hated it here. She was a city girl, like me and Leda. He always said she left him because she couldn't live in this state. And Leda and I couldn't live here now, even if we wanted to. The place isn't fit for dogs. Look!'

She pointed up at the ceiling, where brown stains of damp showed on flaking plaster, and at the cracked glass in the rotten window frame, the threadbare rugs and old furniture, at the oil lamps in readiness for power failures.

Attis sighed.

'I did my best for him,' he said. 'There's just no money in poetry.'

'But there's money in the poems of dead poets, isn't there?' asked Frona. 'And now he's dead and made his money, someone's trying to steal it!'

'Steal it?' The agent seemed shocked. 'What on earth makes you say that?'

'That does!' She pointed at the metal case at the priest's feet. 'Someone who knows what was in his will has stolen his remains to invalidate it, and keep us from our inheritance!'

Papa Tomas looked up from his plate with interest; Maria halted in her rearranging of the crackers.

'What someone?' asked Attis. 'Why?'

'Some enemy. Someone who has an interest in keeping the money locked away.'

She looked hard at the agent, and made her meaning clear.

'Frona! Surely, Frona, you can't be accusing me?' In apparent hurt and indignation, Attis's face grew red. 'Why would I do such a thing, to you of all people? No one could have worked harder on Santos's behalf, on behalf of his estate, and in your interests! Tirelessly, I have worked! I've sold rights to dozens of countries, and overseen the royalty payments in a fair and businesslike manner. The accounts may be frozen, but I can assure you that all the monies that should be there, are there! And might I remind you, I am myself a beneficiary of the will? It grants me a one-off sum, if you remember, which at the time of his death Santos simply didn't have, a very generous gesture which four years ago his estate could not possibly have paid. Maybe he was a better businessman than he seemed. In willing me that sum, he willed me an incentive to make the money – which I may say I have done, alongside a considerable sum for you, and Leda. So I cannot for one single minute see why you

74

think I should want to keep his money from myself, or you, especially in such a bizarre and ghoulish fashion! Why in God's name would I do something so heathen as to dig the poor man up, and hide his bones? I may be many things, Frona, but a grave-robber I most certainly am not.'

Frona sighed.

'I'm sorry,' she said. 'I appreciate all you've done. But if not any of us, who?'

'Bad eyes,' murmured Maria, 'bad eyes.' She made crosses over her heart, and glanced at the darkening window as if an unwelcome face might be watching. The priest made crosses too, and sipped more brandy.

'Does it matter who?' asked Attis.

'What do you mean?' Frona picked up a ram's-head poker, and shifted the charred logs to shake off their ash. Small flames flickered, and died again as she placed a fresh pine log in the grate.

'We've exhumed the bones in Santos's grave. Doesn't that meet the terms of the will?'

'Not if they're not his bones.'

'But we could say they are.'

'Say that those pig bones belong to my brother? That will bring shame on him, and on us, his family.'

Papa Tomas nodded enthusiatic agreement.

'But what if the bones were blessed?' asked Attis. 'Think about it, Frona; I'm trying to help you, and Leda. A blessing would surely make it right. You'd make it right, wouldn't you, Papa, for a consideration?'

But Frona shook her head.

'We can't do that,' she said. 'Where are Santos's bones? Someone has desecrated my brother's grave, Attis! That's more important than any amount of money! We should be going after this grave-robber, this criminal!'

'Just so,' said Attis, carefully, 'Just so. And with money, you could hire an investigator to track him down. You're quite right that a criminal act has been committed here, for reasons we don't know. But without money to pay someone to find out, the truth may never be discovered, and poor Santos's remains may never be found. So here's what I suggest. Papa, we'll need your help. We must inter the bones as if all is as it should be.'

But Papa Tomas shook his head.

'I don't think I could do that,' he said. 'I'm sorry – I'm sorry for you all, and I really do wish to help – but I really couldn't.'

'What if, then,' suggested the agent, 'we inter no bones at all? An empty box. That removes your objection, surely, Papa? I know in the family's interests we can rely on your discretion and your silence. When Santos's remains are found, maybe you'd conduct a quiet ceremony to bring him home. And when the money in the accounts is released, Frona, you can hire someone to discover the truth.'

'And what about local tittle-tattle?' asked Frona. 'How will we keep a leash on that?' She looked across at Maria, but Maria was busy, wiping dust from an unopened bottle of wine.

'Papa Tomas has considerable influence. Papa, you could help us there, too.'

The priest looked doubtful.

'What will I tell them?' he asked. 'That there was some trick of the light? I'm afraid the rumours will persist. And what about the bones, here, in the case? What if they *are* Santos's bones, transformed? To dispose of them without proper ceremony would be a sin.'

'We could re-bury them,' said Attis, 'somewhere they won't be found.'

'But what if there has been some kind of . . .' objected the priest.

'This is all superstition,' interrupted Attis. 'Do you really believe Santos has been magicked into a pig?'

'A possibility, in the minds of some, is all I'm saying.'

By the table, Maria crossed herself again.

'So clean the bones with holy water, and bless them,' said Attis. 'When Frona has money to pay an investigator, no doubt we'll prove there's been no magical transformation. Can we agree, then, to this plan? Our story is, the observers were mistaken and the reports are malicious gossip. The case will be placed empty in the ossuary, and I'll contact the lawyer and tell him to call the bank to release the funds.'

'How long will it take?' asked Frona. 'When do you think the money will come through? I want my brother's remains found, and brought home to his final rest.'

'These things take time. Two weeks, at least; perhaps as long as a month. But, since we know the money is coming, we can start to move ahead. When I get back to town, I'll make enquiries of my own, and find the most efficient man I can to take on the job. Now, if we're done, I'll go and find poor Leda. She'll be desperately cold and miserable, out there all alone in the dark.'

Like wildfire, like a virus, the news spread; the women carried it like contagion, and every mouth that repeated the story built on it, embellishing and embroidering, until only the smallest kernel of truth remained at the tale's heart: that the poet's bones were not human, but had been transformed into a beast's. Some said he had been dug up and replaced by malicious hands; others that the matter was far more sinister, and that the devil was at work. First he was a mere pig, of average size; but with each telling he grew, until he had become a massive boar, with tusks so long they'd go straight through a man. The poet was destined to become a legend and his transformation a myth; and the news came quickly to the ears of Maria's old mother, Roula.

Roula claimed now to be in her ninetieth year, but Maria was known to be only seventy-one, which made Roula's claim impossible, as she had been married at thirteen. Housebound for two years, she was confined to the *salone*, propped up with cushions in her bed, and waited on and cared for by her daughter.

The tale was brought by Maria and seconded by the neighbour, who had also been amongst the women at the grave.

With a shawl around her shoulders and a tray across her knees, Roula was spooning broth into her toothless mouth and sucking on bread soaked in the soup.

Maria and the neighbour told each other the story, then told it slightly differently, again: poor Santos's bones a boar's, Frona angry and upset, Leda brought home silent with the shock, Papa Tomas refusing to speak of the matter at all.

'The devil's amongst us, here in Vrisi,' wailed the neighbour. '*Panayia mou, Panayia!*'

Old Roula lowered her spoon, and regarded her daughter and the neighbour through milky eyes.

'Eat your broth, Mama,' said Maria.

'Where will the bones go now?' asked the neighbour, in excitement. 'Not in the ossuary, surely? They must burn them, to purge the devil.'

'They say they'll get to the bottom of it,' said Maria to the neighbour. 'They're hiring an investigator to look into it. Don't say anything, but they believe that it's an enemy, trying to rob them.'

'An investigator?' asked the neighbour. 'What kind of investigator?'

'A detective of some sort, I suppose. Someone who'll make enquiries.'

'An investigator?' asked Roula. 'Here in Vrisi?'

But her daughter and the neighbour both ignored her and went on with their speculation.

Roula spooned more broth into her mouth and sucked on the sodden bread.

'I used to know someone you might suggest,' she said, after she swallowed.

'Have you finished your broth?' asked Maria, taking away Roula's bowl. 'You used to know a lot of people, Mama. But as you're always telling me, most of those you used to know are dead. It's getting late, for you. Come on, and I'll get you ready for your bed.'

For the second time that month, the moon was full – a rare blue moon – and the wind had shifted to the north, sweeping away the clouds to leave a night of remarkable beauty. Moonlight flowed in through the curtainless window, a delicate light with the dim glow of pewter, casting shadows with the soft look of gauze.

In her sleep, Roula was restless, shifting uneasily between drowsing and the strangeness of her dreams. In her dream, a dog was barking, though not the skinny hound her son-in-law kept now (which was a nervous dog, prone to crafty nipping of goats' hocks, and always appearing where it was least expected, like the sly son-in-law himself). No: the bark belonged to Antonio, her father's dog when she was a girl; Antonio, long-haired, sand-brown and kind-eyed, a pastoral dog by nature and biddable with the herd. Antonio was barking a warning, running up and down the yard as he had when someone drew near, his chain rattling as he dragged it through the dirt.

In her dream, Roula listened, waiting for whatever had disturbed Antonio – a rodent or a cat – to move away; but the dog barked on, and, since no one else got up to go and settle him, she threw off her warmthless blankets, and putting both feet to the floorboards, stood up.

She stood easily and confidently, independent of her sticks, and felt the sensation of woollen bedsocks under her soles; and she felt too the bones of her legs and feet doing their work as they used to, and her muscles strong and useful, without all their aches and pains, without the danger of their failing.

Antonio still barked, and Roula walked quite naturally to the door. Though she wore only her nylon nightdress and a crocheted bed-jacket, the night – to her – wasn't cold. With newly dextrous fingers untroubled by their arthritic joints, she unfastened the bolt, turned the key and opened the door.

As the bolt was drawn, Antonio become silent, hoping for some ally to join him, but his silence was short, and he began to bark more ferociously, as if whatever – or whoever – was troubling him was growing nearer. And then someone snapped their fingers, and said a word, and the dog fell silent; and Roula heard the familiar, forgotten sound of his chain curling on itself as he lay down.

Curious, in her stockinged feet she stepped into the night, into the light of the blue moon, which to her mother had always been taboo, because of its dangers of madness and bewitchment; and, sure enough, it was playing its tricks, turning her long, grey hair – let loose for night – back to the splendid, shining black of her maiden days. She walked along the path from door to yard, delighted with the freedom of her restored body, stepping over the stones with the hem of her nightgown lifted over her toes. She blessed her obedient limbs, and with the easing of old age's miseries, her spirits lifted; the bad temper and dissatisfaction which coloured her latter days left her, replaced by the *joie de vivre* she had felt throughout her youth.

She rounded the house corner, and there indeed was dear Antonio, lying head on paws. As he saw her, he lifted his big head and wagged his tail, not in great excitement but as if only minutes had gone by since he had seen her last. Roula wondered at how fondly she remembered him, and at how clearly memory presented him to her now, as many years had passed since he had even crossed her mind; but here he was, a welcome visitor from the foreign land of dreams, where time was an irrelevance, and the remotest yesterdays might put in an appearance as readily as last week.

The hens, in their coop, were restless, shuffling and fluttering on their perches, making low noises of unease, as if they sensed some predator. The night smelled of pine and cold wind; and there was a sweetness in the air she couldn't name, familiar and agreeable as spring flowers, yet lost as the days of childhood, a perfume she had known but knew no longer.

And seated on an orange crate between coop and dog, was a man, with his back to her, who, like the sweetness in the air, was forgotten yet remembered, strange yet familiar, a figure who had long ago vanished from her memory. He heard her footfall and turned his head, and, seeing her, smiled and at once stood; and, though the moonlight cast dark shadows which concealed his features, she knew his face immediately, and was glad beyond expressing to see him.

'Roula,' he said, in a voice which hadn't changed. 'Roula, let me look at you.'

He held his hands before him, and she took them in her own, and in her dream could feel their warmth and comfort.

'Hermes,' she said. 'It's you.'

They smiled in delight at their reunion. Inside the coop, the chickens fluttered and flapped. Antonio lay his head down on his paws, and whined uncertainly.

Hermes kissed her on the cheek, and as he bent close, she

recognised the sweetness as his fragrance and picked out its individual components – the bitter orange of neroli, the honey fragrance of immortelle, the earthy tang of vetiver – which, all combined, seemed the scent of very heaven.

'So beautiful still,' he said, and by the light of the blue moon, it was true; she had become how she had been when she had known him.

'I was looking at the stars,' he said. 'Such a clear night, and the stars so magnificent.'

Hand in hand, they looked up at the constellations, and watched until a shooting star crossed the sky.

'Quick, make a wish,' he said.

'I wish for a painless death,' she said, with no hesitation. 'I wish to die in my sleep.'

He squeezed her hand as if the wish were acknowledged, and turned his face from the sky to look at her; and with him too, it was as if the years had never been. He appeared the same, handsome and noble, smooth-skinned.

'Why are you here,' she asked, 'after all this time?'

'The years pass, don't they?' he said, with a touch of sadness. 'Before I know it, my friends are gone.' Then he added, more brightly, 'I came to see you, that's all. But now I'm here, I sense perhaps my being here is timely.'

'In what way, timely?'

'We must wait, and see. Come, I'll take you back inside. This night air can settle on the lungs.'

'Before I go,' she said, 'let me say goodbye to Antonio.'

She let go of his hand and crouched down beside the dog, who looked at her with grateful, loving eyes as she stroked his head and murmured affectionate words; and as she took her hand away, he licked it, and she felt the dampness of his tongue.

Hermes led Roula down the path, and followed her inside to the truckle bed, where she lay down, still lithe and free from pain. Leaning over her, he covered her with the blankets, which seemed, for once, as soft and warm as cashmere. Like a child, she lay content. He bent down, and kissed her forehead.

'Sleep,' he said. 'And wishes shall soon come true.'

And he was gone.

She opened her eyes as dawn was breaking, and remembered Hermes, and the dream. But her hands were once again an old woman's, the rough blankets were scratching her chin, and the pains and aches of every day were already pinching, in hips and knees and hands.

Nine

On the morning after the exhumation, Attis left the bedroom he had slept in and went quietly into Santos's old study. With his back to the smoking fire, he folded his arms and lowered his chin to his chest, so if anyone had intruded on him, they would have believed him to be in a moment of quiet reflection, though in fact he was listening for any movement on the floor above. Along the hall, Maria clattered plates and pans, and ran water into the sink. She spoke a few words he couldn't catch, and he waited to hear a reply; but none came, and he concluded she was talking to no one but herself. Only when he was certain he would not be disturbed, did he begin.

He sat down at the poet's table, on the cushion-seated chair which had been Santos's favourite. Though Frona had wanted to keep the place as Santos had left it, in truth nothing was as it used to be. When Santos was master of his own sanctuary, Maria had been banned from the room, except to tend the fire. In his absence, her tidying and cleaning – incompetent though it was – had changed it beyond recognition.

In each long side, the table had two drawers, where cutlery and utensils had once been kept. He opened the right-hand drawer, which faced him. On a lining of discoloured newsprint, it held stationery supplies – a stapler, a pot of paperclips, a pencil-sharpener, scissors – all ordered in a way Santos would never have managed. There was a bone-handled hunting knife, a medallion of no value on a chain, a well-used pack of playing cards. Attis closed the drawer, and opening the left-hand side, found nothing but a telephone directory, several years out of date.

He listened. Overhead, a floorboard creaked. He stood, and rounding the table, slid open the drawers on its far side. In one, the household utility bills of years past were fastened in packets with elastic bands; the last held a backgammon set from Santos's boyhood, and an appointment diary for the year he died.

Attis flicked through the little diary's pages. In the earliest months of the year, there were a few entries in Santos's distinctive hand: appointments with Attis himself, a wedding, several days where there were only initials or times, and phone numbers. The empty pages reflected Santos's life and his disinclination to be sociable; even if he'd marked a date in the diary, he could never be relied on to appear where he should be. Notoriously forgetful of engagements, he had caused Attis some embarrassment over the years, until Attis had developed a strategy which was often successful: he wrote a letter of reminder to Santos two or three days before a meeting, or a reading, or a dinner. To phone him and remind him had been pointless; Santos would make a scribbled note on some scrap of paper, and blank the phone call and the note from his busy mind. The diary's last entry – a name, and a number – had been on a date just after his death. Beyond that, the pages were empty.

Attis slipped the diary into his pocket, and considered. Moving the chair out of the way, he bent to see the underside of the table, then pulled the right-hand drawer from its runners and lifted it over his head to see its base, but found nothing but a few fading carpenter's marks. He returned the drawer to its runners, and slid out the left, holding this drawer, too, up over his head.

A brown envelope was taped to its base.

Over a wide aluminium bowl filled with water, Maria was using a paring knife to dig a weevil from a potato.

'Maria, *kali mera*,' said Attis from the kitchen doorway. 'I'm walking down to the village to get some air. Tell Frona I'll be back before too long.'

'Don't you want breakfast?' asked Maria. She dropped both knife and potato into the water, and wiped her hands dry on her apron. 'There're plenty of eggs. Sit down, and I'll put the coffee on.'

'Don't trouble,' said Attis. 'I'll get coffee at the *kafenion*.'

'Is their coffee better than my coffee, then?' asked Maria. 'Sit, and eat. The eggs are fresh this morning.'

'Thank you,' said Attis. 'Maybe later.'

Maria heard the front door close, and remarked to herself on the folly of paying good money for bad coffee; but there were weevils in the potatoes, and with her mind on dealing with them, Attis and his unwanted breakfast were soon forgotten. When Frona came downstairs a short while later, she at least seemed to have some appetite, and accepted not only eggs and coffee, but a bowl of goats' milk yogurt besides.

Frona asked after Leda.

'She came down a while ago, all wan, poor chick,' said Maria. 'I made her some tea, but she wouldn't take anything else but a slice of bread. She said she'd eat upstairs. This business is hard on her, *kalé*.'

'It's hard on us all,' said Frona, with a sigh. 'I think the best thing for Leda is to get her out of here, and back at college. I worry how she'll cope, after yesterday. When Santos died, for a whole month she barely spoke.'

86

'Ah, but look how she rallied after that,' said Maria. 'The young are strong. She'll take it in her stride.'

'Do you think so?' Frona pushed away her half-eaten eggs. 'If it were me, I think the shock of those horrible remains would scar me for life.'

Frona was still drinking coffee when Maria went upstairs to make the beds. In Santos's old room, at the foot of his brass bed, Attis's small suitcase was fastened and locked, ready for his journey back to the city. In Frona's room, next door, the bedsheets and blankets had been straightened. Maria looked hopefully for the indentations of two heads in the pillows; but the pillows had already been plumped, and the evidence she sought wasn't there.

Down in the kitchen, Frona was washing the breakfast dishes.

'He's off today, is he?' asked Maria.

Frona laid a chipped plate on the drainer.

'Who, Attis? I believe so.'

Maria tied a cotton apron over her black dress, and sitting down with a blunt paring knife, began to clean a handful of wild greens.

'You could ask him to stay, another day or so.'

Frona turned from the sink. Beneath her eyes, the skin was grey and swollen from lack of sleep.

'Why would I do that?' she asked. 'We're leaving ourselves, tomorrow.'

'He could give you a lift.' Maria snapped the stalks from leaves of chervil, releasing the scent of aniseed.

'We don't need a lift. I'll ask Hassan. Where is Attis, anyway?'

'He said to tell you he'll be back soon,' said Maria. 'He watches you, *kalé*. I've seen him, watching you.' With the tip of the paring knife, she tapped the corner of her eye.

'Don't be ridiculous,' said Frona, turning back to the dishes. 'Attis has no interest in me. Not in that way.'

'You're wrong, *kalé*. It's in his eyes.'

'He must be mad, then,' said Frona. 'Maybe he's after my money.'

'You don't have any money,' said Maria. 'But he does. He's getting long in the tooth, but he'd take care of you. There'd be no more money worries, with him. If I were you, I'd give him a chance. You're getting no younger yourself, and at your age, there may not be many more offers.'

Roula sat in the chair where Maria had left her. The rugs she was wrapped in gave her no warmth; a breakfast of rusks and milky coffee had not tempted her failing appetite. Outside, her son-in-law called the dog as he set off to tend the goats, and she envied him his task; the morning's predictable inactivity was wearying, and she closed her eyes to doze an hour of it away.

There was a knock at the door, and thinking the unwelcome neighbour had come calling, she feigned sleep. But there was no shrill call of *Kali mera*, no shout for Maria; instead, she heard the door quietly open, and sensed someone approach her in her chair.

She opened her eyes. The fat man stood before her.

'Hermes!'

Smiling, he bent to kiss her cheek, then took her aged hand and kissed that too.

'My beautiful Roula,' he said.

'I saw you last night, in my dreams,' she said.

'I'm flattered,' he said. 'I brought you a gift.' From his holdall, he produced the jar of medlar jam he had bought in Seftos. 'I made a detour for you specially, because I remembered how partial to this you are.'

'Put it on the table for me, would you?' she asked. 'Then

88

come and talk to me. They're looking for an investigator, so it's good you're here. There's been a discovery. A scandal!'

The fat man's smile grew broader. He pulled up a chair close to hers, and Roula told him of the pig's bones in the poet's coffin.

'Intriguing,' he said. 'I come to bring you medlars, and you offer me a puzzle in return. Shall I see what I can discover, to satisfy your curiosity?'

'I wish you would,' said Roula. 'You'd bring a little sparkle into my day.'

The morning's brightness was subdued by the towering pines, and on the road, the sun made little impact on a day which carried echoes of the long and snow-bound winter.

Attis's corduroy jacket was unsuitable for the cold; he wore it for its youthful look, though the sweater beneath was not a style a younger man would choose. He walked with his hands in his pockets; they were warmer there, and kept the envelope he had taken from Santos's study secure. Down below, the village came into view: the whitewashed houses turned drab over the winter, the narrow lanes running between them, the dome of a grandiose church. Parts of the hillside had been cleared of trees to become smallholdings, marked out by flimsy fences of chicken-wire and planks, of corrugated iron and rusted stakes, and in places by part-collapsed walls. Tethered goats nibbled at piles of hay; hens pecked around their hooves for seeds fallen from the dried grasses.

The road wound in its descent – a bend to the north, a curve to the south – hiding the stretch below from the walker above; so it was not until Attis had covered two thirds of the distance between the poet's house and the village that he saw there was someone on the road ahead.

An old beehive had been abandoned at the roadside, and a

man was making use of it as a seat. No archetypal villager, or farmer, the man seemed out of place in this rural spot, where cashmere overcoats were beyond the means of all. His grey suit, though well cut, did not quite disguise his heaviness, and his glasses suggested a role in education or central government. Most striking of all were his shoes, so inappropriate for the season; he wore old-fashioned tennis shoes, whose white canvas was spotted with mud and marked with the wet.

The man's demeanour suggested he had been there for some time, and Attis thought he might be waiting for a late-running bus. If so, he seemed untroubled by his wait, his attention on a book open on his lap. He seemed absorbed in his reading; and yet, as Attis appeared in the road, he looked up as if he had sensed Attis's approach and watched him as he drew close, until Attis was within earshot, when the stranger gave a bright smile, and spoke.

'*Kali mera*,' he said.

'*Kali mera sas*,' replied Attis.

Attis was going to walk by; but as he drew level, the stranger closed his book, picked up the navy holdall at his feet and stood, revealing himself to be tall, though even his commanding height could not disguise the fatness of his stomach. He fell in beside Attis, matching his stride.

Startled by the stranger's adoption of his company, Attis stopped in the road, intending to let the fat man go on alone; but the fat man stopped alongside him, and before Attis could speak, himself spoke out, declaiming several lines of poetry Attis knew very well.

> '*Our glories with our passing shall not fade,*
> *But burn on like the incandescent stars*
> *Which vanish imperceptibly into dawn*
> *And yet like souls of men will never die.*'

Attis turned, and faced the fat man, who smiled.

'It's beautiful, isn't it?' he said. 'The work of the incomparable Volakis, of course. Such a marvellous poet; such a tragic and untimely death. I'm here to visit an old friend, but whilst I'm in Vrisi, I thought I'd take the opportunity to pay my respects to the poet, and see something of the place which inspired so much of his work.' He held up the book he had been reading. '*Songs from Silence*. I give copies to everyone I know. Have you read it?'

Attis gave a tight smile.

'As a matter of fact, yes,' he said. '*Kali mera sas.*'

'Before you go,' said the fat man, touching his arm, 'I wonder if you could tell me whether this is the road to Volakis's house? The climb is steep, and I'm reluctant to go on without confirmation I'm on the right track.'

'This is the road,' said Attis. 'A kilometre or so more, and you'll find the gate.'

'I'd like to take a few photographs, if I can,' said the stranger, as Attis turned away. 'Pictures always help to sell an article.'

Attis turned back to the fat man.

'An article? What article?'

'I place a few pieces, here and there, on a freelance basis.' The fat man slipped the book into the holdall. 'My specialism is the ancient poets. I'm considered something of an expert on Panyassis of Halicarnassus, though interest in him is very limited these days. But I'm a great admirer of our modern poets, too. I've published commentaries on several. Seferis, of course. And do you know any of Elytis's work?'

He raised his face to the sky, and with closed eyes, recited from memory,

> *I spoke of love, of the rose's health, of the ray*
> *That by itself goes straight to the heart,*

Of Greece that steps so surely on the sea
Greece that carries me always
*Among naked snow-crowned mountains.**

I admire Dimoula too, and Patrikios . . . But I think of all of them, Volakis had the edge. He was a great loss to our national literature. I thank you for clarifying that I haven't lost my way. I shall go on, and find the house.'

'Just a moment,' said Attis, as the fat man turned to go. 'Do you have a publisher for your piece?'

With shrewd eyes, the stranger looked at him.

'If the article is worthwhile, it will no doubt find a place in one of the academic journals.'

'Have you thought of aiming for the national press?'

The fat man laughed.

'To be blunt,' he said, 'admirer though I am of Volakis, his work and his ideas are not daily reading for the man in the street.'

'Perhaps not,' said Attis. 'But what if you had some insight into the man from one who knew him? That would be a story with mass appeal, wouldn't it? Enough appeal to tempt even the nationals.'

The fat man appeared to consider.

'Perhaps so, yes. But where would I be lucky enough to find a personal acquaintance of Volakis who would talk to me, and provide that insight? I believe the family is very private, at Volakis's request. He was not, I think, a man who sought publicity.'

'No, he wasn't. But publicity's always useful, even after a writer's death. The estate – the poet's family – always benefits from an increase in sales.'

'The family? Or the publishing business?'

---

* From *Burnished Day*, by Odysseus Elytis.

'Without the business of publishing, the world would never have seen Volakis's work,' said Attis, defensively. 'Without a publisher, a poet may be as brilliant as he likes, but his work will never be read.'

'Quite right,' said the fat man, genially. 'I meant no offence.'

'You didn't answer my question,' said Attis, 'whether you might interest a wider audience in your piece, if you'd a good source on the poet's life.'

'I should be honest and tell you that a source on the poet's death would be more appropriate to my skills. I don't wish to mislead you. I am not a professional journalist, and my interest in the arts is a sideline only. If you are looking for someone to promote Volakis's work, I, as a mere amateur, am not your man. I work as an investigator. That is where my talents lie.'

Attis's eyes lit with interest.

'Investigators come in many flavours and colours,' he said. 'Insurance investigators, tax investigators, investigators of water leaks: which of the breed are you?'

The fat man smiled.

'I investigate anything which has a bad smell about it,' he said. 'I specialise in wrongdoing, underhandedness and deceit.'

He looked into Attis's face, as if seeking something there. Attis was uncomfortable under his scrutiny and looked away.

'Fraud, then,' he said. 'Is that something you could look into?'

'Fraud, embezzlement, extortion: all manna to me,' said the fat man, cheerfully. 'Though I should warn you, my findings are not always welcomed, even by those who have sought out my services.'

Attis considered.

'I'm on my way to the village to make a phone call,' he said. 'If you come with me, I'll buy you coffee, and we can talk. I have a proposition which may interest you. They call me Attis Danas.'

He held out his hand, and the fat man shook it.

'I will listen to any proposition, though I do not guarantee to go along with it,' he said. 'Hermes Diaktoros, of Athens. The name – Hermes Messenger, in more modern parlance, as I'm sure you're aware – is my father's idea of humour. He's something of a classical scholar. And in the spirit of my name-sake, I call these' – he indicated his white tennis shoes – 'my winged sandals. You know your way about here better than I. Please, lead on.'

But despite his suggestion that Attis should go ahead, the fat man's pace on the road was surprisingly quick, and Attis found himself hurrying to keep up.

'Are you a resident of Vrisi?' asked the fat man, as they walked.

'I? No.' For a moment, Attis was silent. 'I should perhaps explain my interest in what brought you here. Santos Volakis was my client. I was his literary agent.'

'Ah.' The fat man nodded with interest. 'So tell me, what exactly does such a relationship entail?'

'Let's find somewhere warm and order coffee,' said Attis. 'Then you can tell me what you offer as an investigator, and if it seems to both of us we might do business, I'll tell you everything you need to know.'

At the edge of the village, a path of steps and stones led down between the houses, leaving the winding road to its longer route. A young girl pegged baby clothes on a line, her fingers red with cold in fingerless gloves; the fat man wished her *kali mera*, whilst Attis passed her by as if she were not there. A man hacked with a mattock at the ground of a small plot; on the doorstep of his house, his sullen wife was polishing a copper pan. The man watched as they went by and gave answer to the fat man's greeting, whilst his wife looked away, her hand still rubbing rhythmically at the pan. By an outdoor oven, a woman was splitting logs and breaking sticks, as her ugly daughter warmed her hands on the oven's flames. The woman smiled enticingly at the passing men, and showed a *tapsi* of chicken and potatoes ready for the oven when the fire burned low: bait for a suitor for the daughter, who, scowling, turned her wide-hipped body away, and wiped her nose on the cuff of her jacket sleeve.

Their path (which the fat man seemed to know, in fact, as well as Attis) began to level out, until it rounded a corner and rejoined the road. The road was wider here, and straight, crossing levelled land where in a gravelled playground, the chains of the swings were broken, and the steps to the top of a little slide were crooked. Lanes led to a school and to the church, before the road passed the village square, where the granite Santos read his wordless book.

The fat man stopped at the foot of the statue, and looked up at the poet.

'It appears the villagers take little care of Volakis's monument,' he said, grimacing at the bird-droppings on the poet's shoulders. 'Do they have no pride in their famous son? A bucket of water and a scrubbing brush would soon restore him to his intended glory. And what of the family? Have they no objections to his state?'

'I'm afraid Santos wasn't always popular in Vrisi, and taking care of his memorial isn't a task many of them would volunteer to do. As for the family, I don't know. They're rarely here to notice, I suppose.'

Behind the statue, across the square, was a pond enclosed by a low wall.

'Here it is,' said Attis, as they drew close to the water, 'the spring which gives Vrisi its name.'

95

They looked over the wall. A trickle of water ran out of the hillside to feed the pond, which drained, at its far end, into a stream which fell steeply down the hillside and was lost between the village's lower houses. At the water's edge, ducks preened on opaque remnants of slow-melting ice.

'Most picturesque,' said the fat man, politely.

'Santos told me that the spring used to be sacred to some god, though which one, I don't remember. There used to be swans here, a nesting pair, but I see they're not here now.'

'Swans are the most beautiful of birds, much admired since ancient times,' said the fat man. 'You'll no doubt know the myth in which Zeus himself chose its form to pursue the unwilling Leda, and that after their copulation, Leda is said to have given birth to an egg. In a less common version of the story, the goddess Nemesis was the object of Zeus's lust.'

'Nemesis?' The name raised Attis's interest, but the fat man seemed not to notice, and carried on.

'When Nemesis became a goose to fly away from him, Zeus turned himself into a swan to follow her. They say it was my namesake Hermes who craftily hid the egg – of hyacinth blue – between Leda's thighs. Other fragments suggest Leda and Nemesis are one and the same, or that Nemesis herself left her egg for Leda to find. The old stories change and grow, until none of us can tell which is the original. Pythagoras, of course, held the view that swans embodied the souls of the great poets when they died. Do you think Volakis has become a swan?'

'I doubt it,' said Attis. 'If he were a swan, he'd be here, at Vrisi's spring. The *kafenion* is over here. Shall we?'

The *kafenion* was of unfinished, amateur construction, with the air of a project abandoned long ago. The side entrance had no door, but was boarded over with nailed-on plywood, and the side walls were unrendered, exposing bricks which were not laid level and the mortar which had oozed between them. In warmer weather, the picture window of its frontage would open to give access to the terrace; but today, the outside tables were empty, the chairs tilted forward to rest their backs on the table edges, and the window was open just wide enough to admit an average man. Attis passed through comfortably, whilst the fat man avoided the indignity of a squeeze by sliding the window back several inches further, and once inside, slid it back into position to keep out the cold.

Inside, the smoke of many cigarettes clouded the air. Men dressed for deepest winter – in flannel shirts and quilted jackets, with fur hats and leather gauntlets on their laps – talked over coffee and each other, their conversation travelling between all tables. A stinking paraffin stove gave off fumes but little heat; the window ran with condensation, in which someone had rubbed a viewing hole so the men could keep an eye on those going by – their own wives, or someone else's.

At the counter, the patron – a man with the ruby flush of high blood pressure, and a knitted hat pulled down over his ears – stood behind bottles of ouzo, cheap whisky and domestic brandy; one by one, he picked duck eggs from a wire basket, and wiped mud from their pale-blue shells with a wet rag.

Attis made for a table by the payphone, whose directory was pencilled on the wall: dozens of numbers and names, some arranged in a ladder as a list, most random notes in many hands, with the pencil that had written them dangling from the phone dial, tied with string to the finger-hole for zero.

'What'll you have?' asked Attis, as the fat man sat down.

'Greek coffee, no sugar,' said the fat man. 'Thank you.'

Attis called out their order to the patron.

'Will you excuse me one moment?' he asked the fat man. 'I have to make a phone call.'

'Of course.'

Attis turned his back, and put his shoulder to the wall so

that both the phone and the number he was dialling were out of the fat man's view.

The conversation around them had died away, as the village men indulged their interest in the strangers. The fat man smiled cordially around their tables, and wished them *kali mera*; they met his friendliness with silence, and averted faces.

Attis deposited coins in the payphone slot, and began to dial a number from memory. Unseen by Attis, the fat man took a out leather-bound notebook, and pulled a little pencil from its spine, and as Attis dialled – enough digits to make his call long-distance – the fat man seemed to think, then wrote in careful print on one of the notebook's lined pages. When Attis finished dialling, the fat man replaced the pencil in the notebook's spine, and put the book away.

Attis waited for his call to be connected. The men around them fell back into conversation, talking of snow, and of impassable roads to the north. When Attis's call was answered, the line, it seemed, was bad; he raised his voice to speak, and blocked his free ear with a finger to hear what was being said.

'Yorgas! It's me, Attis. How are you, *pedi mou*, how are you . . . ? Cold, very cold, we'll be snowed in if I don't get out today . . . Listen, I want you to be the first to know. I've found something very special at the house . . .' He laughed. 'Yes, very good news, very good . . . I think you'll be very pleased . . . I don't know. Here, let me have a look . . .'

Holding the receiver between chin and shoulder, he reached inside his jacket for the envelope from Santos's study. With a glance around the room – where the coffee drinkers were discussing the council's incompetence, and the fat man seemed interested in the patron's coffee-making – he lifted the envelope's flap and half-withdrew several folded sheets, typewritten but with the ink-marks of hand corrections. He slipped the envelope back into his pocket.

'I don't know yet,' he said, into the phone. 'I haven't had chance to look. Under the circumstances, it's tricky. My best guess is twenty, twenty-four. And a brilliant title – *The Odes to Nemesis*. Listen, with luck I'll be back in town by nightfall. Why don't you meet me at Georgio's, and we'll take a look together, see what we've got . . . 9 o'clock is fine . . . Of course. My regards to your good lady . . . We'll speak later.'

He hung up the phone, and remained for a moment leaning against the wall. As he sat down opposite the fat man, he composed his face to disguise a self-satisfied smile.

'So,' he said, 'now we can get down to business.' He looked around at their company, aware that, in spite of seeming absorbed in their own banter, the village men would eavesdrop if they could. 'Where should we start?'

'You were going to tell me . . .' began the fat man; but the patron was approaching with a tray. The fat man stopped speaking, and he and Attis sat silent as the patron placed coffee and glasses of water before them. When the patron moved away, the fat man, too, seemed conscious of others' interest in their talk. When he spoke again, he kept his voice low.

'You were going to explain to me the nature of your relationship with Santos Volakis,' he said. 'I don't understand what is involved in being his literary agent.'

Attis sipped at his coffee, and replaced the cup on its saucer.

'In principle, it's simple,' he said. 'I'm a businessman; Santos was an artist, a creative. I handled his business affairs – dealing with publishers, in the main, often his publicity too, requests for public appearances, commissions, interviews. My job was to sell his work, and get it out to the widest possible audience. Which was not always easy, I have to say; the market for poetry has always been quite limited. My fee was 15 per cent of his earnings, which was not, believe me, a great amount for the effort I put in.'

'And had you worked together a long time?'

'I was the only agent he ever had; his first, and his last. I'm one of the best in the business, *Kyrie* Diaktoros, though I say it myself; the solidity of my reputation gives the stamp of quality to my clients. Santos never had reason to go anywhere else.'

'And was that the extent of your relationship – a professional one?'

Attis did not answer immediately, but took another sip of his coffee. Allowing him time to consider his response, the fat man reached into the pocket of his overcoat, and took out matches and a pack of cigarettes – an old-fashioned box, whose lift-up lid bore the head of a 1940s starlet. He slid the cover from the matchbox; but instead of taking out a match, he looked inside, then tipped from it into the palm of his hand an object of yellowing ivory.

'I don't wish to interrupt your thoughts,' he said, 'but I had quite forgotten I had brought this with me. It's a novelty which is, in my experience, unique. I acquired it very recently in Crete, as a gift from an elderly gentleman who wanted it protected from his daughter's zealous house clearance once he is gone.' He held up the object between his thumb and fingertip. Small, and discoloured with age, it was plainly the tooth of some creature, serrated on its edge and pointed like a fang.

Attis looked at the object with little interest at first; but recognising the uniqueness of its features, he leaned forward to inspect it more closely.

'What in heaven and earth is it?' he asked.

'Well,' said the fat man, offering the object to Attis, 'I couldn't vouch for its authenticity; but I am told it is that great rarity, a hen's tooth.'

Attis was about to take the object, but withdrew his hand.

'A hen's tooth?' he asked. 'How could it possibly be a hen's tooth?'

The fat man smiled, and dropped the ivory back into the matchbox. He held out his cigarettes to Attis, who shook his head to decline; choosing one for himself, he produced a slim, gold lighter, knocked the tip of his cigarette on the table, and lit it.

'I must assume some prank or practical joke played on the old man,' he said. 'But even so, it's an intriguing object, and a clever forgery, if forgery it is. I shall treasure it regardless, as its previous owner did, because it reminds me of the greatest rarity in my profession: willingness to part with the truth. Here.' He closed the matchbox, and placed it before him on the table. 'Let us leave it here between us, as a reminder that hens' teeth – and truthfulness – may both be found, if one searches long enough.' He drew again on his cigarette. 'So. We have wandered off the track. You were telling me, I think, about your relationship with Santos.'

'It was, at first, very formal and businesslike,' said Attis. 'He came to me as a young man, an innocent, naive.' He gave a small smile, as if the memory amused him. 'He had already had his first volume of poetry published, without the benefit of an agent to help him through the minefield of contracts. He felt – quite rightly – he hadn't got himself a very good deal, and so he came to me and asked me to sell his second collection. Which I agreed to, of course; the quality of his work was unmistakable. I sold it to the same publisher who had his first poems, but on much better terms. We started small, a few hundred copies; but sales have grown, from there.'

'A few hundred? It seems a very modest quantity.'

'A common enough beginning, especially for a poet. And his work was well received; the critics liked it, and a few academics. I used my contacts, and word got round in the right circles; the book went to reprint very quickly. Santos was impressed, and we stuck together, after that.' The patron was carrying tumblers of spirits to a nearby table; Attis raised a finger and caught his eye. 'Will you have another coffee?' he asked the fat man. 'Or will you join me in something stronger, to take off the morning's chill?'

'A Metaxa, then, if you're having one. Was Santos happy with his modest success?'

Attis gave their order to the patron, and waited whilst the empty cups were cleared and the fat man's ashtray was replaced with a clean one. When the patron left them, Attis shook his head.

'No, he wasn't happy,' he said. 'Not in the end. He became more and more dissatisfied.'

'And what about his family? Did he not have a wife? Was she content to live a life of poverty whilst her husband served his muse?'

'He was no longer married. His wife left him, some years ago. I imagine Santos was a hard man to live with. He could be arrogant, at times, and temperamental, often. And if you're going to be investigating any part of his life, I must tell you – I would say in confidence, but the facts are common knowledge, in certain quarters – he had something of a reputation as a womaniser. They say, don't they, that the quiet ones are the worst? Well, women were drawn to Santos – they loved that romantic image of the brow-furrowed, brooding artist – and he saw no reason to resist. He'd look into their eyes, and whisper a few well-chosen lines of poetry – his own or someone else's, they didn't know, or care – and make another easy conquest. And yet he loved his wife. I believe he thought she would tolerate a few short-lived infidelities for the privilege of being married to the nation's greatest living poet, but she didn't see it that way. She put up with him wandering for a while, then ran off with one of his fellow poets – a man with half Santos's talent, but less inclination to reap the more dubious benefits of literary success. I believe she's in America with him now. She and Santos had a daughter, Leda, who has been raised to a large degree by his sister, Frona. Frona's done a marvellous job with Leda. Frona, too, is divorced.'

'Well, well,' said the fat man, knocking the ash from his cigarette. 'A family of partings. Did his divorce not affect his work?'

The patron brought their tumblers of Metaxa. Attis raised his glass to the fat man.

'*Yammas*,' he said, and drank. 'His divorce did affect his work, yes, but perhaps not in the way you'd think. You'll think me cynical – probably I am – but the loss of her was the making of him as a poet. His work after she left him has a poignancy, an ethereal quality not found in his earlier poems. The best work comes from a suffering pen; that is the nature of art.'

Over the rim of his glass, the fat man regarded him.

'That seems very cold,' he said, 'to wish suffering on your clients to improve their poetry, or prose.'

'I don't wish anyone suffering. All I'm saying is, in my experience, pain makes a good artist great. And is it not the function of art to express the human condition?'

'So you may barter the human condition for cash?'

Attis gave a tight smile.

'You're hard on me, *kyrie*. As I said, I didn't bring Santos's misfortune on him; he needed no help from me there. I merely made the point that, having suffered the misfortune, his work was immeasurably improved. He had in any case a great talent; but he was a gifted man who even to early middle age – he was forty when we lost him – had never known financial success. He struggled for money, always, because he was dedicated to his art. He wasn't modest about his talent; he knew he had it; he was proud of it, and carried himself accordingly.

That didn't always make him popular. These are country folk, as you can see; they're not ones for poetry when there's work to be done. They value hard labour, and Santos put himself above that. They mocked him for it, pulled his leg, and that hurt him. His art made him poor; he would have done better, he used to say, as a farmer, and he was right. I told him time and time again that such is the way of the world, and he knew what I said was true – that the great poets are only great when they are dead.'

The fat man raised his eyebrows, and stubbed out his cigarette.

'So how did he die?' he asked.

Attis shook his head.

'Such a stupid thing. He choked on an olive. His death was mundane and unglamorous; but, let me tell you, as a plan to advance his career, it was a masterstroke. With that sorry death, *voilà* – he was famous. His work began to sell, and sell, and sell, reprint after reprint. He would have been a wealthy man, if he were with us now.'

'But he's made you wealthy?'

'I've done well enough. His family is still waiting, though, to see the benefit.'

He drank again; the fat man looked quizzical.

'Such a boost in sales hasn't made them money? How could it not?'

'There was a clause in Santos's will. No money was to be paid from his estate until his bones – as he so poetically put it – had seen the light of day. We assumed that to mean following his exhumation, and we expected his bones to see daylight yesterday. Unfortunately, that didn't happen. Let me be honest again – if you're worth your fee, you'd find out for yourself, anyway – that clause affects me, too. As far as ongoing earnings are concerned, I have no financial interest in the first book, as he agreed that contract before he and I met. The royalties on his other work are paid direct to me. I take my cut, and Frona and Leda's share – by far the greater share, I have to say – goes into the estate's account, which remains frozen. But, though my share of the royalties is unaffected by the will, he did leave me a legacy, a one-off payment, which I've not yet received.' He glanced at his watch. 'I'm pressed for time. I have an appointment back in the city, and they're forecasting more snow. You should think about leaving yourself, unless you want to spend the week in Vrisi.'

'Well,' said the fat man, 'if our time is short, perhaps you should use it to explain to me what exactly you want me to do, if you wish to use my services. If you're wondering if I am capable of doing the job, I can provide references, of course. But I feel you are someone who prefers to make up his own mind, rather than relying on the opinions of others. If you feel you can trust me, set me your task. If not, we'll shake hands, and I shall leave you.'

He reached out, picked up the matchbox containing the strange piece of ivory, and slipped it in his pocket with his cigarettes and lighter as if preparing to leave.

'I'll give you the job,' said Attis, draining the last of his brandy. 'But if I hire you, I must tell you things I don't want anyone to overhear. Would you mind – though I know it's cold – stepping outside?'

'Gladly,' said the fat man, draining his own glass.

Attis signalled to the patron and laid money on the table to cover the bill. As he put away his wallet, the brown envelope showed in his pocket.

'As far as my fee goes, by the way,' said the fat man, as he stood up, 'I use an unconventional scale of charges. The more interesting the mystery, the less I charge, so if it really taxes me, I'll solve it for no payment. A more mundane problem would be poor use of my time and talents, and so the fee might be substantial. Do you agree to my terms?'

'I'll agree to anything,' said Attis, 'as long as it clears up this affair.'

Outside, the sky had lost any shade of blue, and was darkening, minute by minute, to stormy grey.

'I'll make it quick,' said Attis. 'Yesterday was the fourth anniversary of Santos's interment, and so his exhumation. The event was happily not well attended – in this cold weather, even the most interfering and ghoulish prefer their firesides to the cemetery. Still, there were more than enough witnesses to provide an embarrassment. It'll be difficult to contain such sensational gossip, but I've enlisted the church's help in that direction.'

'Were the bones not clean, then?' asked the fat man. 'I know how superstition persists, in these rural communities, on the correlation between the whiteness of a man's bones and the purity of his soul.'

'Worse,' said Attis, rubbing his chin as he considered whether to go on. 'Far worse. Listen. Before I speak, I must have your absolute assurance of discretion.'

'It is my nature to be discreet. You may rely on that.'

Attis shrugged.

'I have anyway no choice but to tell you, because you have to know. Whether the bones were white or not is of no relevance. They were not Santos's bones.'

'How can you be sure?'

'Because . . .' Attis looked anxiously around, concerned even in the open at the possibility of being overheard. 'They were clearly the bones of a pig.'

The fat man's face showed his apparent surprise.

'A pig? How should a pig's bones be in a poet's coffin?'

'That, my friend, is for you to tell me. But my guess is, they were put there by someone who wishes to keep Santos's heirs from his money. Yesterday should have been a pay day they've looked forward to for years. So Frona and I have come to a decision – rightly or wrongly – to cover up the swap, and let the family claim what's theirs regardless. But it's essential we find out who's played this cruel and despicable trick. If word gets out, Santos's reputation will be damaged, and that will affect sales.'

'And if the lawyers who drew up the will find out its terms have not been met, what will happen then?'

'No doubt they will contact the bank, and the accounts will remain frozen.'

'And the family will be short of a good deal of cash.'

'Yes. I'm ready to help them, because it's so unfair.'

'Not because you look forward to your own cut?'

'That too, of course. But I'm very fond of Frona. I don't like to see her struggle when there's money in the bank.'

'Nonetheless, the terms of the poet's will have legal standing. I should like to see this document.'

'I have a copy at the house. You're welcome to it, if you'd like.'

'Thank you. The problem is altogether intriguing, yet it is difficult to know where to start. If I stay here in Vrisi, I shall be conspicuous; yet the solution to the problem must be here, in part at least. Someone, as you say, has swapped Santos's bones; are you thinking that to make the swap, they must have come to Vrisi?'

'I assume so, yes.'

'Assumptions are always dangerous,' said the fat man. 'I have no dealings with them. Here is my suggestion. I shall take on your mystery, but I think it would be better to delay a while, until the incident is forgotten and no connection made between it, and me. In the meantime, if there are developments, you may summon me through the newspapers; put a notice in the personal column of the *Ethnos*, and I shall see it. I may not be free to come immediately, but rest assured, I shall get here as soon as I'm able.'

'Here, take my card,' said Attis. 'If you have questions, please ring me.'

The men shook hands; but as Attis was walking away, the fat man called him back.

'One more question, an important one,' he said. 'If Santos's bones weren't in his grave, where might they be?'

'I've no idea,' said Attis. 'That's the question that troubles Frona most of all.'

'It troubles her, but it doesn't trouble you?'

'You're putting words in my mouth,' said Attis. 'I didn't say it didn't trouble me. And rather than asking me where they are, perhaps, with respect, you should earn your fee, and find them.' He hesitated. 'There's something I'm reluctant to part with, but which may be of help to you. I must confess, I've no business having it in my possession at all. I found it at the house. If I give it to you, will you give me your word you'll return it to me as soon as possible, so I can replace it?'

'Of course.'

Attis reached into a pocket, and handed over the small diary from Santos's desk; as he did so, the fat man glimpsed again the brown envelope produced during Attis's phone call.

The fat man produced the diary, and glanced through the pages.

'There's very little to go on,' he said. 'What do you make of these initials, and these phone numbers?'

'I'm afraid they may relate to Santos's – liaisons.'

'And there's almost nothing at all after the date of his death.'

'Isn't that what you'd expect?' asked Attis.

The fat man smiled.

'It is indeed,' he said. 'Under the circumstances, I would expect no different.'

The fat man went back inside the *kafenion*. At the counter, the patron was polishing glasses.

'I wonder,' said the fat man, 'if you might be able to give me breakfast?'

'There're eggs,' said the patron. 'You'd have to wait a little while for bread. My daughter's not gone yet to the baker's.'

'I don't mind a short wait,' said the fat man, 'but the weather is deteriorating, and if I don't leave the village soon, I may be here much longer than I intended.'

'Take a seat,' said the patron. 'I'll send her now.'

The fat man returned to the table he and Attis had left. Laying his holdall on a chair, he stood at the payphone and scanned the numbers pencilled on the wall. Finding the one he needed, he pressed a coin into the slot, and dialled the number.

'Taxi?' asked the fat man, when the call was answered. 'I need your services. There is a document which needs collecting from the Volakis property. Then I would be obliged if you could pick me up at the *kafenion*, on the hour.'

With the pick-up arranged, he replaced the receiver and wrote the taxi's number in his notebook. He drank another coffee with his breakfast: an omelette of duck eggs, bright yellow and well seasoned, filled with buttery and melting *kasseri* cheese and a handful of wilted spinach; on the side were curling slices of air-dried ham, burgundy-dark and lined with soft, white fat. The fat man ate with relish, mopping up the olive oil the eggs had been cooked in with bread fresh from a wood-oven, and for dessert, he enjoyed a piece of *galakto-bouriko* – milk pie – cut from the baker's tray: crisp filo filled with milky semolina custard, which oozed pleasingly between the pastry sheets when he cut it with his fork.

With a fingertip, he picked up the last crumb of syrupy filo from his plate, and finished the water in his glass. Glancing at his watch, he approached the counter to pay his bill.

'You'd better go, if you're going,' said the patron as he handed the fat man his change. 'There's lively weather coming. There'll be snow by afternoon.'

'I hope I haven't left it too late,' said the fat man. 'I felt I must do justice to your excellent food, and to the skills of the baker who made the *galaktobouriko*.'

The patron smiled.

'Thank you,' he said. 'I like to cook, and the baker is my eldest brother; he took the business on after my father. Simple food, well cooked; in our family, it's a code we live by.'

'You are to be congratulated,' said the fat man. 'I shall be back here, before long; be assured you shall have my custom again then.'

'It'll be my pleasure.' The patron offered his hand, and the fat man took it. 'I'm always happy to cook for someone who appreciates it. Maybe I'll see if we can find something a bit special, when you're back. You have business here, then, do you?'

'My business takes me to many places, and this is only one port of call. I shall have covered a lot more ground, more than likely, before we meet again.'

'Greek coffee, no sugar,' said the patron, with a wink. 'I'll remember how you take it.'

Outside, a silver car drew up, a 'For Hire' sign unlit on its roof. The driver gave two short blasts on the horn.

'*Kalo taxidi!*' called the patron, wishing the fat man a good journey as he left. His other customers lapsed into silence, until the fat man closed the *kafenion* door behind him; then their earnest discussion of his business in Vrisi began.

The taxi's paintwork was clean, but there was rust on the sills and wheel arches, and one of the hub caps was tied on with string. The fat man opened the rear door, but as he was about to climb in, the driver stopped him.

'Sit here, my friend, sit up front with me,' he said, and so the fat man closed the rear door and climbed into the passenger seat, placing his holdall between his feet on a piece of well-swept Persian carpet.

The taxi's interior was warmed to an exceptional degree, the fan blasting out hot air as the diesel engine ran on. The red vinyl of the rear seats was covered with hand-woven blankets, and on the parcel shelf was a bouquet of peach-coloured plastic roses; the over-heated air was potently sweetened with freshener sprayed from a can. A clean-bladed shovel lay length-wise across the seats, along with a flask, a package of food and a fur hat.

The driver held out his hand. He was a once handsome man with a long, grey ponytail and a carefully trimmed goatee; he wore blue jeans and a quilted jacket in burnt orange, and on his hands were a rally driver's gloves, with circles cut in patterns from the tan leather.

'Hassan,' he said, as the fat man shook his hand. 'We're travelling companions, and so we should be friends. Where're we going together?'

The fat man asked to be driven to a town with a station, and Hassan for a moment looked doubtful.

'With the weather coming, that might be tricky,' he said. 'Still. I enjoy a little adventure. Let's go.'

He put the car in gear, and revved the engine hard so the wheels span on the road, until the car leaped forward with the back end snaking as they moved off.

'I am Hermes Diaktoros,' said the fat man, gripping the arm-rest of the door as they took a corner too fast. 'From Athens. But you, from your name and accent, are not from here, I think.'

'Not I,' said Hassan, as the car passed the last houses in the village. Rounding a blind bend, Hassan swerved to avoid a black-clad woman, and the fat man briefly closed his eyes as a collision with a wrought-iron fence seemed inescapable. Hassan laughed, and gave the fat man a nudge. 'Nervous passenger, eh? You're safe with me, friend, perfectly safe. Ask anyone who knows me, they'll all tell you the same: I've never had an accident, in all my years of driving. And this weather threatening doesn't trouble me. I was raised in Turkish mountains, real mountains, with real winters. You Greeks know nothing about winter! To see a real winter, you have to go to Turkey.'

They began to climb, and the car approached the first of the hairpin bends which took the road out of the village and up the mountainside. Under the overhanging pine trees, the morning seemed dark as evening.

'Is there no danger of ice?' asked the fat man, as they approached a bend which overlooked a precipitous drop.

'Not cold enough for ice,' said Hassan. 'It wants a few degrees colder yet, before we need to trouble ourselves about ice.' He changed down a gear, and took the bend at speed; there was a slight twitch on the back end as the rear wheels lost traction. 'I wanted to drive professionally, in my youth, but that's an expensive hobby. My wife wouldn't put up with the expense.'

'Is your wife a Turk also?'

'My wife is a Greek. We aren't together, now.'

'I'm sorry.'

'I'm sorry too. She fell for the sweet words of another man, and put the cuckold's horns on me. My fault; there's no woman on this earth who can be trusted. I didn't watch her close enough, and I paid the price.'

Hassan fell silent. They passed the shrine at the chapel of St Fanourios, though too fast to make out the skulls; neither Hassan nor the fat man made crosses as they went by. Then Hassan found a smile, and turned to the fat man; the fat man would have preferred him to keep his eyes on the road.

'So what was your business, in the village?' asked Hassan. 'We don't get many visitors, this time of year.'

'I was in the area, and wanted to see the birthplace of your poet,' said the fat man. 'His work is wonderful, inspiring. Have you read him?'

'No.'

'Did you know him?'

'I knew him, yes,' said Hassan, shortly. 'Why do you waste your time on him? Poet, and *poustis*, the two are one and the same. He was all posing and sensitivity, never knew a day's work in his life. But you remind me, speaking of him . . .' He lowered the sun-visor over his windscreen and took down an envelope, which he handed to the fat man. 'They gave me that for you, at his house. Anyway, I'm not one for literature, though if I were, I'd stick to the Turkish poets. The world's best poets are Turks. Fuzuli, for example: you must have read Fuzuli, if you're a poetry-loving man.'

The fat man tucked the envelope into his holdall.

'No, I'm afraid I haven't. I have travelled a little in Turkey, but I know shamefully little of its culture. You yourself seem such a patriotic man – what persuaded you to come from Turkey to a little spot like Vrisi?'

'My wife,' he said. 'I came for love. I was in the merchant navy for a while; we met when the ship I was with put into Nafplio. She was working in a *kafenion* there, helping out some relative. One thing led to another, as things do. I stay now to see my kids. But I shall go back home, where I belong, some day.'

'There's no hope of a reconciliation?'

'That's something you must ask her.'

The taxi driver became melancholy, and thoughtful. They drove on in silence for a while, the fat man always gripping the arm-rest of his door.

'I had an excellent meal this morning, in the *kafenion*,' he said, at last. 'The patron there is a good cook, and his brother the baker likewise.'

'You're right there,' said Hassan. 'You should try his *mezedes*. Of course the Greeks can't compete with Turkish cooking – all Greek cooking is adapted from Turkish anyway – but his *mezedes* are good, by Greek standards. Especially tasty with a glass of ouzo, I'm told, though I myself don't drink. If you come back to Vrisi, we'll go there together and eat *mezedes*.'

'I would like that,' said the fat man.

'And then I'll make you some Turkish specialities, give you some real food. You'll think you've died and gone to heaven.'

The fat man smiled.

'That would be excellent, too,' he said.

The road had reached its apex, and they began their descent on the mountain's far side. With the downhill gradient, Hassan's speed increased.

'We'll stay ahead of this weather easily now,' he said; and changing up to the highest gear, he took his foot off the brake, and allowed the taxi to pick up more speed still.

Not wishing to give offence, the fat man forced his eyes to remain open; and to take his mind off the danger he saw in the roadside chasms, he hummed himself a tune: the melody was Hatzidakis's famous *Swans*.

Ten

There was trouble with the engines, and the island's ferry was severely delayed; she docked in Seftos harbour three hours after her scheduled time, as night was closing in and the lights along the quay were coming on.

The passengers were few. Strong winds had been forecast for the crossing, and the journey had been rough; the women had made dramas of their seasickness, groaning and puking into waxed-paper bowls, whilst the indifferent men smoked and played cards, drinking coffee from cups which slid across the table tops as the boat rolled.

The hermit was amongst the first to disembark. The evening was damp, with lamplight reflected in broad pools of rain-water. Against the harbour wall the sea was choppy, rocking the moored boats which tugged at their anchor-lines. Fragments of old tunes squeezed from an accordion drifted from the *kafenion*; behind its condensation-fogged windows, inebriated men laughed loud.

The hound tied to the trestle-table outside the general store sniffed the air, raised his head and whined. As the hermit approached, the dog leaped to his feet and strained in a frenzy towards him, springing from the ground in his excitement.

The hermit smiled, and rubbed the dog's head vigorously. He let himself be pawed and licked, until the dog was calm. Leaving both his haversack and the dog at the shop door (where the dog whimpered his distress in fear of losing him again), he made his way inside, between the sacks of rice and lentils.

The shopkeeper sat on his stool behind the counter, a bottle of *tsipouro* at his elbow, a measure in a glass close to hand. A dim bulb cast shadows on shelves of chocolate bars and tinned squid, on shaving cream and boxes of incense. The cheese fridge hummed; the despondent linnet hid its head under its wing. On the radio, a young man sang of homesickness, of missing his dear mother and the island of his birth.

'*Kali spera*,' said the hermit to the shopkeeper.

The shopkeeper was eating roasted peanuts. He looked up from the shell he was cracking and at his customer, struggling to put a name to the face.

'*Mori!*' he said, at last, dropping the peanuts back on to their plate. 'It's you, our hermit! *Kalos tou, kalos tou!* Well, you've certainly smartened yourself up on your travels! Have you been at the barber's all this time? No offence, friend, no offence. And new clothes too: *kalo risiko, kalo risiko*. Did you come in on the ferry?'

'I did, and it was hours late,' said the hermit. 'Why do they publish a timetable at all?'

'It'd be the engines, was it?' asked the shopkeeper. 'She's an old vessel. It's a miracle they keep her afloat, especially in such weather.'

'I believe it was the engines, yes, but that's irrelevant. It's late, and it'll be dark, now, before I get across, so I'll take what I need, and be gone. The dog's in good health, by the way. Thank you for taking care of him. I'm obliged to you.'

The grocer waved his hand.

'Not at all,' he said. 'My kids got quite fond of him. They've given him a few treats, so he hasn't gone short, though he eats the same as two grown men. It's a mystery to me how you afford to feed him.'

'He feeds himself, where he can hunt,' said the hermit, finding his wallet. 'He catches rabbits. He's fast, and they're stupid. I remember I promised you something for his good care.'

He handed over two banknotes; the shopkeeper pocketed them, and held up the bottle of *tsipouro*, but the hermit shook his head.

'Will you cut me some cheese?' he asked. 'And I'll take some ham.'

The shopkeeper moved to the fridge, and loaded a block of smoked cheese on to the slicer. As he cut, he glanced covertly at the hermit, who was selecting ground coffee and canned milk from the shelves.

'You been far, then?' asked the shopkeeper, with apparent disinterest, as he wrapped the sliced cheese in waxed paper.

'A fair way,' answered the hermit. 'I'll take a kilo of sugar, whilst I'm here.'

'Family, was it?' asked the shopkeeper, fastening the parcel with an elastic band.

The hermit turned from the shelves.

'Business,' he said. 'Have you heard the forecast?'

The shopkeeper sucked in his breath, and as he replaced the cheese with a leg of ham, he shook his head.

'Not good, not good at all,' he said. 'They say there's been more snow, to the north. No danger to us, this far south, thanks be to God. But they say there'll be storms blowing through, the next couple of days. You'll have to wait it out, hermit; you'll have to stay here with us, until it passes.'

'I'll do all right,' said the hermit, placing a tin of pears by the cash register. 'I need batteries – big ones, for a torch – and I'll take a can of butane for the stove.'

The shopkeeper stopped the slicer, and looked with incredulity at the hermit.

'Are you mad, friend?' he asked. 'You can't be thinking of going over there, tonight? Take a bed at the taverna, relax, have a drink or two, and go tomorrow, in daylight at least.'

'I know my way well enough,' said the hermit, 'and you say it'll be worse tomorrow. So. What do I owe you?'

'Well, don't expect me to come after you when you're sinking,' said the shopkeeper. He took a pencil from behind his ear, and on the back of a supplier's invoice began to list the hermit's purchases, adding a price he thought appropriate after each item. 'A night crossing in this weather wants a lot of care, and – no offence, friend, no offence – your experience is not what it might be. Better sailors than you have come to grief on a sea like this. She's like a woman – respect her moods, or take the consequences. Stay here tonight, I tell you. You'd be a fool to go.'

'The risk is my own,' said the hermit. 'If you don't see me for a while, assume the trip didn't go well, and look for me on the seabed.'

The shopkeeper shrugged.

'Two thousand nine, then,' he said. 'Don't say I didn't warn you. Call it two eight, for cash.'

The hermit handed over three thousand-drachma notes.

'Keep it,' he said. 'I'll take a tin of something, for the dog.'

'There's corned beef,' said the shopkeeper. 'Or Spam. That animal likes Spam.' He gave the hermit a tin from the shelf behind him. 'I didn't keep your newspapers, by the way. I thought you'd have no trouble finding newspapers, wherever you were. I'll keep one back for you again, from tomorrow.'

The hermit gathered up his purchases.

'I mean it, about taking care,' said the shopkeeper. 'It's a bad night to be out there, in your small boat. What's your hurry, that you must get back tonight? I'll tell you what, I'll get the wife to mind the store, and I'll keep you company. We'll go and have a drink together, you and I. What do you say?'

'I appreciate your concern,' said the hermit. 'But I've been away much longer than I intended, and I feel the need to return to my own quiet corner. I get tired of the world's ways, and its people.'

'Don't we all, my friend?' said the shopkeeper, taking a drink of his *tsipouro*. 'Don't we all?'

Outside, the hermit whistled his dog to heel, and heaved his haversack on to his back. At a berth along the quayside, he crouched to pull his boat in close; the dog jumped aboard, and padded, tail wagging, to the stern. The boisterous water rose and fell, its wave peaks splashing the roadway as they hit the harbour wall. Beyond the beacon at the harbour's end, the sea was dark.

By the light of a streetlamp, the hermit stepped into the boat, and stashed his small cargo under the seats, covering it with an oil-stained tarpaulin. He lifted the bench cover, and changed from his new shoes into a worn pair of boots.

In the deserted harbour, his engine sounded loud. With the navigation lights glowing red and green, he hauled in the anchor, cast off the mooring rope and headed out to sea.

Beyond the headland, where no land provided shelter and the wind could build its strength, the roughness of the sea was intimidating. He should, he knew, go back; yet the prospect of capsizing and going down seemed preferable to the shop-keeper's smug self-righteousness if he should return.

He gripped the tiller tight beneath his arm, and trained a torch-beam on the shoreline to gauge his distances; but the torch-beam found only water, and with no choice but to sail on blind, he gambled as he steered by wits and senses.

He wore no watch, and lost all track of time. The dark pressed in on all sides: ahead, behind, to port and starboard, there was no sign of lights, or land. The first wisps of panic entered his mind; the dog, becoming troubled, left his accustomed station at the prow, and lay down on his master's feet.

Then, the hermit began to doubt that he was alone.

A memory possessed him – a room, a bed, a bottle – and his sense grew, that the man who had lain in that bed was here, now, in the boat. Afraid to look, and as afraid not to know, he flashed the torch beam to the prow.

No one was there.

The dog whined. The hermit kept the torch trained on the prow, as if its light could keep his fears at bay; and with his free hand, he dug deep into his pocket for the scrap of paper he had put there.

The paper was folded in four, and he didn't trouble to read it. Wanting neither the paper nor the memory, he let the paper go, and in an instant it was carried away, lost in the dark. But the memory was different. Darkness was its friend, and helped it put down roots; and once the roots were strong, the memory began its virulent growth.

Death

Eleven

Winter had not finished with Vrisi. As the fat man sped away with Hassan, a fresh snowfall began – weighty flakes, at first, which fell grey through the air but became, on landing, white, and brightened the patches of gritty snow remaining from the last fall. Then, as the temperature dropped, the snow became a mist icy and fine as dust, and seemingly harmless; but this white powder blew into every cranny, and crept in under the doors, blowing off the roofs in ash-like clouds which flew wet in the faces of those passing, and quickly formed soft drifts of uncertain depths.

For three days, snow fell. Trodden down on house paths and steps, it froze into perilous ice, clear yet distorting as the glass in old windows. The housewives scattered salt, crackling the ice as it split; they hacked at it with their broom handles, and swept the shards away. The north wind grew in strength, until even the livestock shivered; the men carried feed heads down, half-deaf under the earflaps of trappers' caps, with the cold burning their thighs through their trousers, nipping their finger-ends red through their gloves. The chickens remained in their coops, pecking at dishes of warm mash, the few eggs they laid frozen solid in their shells. Ducks slithered on the pond's new ice; there was ice again on the water butts; icicles hung long from leaking gutters, and forgotten washing froze brittle on the lines.

The people stayed indoors, close to the fires, though the snow found its way down the chimneys, hissing as it dropped on the burning logs. Wrapped in their outdoor clothes, they ate pulse soups and broths, and the women warmed their hands on honeyed tisanes. The men kept glasses by their coffee cups and used alcohol to fight off boredom, until the pressure of being at home grew too much; then they went to the *kafenion*, where more alcohol led to risky bets on hands of cards. The more they drank, the more they lost; their curses grew angrier and bluer, ringing loud through the afternoons.

The roads were slick and treacherous, and, as the snow's depth grew, impassable except on foot. For a day, they stayed that way, until the men rigged a makeshift plough to a tractor and ploughed the snow into roadside mounds, which grew higher with each day's clearance.

During the night of the third day, the wind changed, and breaks appeared in the clouds; the morning which followed brought clear skies, and the thaw at last began. Snow slid from the roofs, and as it melted, revealed the buds of a new season's growth. Vrisi's spring ran fast with melt-water, which filled the pond where the ducks dabbled and dived.

But where the snow was deep, the thaw was slow; and where the banks of ploughed snow were in shadow, they lay, slowly shrinking, for over a week.

The phone rang.

Driven to bed by boredom and the hope of warmth, Frona lay the book she was reading on the blankets, and turned the bedside clock towards her to read its face.

The hour was not late, but as she went by the closed door,

Leda's room was silent. In Santos's study, Frona answered the call.

'*Oriste?*'

No one spoke, but at the end of the line, someone was listening: Frona was sure of it.

'*Oriste?*' she said, again. 'Who is this?'

The caller held on a few moments longer, not quite silent, breathing with care, until the receiver was replaced and the line went dead.

'Who was on the phone last night?'

Frona was clearing breakfast. Leda had eaten almost nothing, but had crumbled a slice of cake on to her plate. The peel of an orange lay on the cloth, along with several uneaten segments of the fruit.

'I don't know,' said Frona. 'A wrong number. Aren't you going to eat that? Shall I ask Maria to cook you some eggs?'

'I don't want anything.'

'Leda, please eat something. You're making yourself ill.' She took a chair next to her niece and, tenderly concerned, scrutinised her face, where the symptoms of insomnia were plain. At the neck of Leda's sweater, her collarbones were unbecomingly pronounced, and her once slender wrists had become skinny. 'Listen, *kori mou*,' went on Frona. 'Listen to me. We're all upset about this business with your father. We all want to know what's happened, and where he is. He was my brother, my only brother, and it's a blade to my heart to think of his grave being desecrated in that way. But Attis has it in hand. With luck, the money will come through now, and life will be much easier for us. We'll find a nicer place, somewhere near the park, somewhere nearer your college. And we'll hire Attis's investigator to find your father's bones. I promise you, Leda, I won't rest until he's home where he belongs.' She made crosses over her breast. 'We'll bring him home, *agapi mou*. You have my word on that.'

Leda turned away her face and closed her eyes. Tears squeezed between the tight-shut lids.

'Don't,' she said. From the sleeve of her sweater, she pulled a handkerchief whose fabric was already damp from her crying.

'Come here.' Frona opened her arms, and Leda leaned into her embrace.

Frona kissed the top of Leda's head.

'I think it's time we went back to town,' she said. 'Hanging round this old mausoleum is getting us down. Your father would never want you to take so much time off college; you know how he would disapprove of that. Remember what he used to say: talent has its place, but hard work pays the bills. And you have talent, Leda. One day you'll be a lovely actress. But you need to work on your talent, not sit around moping. We must go home, and you must work, and make him proud of you. Make us all proud.'

Leda shook her head.

'I can't go,' she said. 'Not until he's found.'

'What can you do, here? Listen to me. The best thing I can do for your father is to take care of you, and that means looking after your best interests. And your best interests aren't here. They're in your life at home, with friends around you, not fretting and worrying about things we can do nothing about.'

Leda dried more tears with her handkerchief.

'How can we go when everything's gone so wrong?' she asked. 'It's all so hard on you! Everything you've done for me, I didn't know – I didn't understand, when I was younger, how difficult it was for you. And now, when it should be easier, it isn't! And I can't sleep for thinking of him, wondering what's happened. Where can he be?'

Frona stroked Leda's hair.

'We'll find him,' she said. 'Attis will see to that.'

'I don't want to hire Attis's investigator. I don't think we should have strangers in our family's business. And you rely too much on Attis. How do you know you can trust him?'

Frona frowned.

'But I do trust him. I trust him because your father trusted him.'

'Did he? Are you sure about that?'

'But our interests are the same, Leda; surely they are.'

'You mustn't trust him. Be careful what you say, and don't discuss our business with him. Why are you so certain he's not involved?'

Wearily, Frona sighed, and squeezed Leda's shoulder as she released it.

'Why should he be involved?' she asked. '*Kori mou*, you think just like your father. You're all imagination and fancy, as he was. We must trust someone, and who else do we have? We need to get out of here. I'll call Hassan, and ask if he can take us tomorrow.'

'Not so soon,' said Leda. 'I don't want to go until he's found.'

'We have to go. I can't be away much longer. I've accounts to prepare for several clients, and I can't just abandon them. We don't have your father's money yet.'

Leda said no more, but rose, and walked out of the room. As Frona picked up the orange peel from the table, she heard Leda slowly climb the stairs.

In the kitchen, she laid the plates on the drainer. Maria wasn't there. Frona lifted the lid of the saucepan on the stove, and stirred a simmering soup of beef shin and carrots.

The phone rang.

She ran to the study, and picked up the receiver.

'*Oriste?*'

No one answered.

'Speak!' insisted Frona. 'Who is this? Speak!'

But no voice spoke, though there was breathing on the line, controlled and quiet.

Intently, Frona listened, as if she might tell from the breathing whether the caller was man, or woman.

'Speak!' she demanded, again; but the caller replaced the receiver, and the line went dead.

Leda's sleep, that night, was restless, her dreams peopled with sinister figures who pursued, and then eluded her; she hurried through dense pine forests on indistinct paths, encountering time and again a tall, well-dressed man she felt she'd met, and yet could not recall, who followed her down a road she didn't know, and had no wish to travel.

The ringing phone woke her. Her room was bright with morning; the bedside clock showed after nine.

The phone rang on, and Frona – already walking to the village – was not there to answer.

The phone rang, and rang. Leda closed her eyes, determined to leave it; then the caller's persistence concerned her, and she sat up in her bed, ready to answer. As she threw off the blankets, the ringing stopped.

In slippers and robe, she went yawning to the kitchen, where she took a cup down from the shelf, and dropped a sprig of sage into the *kafebriko* to make tea. With the last match in the box, she lit the gas.

The phone rang again.

But in the study, hand over the receiver, she hesitated: the memory of her dreams made her afraid, that someone – something – malevolent was on the line, and in the cold, she shivered.

The misgiving passed, and she picked up the receiver.

'*Embros?*'

No one spoke.

Leda listened. Beneath the apparent silence, were the small sounds of someone's breathing.

'Who is this?' she asked. Still no one spoke, and, frowning, she lowered the receiver towards its cradle; but as she was about to cut the call, she heard a voice.

She put the receiver back to her ear.

'*Oriste?*' she said.

'Leda,' said the voice.

The outlying churches and chapels had been neglected during the snow; so, when the road was safely passable and held no danger of slipping to old, slow-healing bones, a widow with a pricking conscience (and the intention to ask for help with a misplaced bank book) set out to light the candles at St Fanourios.

The warmth of kinder winds was doing its work, and on the road, the snow was all but gone, except for the deepest of the plough-raised banks.

The widow intended first to light the lamp over the glass-fronted shrine of skulls, who greeted her with their macabre grins of welcome. She struck a match; and as its flame flared, a spitting piece of phosphorous flew up. To avoid it, she turned her face away, and as she did so, her eye was caught by an object in a melting snow-bank.

She thought, at first, she was mistaken. She dropped the match, and moved closer to investigate.

There was no doubt of what she had found.

She made no close examination of her discovery, but called, ashen-faced, on the saint whose service she must now neglect, and hurried, almost running, down the road, through the

129

village to the *kafenion*, from where a priest and a policeman might be called.

The men, at first, smiled behind their hands in disbelief and refused to accept her story; but when her tears began, the patron went to the phone. He dialled the number for the police, as she told them again what she had seen: a limb, the lower part of a leg, and a man's foot with the shoe still on it, his trousers soaking wet with melting snow.

Midday, and the sunshine had brought the first bees from their hives. A grey police car drew up in the yard of the poet's house; the two officers who climbed out slammed the doors, and put on the berets they pulled from their shoulder-tabs. As they approached the house door, their blouson jackets swung open to show holstered handguns.

Under a bush, a watchful cat crouched.

By daylight, the old place's many flaws were plain; the drainpipe hanging loose from the wall, the untidiness of the overgrown garden, the dirtiness of the unwashed windows, all showed the owner's neglect. The policemen took up positions on either side of the doorway, matching each other's manly stances: feet apart, hands clasped over the groin.

'What a dump,' said the younger man, a recent recruit, called for the first time to perform this duty. 'How do they live in a hole like this?'

His colleague was a veteran of the cities; he'd worked the squalid brothels and the dope dens, cleared out the dross from filthy squats, uncovered bloated corpses on the wastelands.

'If this is the worst you ever see, you'll die a happy man,' he said, and rapped on the front door. In the pine trees, a jay cackled. The policemen listened; across bare tiles, footsteps approached them.

Leda opened the door, and the policemen moved forward to stand shoulder to shoulder before her. Seeing a pretty face, the younger man started to smile at his good fortune, then recalled the reason for their visit and assumed a serious expression, though his body betrayed his true thoughts with a blush which spread from neck to cheeks.

'*Kali mera sas*,' said the senior man, respectfully.

'*Kali mera*,' replied Leda.

'*Kyria* Kalaki?' he asked, though he knew full well she wasn't; he'd asked about the house's occupants in the village.

'*Despina* Volakis,' said Leda. '*Kyria* Kalaki is my aunt.'

'Is your aunt here?' asked the policeman.

'She's gone visiting,' said Leda. 'There's only me in the house.'

'No one else here at all?'

Leda's expression grew puzzled.

'Only Maria. Can I ask your business here?'

She looked from one policeman to the other; the younger man, in spite of himself, flashed her a smile.

'Please, fetch this Maria,' said the senior man. 'And perhaps we could come inside.'

Leda frowned.

'What's this about?' she asked. 'Has something happened to Frona?'

'Fetch Maria, please,' said the policeman, and as if entitled he took a step across the threshold, so Leda, persuaded by his confidence, moved back to let them pass.

The senior man stood at the centre of the hallway, whilst his companion, smiling abashedly, took up a position behind him.

'Is this about Maria?' asked Leda. 'Has she done something wrong?'

'No, no, she's done nothing,' said the policeman. 'If you wouldn't mind . . .'

Leda left them. The two men looked around the hallway, taking in the ornaments and artefacts – the watercolours and sepia photographs hung in old frames, the chess set carved from olive wood on the dowry chest, the tusked boar's head glowering from the wall. They waited. Somewhere, above the sounds of domesticity – rattling saucepans, an oven door closing – a clock ticked.

Leda brought Maria from the kitchen, the old woman wiping her hands dry on her housecoat.

'I don't have time for policemen,' she was saying. 'I haven't time to chat to anyone, in the middle of cooking. Don't offer them coffee, whatever you do. If you offer them coffee, they'll never go.'

Her voice was loud. When she realised the policemen had heard her every word, she fell silent, but seemed indifferent to any offence she might have caused.

'Is there somewhere we can sit?' asked the senior officer, of Leda.

'We'll go in my father's study,' she said and led the way, pointing the men to the old horsehair sofa, herself standing with Maria before the fire.

'Perhaps you'd like to sit yourself,' said the policeman, indicating the poet's chair at the table.

'I'll stand,' said Leda. 'So, what's this about?'

The younger man cleared his throat and leaned forward over his knees, as if he were about to speak; but it was the senior man who said, 'It's about your father.'

The younger man looked at his feet, afraid to meet Leda's eyes.

'I'm afraid I have bad news,' said the senior man.

'Bad news?'

The policeman was a little rattled. In his long experience, families had usually, by this stage, got the message; an unexpected visit from the police was, in many cases, message enough, and for those who resisted the implications of their presence, the request to take a seat confirmed the worst. Never had it been necessary to say the words; women moved directly to weeping and wailing, whilst men jumped to the 'how' and 'when'. But here, it seemed, he must be more explicit.

'A body has been found,' he said, cautiously. He paused, certain of the onslaught now: the screaming, the tears, the damning or the invocation of God.

'Yes?'

The young man, too, was puzzled, and lifted his head; the business was turning out much easier than he had thought.

'Well,' said the senior man, awkwardly. 'The body is that of your father, Santos Volakis.'

To the policemen's shock, Leda laughed.

'I doubt it,' she said. 'My father is already dead, and has been these four years.'

The policemen stared at her; the younger man blushed at what he assumed was their error, and prepared to rise, and leave.

But the older man gave a patronising smile.

'I'm sorry, *despina*,' he said, quietly, 'but there really is no doubt. We've heard an account of your father's exhumation, and we know his bones were not found in the grave. And it's my sad duty to tell you that we've now found a body we're quite certain is his.'

Leda's composure was fading; the colour was gone from her face, and she reached for Maria's hand, her own hand trembling.

'What makes you sure it's him?' she asked, in a voice no more than a whisper.

'He was carrying his identity card,' said the policeman. 'He had all his papers with him. The body we've found – there's

133

no doubt of it – is that of Santos Volakis. And we're here to ask you, if you feel able, to identify his remains.'

'He's been alive?' whispered Leda. Maria squeezed her hand. 'All this time, he's been alive?'

The policeman gave a small shrug.

'It would seem so,' he said. 'Until recently, at least.'

'How recently?'

'I couldn't say, exactly.'

'No.' Leda shook her head. 'No, no, no! It isn't him! It can't be!'

She turned to Maria, who hugged her to her chest, as Leda muffled her sobbing on Maria's shoulder.

'You may bring Maria with you, if you wish,' said the policeman, more kindly. 'We'll drive you there, of course, but we must go now. There's to be a post-mortem, and the van to collect the – remains – has already been despatched. An identification is needed to complete the paperwork, so we shouldn't delay too long. And there's something else; I'm sorry to have to tell you, but your father sustained some injuries before he died. It won't be an easy thing to do, and you must prepare yourself. With the age of the corpse and the injuries, identifying your father won't be a pleasant task.'

Twelve

In the police station at Polineri, a grey-haired man leaned on the unattended reception desk, and watched as the policemen led the women across the car park. Leda wore the black overcoat she had worn for her father's funeral, fetched in haste by Maria from one of the old wardrobes; with the sleeves too short and the fit too tight, the coat regressed her to the adolescent she had been on that occasion. The reek of camphor was in the fabric but had not deterred the moths; tiny holes peppered the shoulders and lapels, with pinpricks of satin lining showing through. Leda walked, head bowed and meek, behind the tall policemen; Maria followed close behind, clutching the handbag she used only for church.

Around the foyer's light-fitting, flies buzzed.

Pouched skin around the grey-haired man's eyes gave him the world-weariness of a bloodhound. He didn't offer his hand but gave the women a brusque bow of his head.

'Ladies, thank you for coming,' he said. 'I'm Inspector Pagounis, currently in charge of this station. May I assume you are *Despina* Volakis?'

'I am,' said Leda.

Maria stood apprehensively behind her, holding on to her handbag as if she might be robbed.

'You can wait,' said the inspector to the uniformed men. 'These ladies will need a lift home. Twenty minutes, and they'll be ready to go.'

The two officers sauntered back to their car, and lit cigarettes. The inspector gathered up a sheaf of forms from the reception desk.

'There are a few formalities,' he said. 'Let's get those completed first.' He took a pen from a stand on the desk. 'Your full name, your address, your date of birth, and your relationship to the deceased.'

He filled out the form as Leda gave the information; when she came to her date of birth, Inspector Pagounis gave a pensive smile, and looked Leda in the face.

'I thought so,' he said, 'I thought so. You're the same age as she would have been, if she'd lived.'

Maria brightened with sudden interest.

'You lost a daughter, *kyrie?*' she asked. 'Ah, what misfortune, what misfortune! Commiserations, commiserations. How did you lose her?'

The inspector's face slipped into melancholy.

'Her lungs,' he said, looking down at the form he was filling in. 'She was unwell, from a baby. We lost her when she'd just turned seven years old.'

'A tragedy, a tragedy!' said Maria. She moved closer to Inspector Pagounis, as if proximity could better feed her craving for the details. 'Did you not try for another?'

'We have a son,' said the inspector, writing Leda's address on a blue form. 'But daughters – daughters are special to a man.' He recapped the pen, and wafted away a fly crawling on his paperwork. 'Damned flies,' he said, and turned to Leda. 'If you're ready, we'd better get on.'

He led the women down dark stairs and along a basement corridor, where their footsteps echoed off the concrete floor.

At the end of the corridor, a man in sergeant's uniform stood on guard at a doorway. Before they reached him, the inspector asked the women to wait, and proceeded the remaining distance alone.

'George,' said Inspector Pagounis to the sergeant. 'Are you ready for us?'

'Ready as we'll ever be,' said the sergeant. He sniffed, then pulled a handkerchief from his trousers and blew his nose.

'It's a difficult job for a young girl,' said the inspector. 'For her last memory to be of him like that . . .'

'With him like that, who could do the job but his close relatives?' asked the sergeant, giving a final wipe to his nose. On the wall by his shoulder, a fly crawled. 'And where the hell's he been, all this time, with them thinking him already buried? The papers'll love it, once they get hold of it.'

'As long as the papers don't get hold of it through anyone connected to this station.'

The sergeant stuffed the handkerchief into his pocket, and gave a shrug.

'You know as well as I do what the press are like. They've a way of getting hold of everything. You and I may say nothing, nor the boys that brought them in, nor the coroner – there's five people already you're relying on not to tell a very interesting tale. And there're all those others, with no professional requirement to keep their mouths shut. I don't see how they'll keep it quiet for long.' He moved his chin to indicate Maria, who held tight now to Leda's arm. 'Old family retainers may be faithful, to a point; but when there's money on offer – well, that would test anyone's loyalty, don't you think?'

The inspector sighed.

'You're right,' he said. 'And happily, the press is not our problem. Let's get on, then. Stay close to her, when we go in.

If she's going to drop, make sure you catch her. Is everything respectable in there?'

'I've done what I can. Which wasn't much, given the state he's in.'

Inspector Pagounis returned to the women. 'We brought him here as being the most convenient to you,' he said. 'The alternative was the city mortuary, but we wanted to spare you the travelling.'

Leda – tense and harrowed – looked at him to acknowledge his remark, but didn't speak. Maria had put her handbag on the floor, leaving both hands free to clutch on to Leda's arm.

'I'm afraid you'll have to wait out here,' said the inspector to Maria.

'I'm staying with her!' objected Maria; but Leda shook her head and freed her arm from Maria's grip, and followed the inspector down the corridor alone.

At the doorway, the sergeant stepped aside. Ready to turn the handle, Inspector Pagounis looked round at Leda.

'Are you ready?' he asked.

'I think so,' she said, and the inspector led the way into the room.

His back, at first, blocked Leda's view. The sergeant followed her in. The room had no window to let in daylight. A fluorescent light burned overhead; dozens of flies crawled on its opaque casing, whilst more were settling on the walls and ceiling, buzzing and droning as they flew. Liberal use of disinfectant had failed to cover the malodour of decay, and Leda raised her hand to cover her nose.

'I apologise,' said the inspector, 'for the smell. There's nothing to be done, no avoiding it. The deceased – your father – has been dead for a little while. Please, step this way.'

Leda was trembling as if she might be very cold: her hands shook and her teeth chattered. Two wooden desks, pushed end to end, had made a bier, and on the bier, a white bedsheet covered a shape, clearly a corpse.

'Please,' said the inspector, encouraging Leda to move closer to him, as the sergeant stayed close to her. The three stood together by the shrouded body, breathing shallowly on the foul air.

The inspector put his hand on the sheet's edge.

'I must warn you,' he said, 'there is some – damage. He fell, we think, and hit his face. And the action of weather – you should prepare yourself for that. Try to see past it, to the facial features. If it's him, you need only nod.'

He pulled back the sheet, revealing the dead man's head and shoulders. The bloodless skin was yellowing and waxen, the lips so pale, there was no distinction from the jaw. Across one eye, a gash had caved in the socket, and livid bruising covered the forehead and the cheek; across the opposite cheekbone, the face had suffered a similar blow and similar bruising. The flesh had swollen from exposure to the weather, so the face seemed oddly too large for the head; but beneath the damage and distortion, the corpse's face could be made out: a bearded man of middle age, and judging by his shoulders, poorly nourished.

For some moments, Leda looked at the body. She gave a nod. The inspector caught the sergeant's eye, and lifted his eyebrows to signal his satisfaction.

'His hands,' said Leda. 'Can I see his hands?'

The inspector peeled back the sheet, folding it discreetly to cover the genitals. The corpse's arms were laid out by his sides. Cautiously, Leda picked up the right hand, flinching at the first touch of its coldness. She studied the hand, its back and its front: its thinness, the dirtiness of its nails, the grime which was embedded in the palm, the silver ring loose on the middle finger. She raised it to her lips, and with tears in her eyes, kissed it.

'I'm sorry for your loss,' said Inspector Pagounis. 'He has the look of someone who neglected himself, in his last days. Was your father a drinker, *Despina*?'

'A drinker? I don't know,' said Leda, quietly. 'I didn't know him at all, in his final years. Do you think you could show me to the toilet? I don't feel well.'

Leda emerged a few minutes later, her face still ghastly from faintness and nausea. Maria hurried to her side and looked intently into her face, and with tear-filled eyes, Leda inclined her head. Maria made speedy crosses over her chest.

'I knew it,' she said. 'I knew it was him. He's found his way home at last, poor lamb.'

The sergeant handed Leda a paper bag.

'His personal effects,' he said. 'This is all he had on him.'

Leda peered into the bag, and reached in for the leather wallet it held. Inside the wallet was her father's identity card, its photograph of a young and smiling Santos. Tucked behind it was a photograph of herself, taken years ago; the Leda in the picture was a mere child. There was a little cash, notes and few coins, less than three thousand drachmas in total.

Leda replaced the wallet in the bag.

'His clothes?' she asked.

'We burned them,' said the sergeant, brushing a fly from his jacket sleeve. 'I'm sorry.'

'Can I go now?' asked Leda.

'One more form to sign,' said Inspector Pagounis. 'Then I'll have them take you home.'

He touched her arm to lead her to the stairs, and Maria started to follow; but the sergeant stopped her.

'A moment, *thea*,' he said. 'There's a small matter, still. I didn't want to upset the young lady. It's about her relative's body. After the post-mortem, someone must arrange collection from the mortuary, and I'd advise a sealed casket for transport. I hate to be indelicate, but the state of the remains has caused us some problems I wouldn't want the family to suffer – the flies swarming like a plague, and the smell of him . . . Well. You know what I mean. You'll be wanting him in your care anyway, I'm sure – the vigil, and the services . . . So I recommend someone should collect him as soon as possible, when the necessary examinations have been done.'

Maria took a few moments to take in his words.

'I'll tell Frona,' she said, and hurried up the staircase after Leda.

'Well, the mystery's solved, at least,' said Maria, shaking her head. 'But my poor lamb, out there in the cold, alone! *Panayia, panayia!* If we'd only known . . .'

She brought the smell of fresh air on her coat, which she hung on a peg behind the door, along with her handbag, which held so little: only coins for church candles, a pocket icon of the Virgin, an embroidered handkerchief. In the lamp before the Archangel Michael, the oil was burning low, and she refilled it from the bottle of first-pressing olive oil she kept especially for the saint. Sitting on a cane-bottomed chair, she unzipped her fur-trimmed ankle boots and replaced them with her rose-patterned slippers.

Reclining on pillows and cushions, covered with the patch-work quilt she had worked herself, when her fingers were still dexterous, Roula was drowsy in her bed. As Maria moved about the room, Roula blinked away half-sleep like a lizard, returning unwillingly from memory's insubstantial realms.

Maria touched her mother on the shoulder.

'Did you hear what I said, Mama?' she asked, as she went into the kitchen and lifted several pieces of salt cod from their soaking water, laying them out on a cloth to dry. 'The mystery's solved. Santos – my baby, my poor baby! They've found him, and he's coming home to us at last.'

Like a dog scenting game, Roula lifted her chin.

'What mystery?' she asked.

Maria gathered tools and ingredients from the kitchen – a pestle and mortar, garlic, oil and vinegar, the remains of yesterday's loaf – and carried them through to the table, close to Roula's bed.

A knock came at the door, and the neighbour, not waiting for an invitation, came in.

'*Yassas*,' she said, lively at the prospect of gossip. 'How are you, *thea*?' she asked Roula.

'Come in, come in,' said Maria, beckoning her to the table. 'Sit, sit. I'm just saying to Mama, the mystery is solved.'

'What mystery?' asked Roula again, as the neighbour pulled up a chair.

'I'm making *skordalia*,' said Maria to the neighbour. 'The grocer had a box of that salt cod. Mama likes cod, don't you, Mama?'

She went again to the kitchen, and returned with a small bowl of water, a knife and a crock of salt, and sat down beside the neighbour to make the garlic sauce.

'Well?' asked the neighbour, eagerly. 'Was it him?'

'Was what who?' asked Roula.

'Santos, Mama,' said Maria. 'My baby, my lamb! I went with Leda to the police station to identify the body.'

She split a garlic bulb into cloves, trimmed their ends and began to peel them, dropping the papery skins on to the cloth. She pushed the stale bread and the water bowl towards the neighbour.

'Soak that bread for me, *kalé*,' she said.

'Did you see the body?' asked the neighbour impatiently, separating white crumb from crust, pressing the softer bread into the water.

Maria dropped a garlic clove into the mortar and began to peel another.

'The police wouldn't let me go in with her,' she said, 'and it didn't break my heart, let me tell you. I didn't want to see him, the state he must be in. You could smell him all over the building.' With the knife still in her hand, she drew three crosses over her chest.

'He must have been there a long time, to stink like that,' said the neighbour. 'Is that enough bread?'

'Plenty,' said Maria, stripping the skin from a third clove.

'It'll be closed casket again, then,' said the neighbour. 'She knew him, though, did she, even in such a state?'

'She said so. I suppose a girl should know her own father, even in such a state as that.'

'Especially as devoted a daughter as Leda.'

'So hard for her! She worshipped him.'

'Deserved or not, she did.'

There was a silence between them all. With six peeled cloves of garlic in the mortar, Maria used the pestle to grind them to a paste, and filled the room with their pungency.

The neighbour seemed thoughtful.

'I suppose there wasn't much left of the face?' she asked at last.

'I suppose there wasn't. I didn't like to ask. She was upset.'

'What a blessing, though, to have him safe with them. The scandal, kalé, of those pig's bones in his grave! What a relief, that they weren't his bones at all! And did the police say what it was he died of, this time?'

Struck by the absurdity of the question, Roula frowned.

'They told her he slipped and banged his face,' said Maria. 'I suppose it cracked his skull.'

'Did neither of you ask them any questions?' asked Roula. Both women looked at her. Maria stopped her grinding.

'What questions?' asked the neighbour, her face creasing with bafflement.

'You asked the biggest question yourself,' said Roula, shortly. 'What did he die of, this time? Even renowned poets don't die twice! If he's only just dead now, he wasn't dead before, was he? But don't you worry. There'll be answers to all questions, soon enough.'

She folded her arms over her stomach, and closed her lips. Maria and the neighbour looked at her expectantly.

'What do you mean, Mama?' asked Maria.

'How will there be answers?' asked the neighbour.

'Someone's been here,' said Roula. 'An old friend of mine. He'll get to the bottom of it. It's what he does, gets to the bottom of things.'

'Who, *kalé*?' asked the neighbour.

'What friend, Mama?' asked Maria.

But Roula gave no answer; she closed her eyes, and seemed to fall back into a doze.

Maria and the neighbour talked quietly as Maria prepared the sauce – squeezing the water from the soaked breadcrumbs, mixing them in the mortar with the garlic, adding oil, salt and vinegar to the right consistency. In the kitchen, Maria dipped the soaked fish in semolina, and heated a pan of oil to fry it crisp. Their talk was of the poet's second death, and where he had hidden himself for so long, and though they had no answers, they enjoyed their speculation. As Maria lifted the last fish from the pan, the neighbour took her leave.

When the door had closed behind her, Roula opened her eyes.

'Has she gone?' she asked, as Maria placed the food on the table. 'The fish looks very tasty. Cut it up small for me, *kori mou*, and put me a dollop of *skordalia* on the side. I'm hungry enough to eat for two. That little food for thought has whet my appetite.'

But Roula's daytime sleeping brought insomnia, interminable nights of wakeful hours where the weight of time's slow passing was intolerable.

Eyes closed, she said a prayer.

'Take me tonight,' she said, 'painless and quick. I need no more time. Let me slip away, and not wake to see another day.'

But another night passed; and with first light falling on the window, she faced again the disappointment of an unanswered prayer.

Thirteen

The dog barked a warning of someone's approach: a fisherman heading for waters where swordfish might be taken,
calling in to the islet on a detour. He was in high spirits, opti-
mistic of a good catch and pleased to be escaping from home,
from his bickering children and the sighs of his discontented
wife. He brought with him four days' worth of newspapers,
all untidy from someone else's reading.

'*Yassou*, hermit!' he called as he came up the beach, the
newspapers under his arm. 'I'm playing postman, for today.'

The hermit made him coffee as the fisherman prattled on:
the fish he expected to catch, the price he would get per kilo,
the second-hand motorbike he might buy if his trip went as
he planned. He smoked a pipe of Swedish tobacco, and as he
smoked, he admired the view and the comforts of the cabin.

'You've made it all very agreeable here,' he said. 'And no
women to nag you. A life free as yours would suit me very
nicely. Maybe I'll come and join you for a while, when I return.'

The hermit offered a biscuit from a packet; the fisherman
accepted, took a single bite himself, and threw the remainder
to the dog.

'Your name was mentioned, the other day,' said the fisherman. 'They say you're putting it to the mechanic's wife.'

He looked expectantly at the hermit, but the hermit, smiling, shook his head.

'You can believe that, if you like,' he said. 'But look at me. I'm no woman's dream, am I? And as you say, I'm a free man. I'd be a fool to complicate my life with women.'

The fisherman put another match to his pipe.

'So what's your interest in the news?' he asked, tapping an oily finger on the newspapers. 'What's it matter to you, what's happening in the world? *Sta'nathema!* Let them all go to hell! It's what I would do, if I were you.'

'I'm becoming ignorant,' said the hermit, dipping the corner of a biscuit in his coffee. 'I lose track even of who's president, and what year it is. When I go over to Seftos, they all think me stupid; I've nothing to talk about but the weather, and the sea. The government might be overthrown, or Athens might sink beneath the waves, and I'd be the last to know.'

'If that damned city sinks beneath the waves, I'll come and tell you myself,' said the fisherman, 'and bring whisky to toast its destruction. And if you can talk about the weather, and the sea, you'll not be behind them over there. What else do they ever talk about? Women's gossip, and old men's tales! Read your papers if you like, but not in hopes of clever chat from a Seftian. I'm going; I've fish to catch. I'll call in on my return; I'll bring you a little something for your dinner. I like this place; it's peaceful. A place like this would suit me very well.'

As he made off down the beach, he waved goodbye without looking back. Inside the cabin, the hermit listened as his engine faded away.

He opened the oldest copy of *Ethnos*, published a week before. The pages were well read, dog-eared and creased, and marked with the stains of a coffee cup, and ink scribbles where the shopkeeper had tested his failing pen. He flicked through the paper quickly, scanning each page's headlines, reading a little news. He put the first paper aside, and scanned the second – dated two days later – in the same way, but found nothing there to interest him. But in the third paper – published four days previously – at page two, he stopped to read.

The headline was bold, and unmissable, set above a half-page article. He read the article with care, and then read it again.

The hermit folded the paper.

The afternoon was drawing on; the light in the cabin was growing dim. The sea was calm, the breeze was mild, and he was growing hungry. He took a fishing line and bait from the shelf, and made his way across the pebbled beach down to the jetty. There, he cast his line into the water, and stood patiently, waiting for a bite.

Reburial

Fourteen

Outside the front doors of his hotel, the fat man paused to consider the weather. Overhead, the sky was clear, but banks of clouds were forming out over the sea. A breeze rustled the branches of a tree bright with a crop of oranges; near its roots, fruit lay crushed and trodden into the pavement flagstones. A woman in a fur coat encouraged a small dog to defecate in a gutter; when she saw the fat man watching, she glared as if he had given some offence and turned her back.

The fat man yawned. His bed had been uncomfortable, the room either too hot, or, when he had turned off the heating, too cold. Though the rate had been expensive, and had included breakfast, he had not stayed to eat; the lack of quality he might expect in the food was implicit in the hotel's other shortcomings.

He disliked this city and was always glad to leave; his business here would shortly be completed, and he'd be free to go. He walked along the dirty pavement to where the side street joined a boulevard. Traffic on the boulevard was heavy, its fumes spoiling the salt scent of the sea. At the intersection of the two streets was a public phone booth – an aluminium box bearing the OTE logo in red. The booth was sited under a balcony where a verdant garden flourished, spreading to the phone booth's roof in pots of ferns.

The fat man stepped into the booth, pleased to find that it had a meticulous caretaker; the floor was recently mopped and smelled lightly of lemons; the receiver, when he picked it up, had been cleaned with lavender polish. He slid the door closed behind him, reducing the traffic's din, and took out his little notebook, turning to the page he had written on as Attis made his phone call in Vrisi's *kafenion*. He had written a series of numbers; now he deposited coins into the phone's slot, and skipping the first three digits as the code for the city he was in, dialled the digits he had noted.

The number rang out several times, until a man's voice answered. The voice was deep and had authority, but there was crackling on the line, and the fat man didn't catch what had been said.

He waited for the man to speak again.

'Yes?' said the man, impatiently.

'*Kali mera sas*,' said the fat man, politely. 'Please forgive me for calling you so early.'

'Who is this?'

'My name is Hermes Diaktoros. I am an acquaintance of Attis Danas. I'm calling you in regard to Santos Volakis.'

'What about him?'

'I wonder if I might beg a few minutes of your time, to discuss a matter of family business.'

'Family business? What family business? Who are you?'

'I'm someone with your best interests at heart, someone who wouldn't want to see you involved in anything illegal. If you're a man of integrity, you'll want to be warned, I'm sure, if you're about to make a deal which might turn sour.'

There was a short silence on the line.

'How do you know Attis?'

'We met in Vrisi. He asked me to look into some family business for him. But before I do so, there are some questions – may I speak plainly, my friend? – which I would like to ask about Attis himself. Discreet questions, of someone who has dealt with him in the past.'

'How did you get this number?'

'From Attis, indirectly. Do you have an office where we can meet? I really think it would be worth your while.'

Again, there was silence.

'Attis is offering you something for sale, is he not, which you would very much like to acquire,' suggested the fat man.

The silence continued.

'It is my strong advice that you talk to me before you hand over any money,' he went on. 'Of course, if you prefer not to speak to me, that is your prerogative, and I shall not trouble you further. *Yassas.*'

He kept the receiver to his ear.

'Just a moment,' said the voice, at last.

'Yes?'

'My office is on Papanikolas Street, number 78. I have a meeting across town I shall be walking to. If you care to walk with me, we could talk. Meet me outside the building at 10.30. But if you're late, I won't wait.'

The fat man looked at his watch and calculated there would be time for breakfast, before he'd need to find a taxi.

'I'll be there,' he said. 'And be assured, I am never late when it's necessary to be punctual.'

Along the boulevard, the fat man stopped at a *periptero*: a wooden kiosk, whose roof was over-painted with advertising for Assos cigarettes and whose every shelf was crammed with goods for sale: sweet biscuits and cigarette lighters, condoms and city maps, chewing gum, lozenges and batteries. In wire racks nailed to a brick wall behind, magazines for many interests – sailing, pornography, farming, fashion – were displayed in Greek and foreign languages, along with all the nation's daily newspapers and outdated international editions: the *Wall Street Journal* and the *Herald Tribune*, *Die Zeit*, a single copy of the English *Sun*.

Framed by displays of postcards of city views, a young woman in tight jeans and a leather jacket with many zips leaned on the counter, flicking through the pages of Italian *Vogue*. She was chewing gum; her heavily made-up eyes ran the fat man up and down, and returned to the photographs of glamorous *couture*.

Attracted by a cover picture of a glazed and golden-baked courgette pie, the fat man picked out a copy of *Yevsi* – Taste – magazine from the racks, and from the newspapers chose that morning's *Ethnos*.

He wished the young woman *Kali mera*, but she gave no reply. There was no room for his intended purchases on the counter where the woman's magazine was spread, so the fat man instead held them out to her, showing their prices. The woman glanced at the magazine and the newspaper, but not at the fat man; eyes back on the pictures of expensive clothing, she stated a price.

'I'd like cigarettes, too, please,' he said, with a smile. 'Do you have any of my brand?' He took a box of his cigarettes from his pocket, and held it up so the woman could see the starlet's pretty face; by contrast, the woman's own face slipped into a scowl as she lifted her chin and tutted, 'No.'

'Perhaps if you looked, you might find a pack or two,' suggested the fat man, brightly. 'Many people tell me they don't stock this brand, and then, when they look, they find a packet or two, hidden away.'

The young woman looked at him with contempt.

'I don't have them, I tell you,' she said. 'Twelve hundred fifty, for those.'

The fat man paid with exact change, and with his magazine and newspaper under his arm, made his way to the pedestrian crossing at the roads' intersection. As he waited for the traffic lights to change in his favour, he heard a bang and a clattering behind him, and the shriek of a woman's angry voice. All around him, pedestrians stopped and turned towards the *periptero*, where the newspaper rack had dropped from wall to ground, scattering dozens of newspapers as it fell. The young woman was moving quickly as she emerged from the kiosk's rear door, but the breeze was quicker. Riffling the light paper of the morning editions, it easily separated the pages of newsprint, and carried sheets of the nation's news high in the air, flying and flapping into the boulevard traffic.

Across the boulevard, the fat man found an Italian café, more appropriate to Milan than to a Greek city, yet somehow lacking an Italian city's style. He took a table with a street view, away from the draught caused by the door's opening and closing, and asked the blonde-haired girl who served him for a Greek coffee without sugar.

'No Greek coffee,' she said, in Scandinavian-accented Greek. 'Espresso.'

His eye had been caught by a display of cakes and pastries.

'Could I trouble you,' he said, 'to tell me what sweets you have on offer?'

She listed them with no interest, her pen held over her order pad to hurry his choice.

'Denmark,' he said, as she finished speaking. 'Am I right?'

'Yes,' she said. She looked at him expectantly.

'I have never been so far north,' he said, affably. 'I am certain the weather would not be to my taste. Though I suppose it is something you could get used to, like the lack of light.'

'Are you ready to order?' she asked. 'If you want a minute, I can come back.'

'No,' he said, 'I'm ready. I think a slice of the lemon tart, with a little whipped cream on the side. It's not something you eat for breakfast every day, but a change of habit is healthy, once in a while. And I'll have one of the croissants too, whichever you recommend; I'm torn between the chocolate and the almond.'

For a long moment, she looked at him.

'I'd have the cherry,' she said, 'if you're asking my opinion.'

'I am, and I will,' said the fat man. 'Cherry it is. And since there are two courses to my breakfast, be good enough to make my espresso a double.'

She left him, and he unfolded his newspaper, reading the headline with little interest: political scandal, though with an original touch – not a minister's affair, but his wife's affair with a boy exactly the age of their own son. Amused, he turned the page, and saw a smaller headline there: *Death of the Lazarus Poet*. Skimming the article for its crucial points, a thought seemed to strike him, and he turned to the classified section in the paper's last pages, where, amongst trysts for illicit lovers, advertisements for deviant sex and a request for a baby to adopt, was a message: *Investigator please return to us urgently. AD.*

The waitress laid his coffee on the table, alongside a slice of lemon tart with a spoon, and a cherry croissant with a knife.

The fat man folded his newspaper.

'Thank you,' he said, with a smile. 'It is most fortunate I have ordered a decent breakfast; my day, it seems, is likely to be quite a challenge.'

* * *

156

The fat man found the address he had been given without difficulty: a white-walled office block on a quiet street, over-hung by the branches of tall plane trees whose roots were lifting and splitting the road and pavements. The building was respectable but not opulent; it suggested modest earnings rather than great prosperity, a business making a comfortable living but not vast profits. A revolving glass door and a glass front on to the street showed a reception desk inside, where a woman typed. There was no sign on the front of the building to announce the offices' business, except for a polished brass plaque – partly covered by the branches of an oleander bush – engraved with the words, 'Bellerophon Editions AE'.

The fat man checked his watch and found the time to be a minute before 10.30. Through the glass, he watched the receptionist pause in her typing to answer the phone on her desk and make a note in pencil before her fingers went back to the keys.

On the street, the three-wheeled blue wagon of a municipal street cleaner – a man whose sagging face told of one hangover too many – pulled up alongside a waste-bin secured round the trunk of a plane tree. Dismounting his vehicle, he tipped the bin's small amount of rubbish into the wagon's back, and as he did so, noticed the fat man and stared at him with curios-ity, as if the fat man were someone he ought to know. The fat man gave him a broad smile, and raising his hand, called out *Kali mera*. The street cleaner responded with a nod, and drove away with his face still full of questioning.

The fat man found his cigarettes, and took one from the almost empty box. Lighting it with his gold lighter, he inhaled deeply. Inside the building, on the modern-looking staircase which curved down behind the receptionist, a man appeared. He descended at a run, his feet light and confident on the stairs; he seemed a man of energy, and as he strode past the receptionist, did not stop but spoke to her in passing, raising his left hand in farewell as his right hand pushed on the revolving door.

The fat man drew again on his cigarette, and watched the man as he emerged. Well built, and not dissimilar in stature to the fat man, his posture was less commanding, his shoulders stooped and somewhat rounded. His appearance was untidy; though his navy suit was well tailored, it was in need of cleaning and pressing; his white shirt was not fastened at the collar; and though his silk tie was a shade of blue the fat man would have admired, it was stained with a double dribble of coffee. He approached the fat man with his hand outstretched, and there seemed about him qualities of openness and cordiality, although he wasn't smiling now. Instead, his expression was wary.

'*Yassas*,' he said. 'I assume you're the gentleman who phoned me?'

'I am,' said the fat man, offering his hand. 'I am Hermes Diaktoros, of Athens. Thank you for agreeing to see me.'

The man's handshake was firm, his hand warm.

'Yorgas Sarris,' he said. 'Please, walk with me. I've an appointment for which I daren't be late.'

He led the way down the uneven pavement, under the branches of the plane trees.

'So,' said Yorgas, as they walked; his walk was brisk and the fat man happily matched it. 'What brings you to my door?'

'To be truthful,' said the fat man, 'I am not entirely sure. Before we go any further, I should ask you whether you have seen this morning's papers.'

'Newspapers? Pah!' Yorgas threw his head back in a gesture of disgust. 'I publish some of the world's finest writers, *Kyrie* Diaktoros. I don't spend my time reading the third-rate drivel that passes for writing in those rags.'

'I respect your point of view,' said the fat man. 'But there is something in this morning's editions which I really think you should see.'

With reluctance, Yorgas stopped walking and glanced at his watch. The fat man took his copy of *Ethnos* from under his arm, and placing his holdall on the pavement, turned to page three and held it out to Yorgas.

As he read the headline, Yorgas's face showed confusion and disbelief. He looked up from the page to the fat man.

'What does this mean?' he asked. 'How can they have found Santos's body? Santos has already been dead four years!'

The fat man's eyebrows lifted in doubt.

'Apparently not,' he said.

'Then what the hell's going on? Please, tell me what you know.' Yorgas turned around, and saw a low wall along the front of a shop selling baby clothes. 'Here, let's sit. You and I must talk.'

'Your appointment,' said the fat man. 'You'll be late.'

Yorgas waved his hand.

'The hell with that,' he said. 'Sit.'

They sat down, side by side, showing similarities between them which suggested kinship.

'I should start,' said the fat man, 'by being honest with you, since I hold honesty in such high value. I obtained your phone number by slightly devious means, through a trick my cousin taught me; the detail of it is not important, but it relates to counting the seconds as a phone dial spins and so calculating what number is being called. Attis does not know I have contacted you. I am acquainted with him because he has asked me to look into the matter of – well, at the time it was the matter of Santos's missing corpse. There was an unpleasant turn of events at his exhumation – perhaps you have already heard? The papers have hold of it now, and so it is in any case public knowledge. I'll leave this paper with you, and if you can overcome your distaste, you may read their version of events for yourself, in full. In summary, the family's belief was that someone had robbed Santos's grave of his remains, and placed there instead the bones of a pig.'

'A pig? That's despicable!'

'Despicable indeed. Understandably, the family wished the matter to be hushed up. Of course there was talk of witchcraft in the village; now it seems the explanation is more obvious. Santos's bones were not in his grave because, for the last four years, Santos Volakis has been very much alive.'

The publisher shook his head.

'What you are telling me – it beggars belief!'

'It does indeed – it's an extraordinary tale, even without its twist. Which is, as you may or may not know, that there was a clause in Santos's will tying up his estate until – I quote, or misquote – *my bones see again the light of day*. That, it now seems, has not happened. So the people who have waited four years for their inheritances may now have another long wait to collect their money.'

'But I don't understand! What does it all mean?'

'Perhaps you can shed some light on that. When Attis phoned you – and I have to admit, I eavesdropped on that conversation – he was offering you something for sale, was he not?'

The publisher looked hard at the fat man.

'Before I answer that question,' he said, 'you'll forgive me, *Kyrie* Diaktoros, if I ask at this point for more clarification on where you come into this.'

The fat man smiled.

'You're a businessman first, of course, and no doubt you're afraid I'm a rival for the goods Attis Danas is offering for sale. I assure you I have no interest in acquiring them. I am employed by the authorities to investigate a wide range of injustices, and

160

I am currently, in what you might call a spot of freelancing, employed by Attis to investigate a matter which has already turned out differently to what we expected. To put it plainly, Attis hired me on the family's behalf to find out what had happened to his client's remains, in order to help them in gaining access to money left to them by Santos in his rather unusual will. That brief, as far as I am concerned, has now changed. I am travelling back to Vrisi this afternoon, and my job, as I now see it, is to discover why Santos has been found dead at a roadside, and – simply because I am interested – I want to know where he has been and what he has been doing these past four years. Someone, somewhere, has been playing a strange game of hide and seek, both with our poet and with his money. And, if I am not mistaken, his work too. Attis has offered you some poems, has he not?'

Yorgas seemed reluctant to answer. The fat man produced his cigarettes.

'Smoke?' he asked, offering them to Yorgas.

'Not for me,' said the publisher. 'I gave it up two years ago. And still not a day goes by I don't miss it.'

'In that case,' said the fat man, putting the cigarettes away, 'I won't tempt you.'

'Attis has offered me some new poems,' said Yorgas, at last. 'At least, maybe not new, but unpublished.'

'And where has he obtained this unpublished work?'

'He didn't say. He wouldn't say. And frankly, I didn't press him.'

'Does the provenance of the work not trouble you? Surely you must have doubts of the identity of their author?'

'There's no doubt whatsoever in my mind. The poems are Santos's work. They are magnificent, and wholly of his style.'

'In short, Attis has struck gold,' said the fat man. 'You have both struck gold, in fact.'

Yorgas threw back his head, and laughed.

'You have the usual view of the world of publishing, *Kyrie* Diaktoros,' he said. 'You think we shall make our fortunes overnight. Alas, it is rarely so, and never so in the world of poetry. The business I now run was my grandfather's enterprise; my father inherited it from him, and I from my father. It's in my blood, and a labour of love. If it weren't, I would've closed the company down decades ago and gone to be a builder, or an architect – a profession where the returns are more dependable than in the business of the printed word. Bellerophon is proud to publish the best of Greece's writers, but the best of Greece's writers aren't the bestsellers. They sell steadily, over time, but none of them's made me rich. My offices are modest, as you've seen, and there's no chauffeur waiting at the door to take me to my appointments. Now, I freely admit to you that Santos's untimely death did me a favour, in the short term; it put his poems in the public eye. But the public eye is fickle and moves on to brighter treasures; like jackdaws, readers always seek the glittering new jewel. So when Attis tells me he has discovered new poems, I'm pleased, of course, but I'm not expecting to make millions, because the boost from Santos's death – forgive me, that sounds heartless in a way I didn't mean – has already run its course. If there are new poems, and if their provenance can be proved, then there may be sales in it, and good sales over time. But this isn't a bonanza day for me, *Kyrie* Diaktoros. It's just another day ploughing a small publisher's long furrow. And besides, Attis and I have so far struck no deal.'

'Are you not really so sure, then, of their provenance?'

'I'm entirely sure of their provenance, but the price he's asking may be beyond us.'

'Really?' The fat man raised his eyebrows. 'He's ambitious, then, for himself and his clients. And yet who could blame him, when Santos is suddenly big news, all over again? The Lazarus Poet, as they're calling him, and a second death, even more interesting than his first. A publisher's and agent's dream, wouldn't you say?'

'I agree, and Attis wants to get the most he can. He's gone away to try his luck elsewhere, but he'll be back. There are few publishers of poetry in this country, and whilst we're all rivals in business, there are gentlemen's agreements we all observe. They won't tread on my toes, and he and I will strike a deal. I'm confident of that.'

'So in fact, you only have to wait a while, and Santos's death – his second death – will bring you similar benefits to his first.'

Yorgas laughed, and waved a finger at the fat man.

'I read your mind, my friend,' he said, 'but you are barking up the wrong tree here. Attis I can't speak for; but my hands are clean. If I've accidently had a piece of luck, then I thank God for it, and I'm grateful; but I'm not the man to go manufacturing luck out of bizarre circumstances such as these, believe me.'

'I may believe you,' said the fat man, slowly. 'But Attis troubles me. His client is newly dead, and by coincidence he turns up a collection of unseen poems. If this is old work, where has it been hidden, and why has it come to light now? And if the poems are new – if Santos produced them before his second death – why wasn't Attis in the know? Because I don't think he was. If he knew why there were pig bones in the coffin, he wouldn't have hired me.'

'You know how it sounds to me,' said Yorgas. 'Looking at it logically, the man behind all this should be Santos himself.'

'The thought had crossed my mind,' said the fat man, 'but it crossed my mind before the body was found. If the plan was of Santos's making, then maybe Attis was a victim of it, in some way. And if that's the case, there must have been another player involved – another player who knows how Santos ended up dead at the roadside.'

'You're suggesting we're being made fools of.'

'Not you, friend. You have your money, do you not?'

'I admit to that. It's I who pay Santos his share – Santos's estate, in recent years – and not the other way round.'

'I admit at the moment to being baffled,' said the fat man, 'but I'll find the answers in the end. And to help me, I wonder if you would do me a small favour? I need to know where Attis found these poems. That's crucial. Perhaps you could dine with him again at Georgio's. Fill him with some decent wine, and then ask questions. If he's involved in something, do your very best to wring it out.'

'Gladly.'

'May I call you tomorrow?'

'You may. You have, I know, my private number.'

'And please, I must ask you to be discreet. Whoever's hand is in this, it's vital we don't tip them off. When I get to Vrisi, things will become clearer.'

'So what do you think?' asked Yorgas. 'Are these poems going to make me wealthy, after all? Discover a big scandal, if you can. The bigger the scandal, the more books I'll sell.'

'Be careful what you wish for,' said the fat man, 'because I might follow that thought to its logical conclusion. The biggest scandal you could wish for would be murder. That would create huge interest in your Lazarus poet, and you, my friend, might easily find yourself with the bestseller you say you've never had, and a perfect motive for the crime.'

Fifteen

The train was over two hours late, delayed at every stop: a late-arriving passenger to be helped aboard; a wait for a gang of labourers to clear the line; lengthy halts for no clear reason at all.

The fat man disembarked from the train, and followed on to the station forecourt an old woman with a cat carrier, which contained not a cat but a chicken, puffed up and broody. Amongst the newer cabs on the stand, Hassan's old taxi was easily picked out; but Hassan didn't see his vehicle as conspicuous, and to draw the fat man's attention, he gave a blast on his horn. Startled, the old woman glared her disapproval, and wandered muttering away with her chicken, down the busy street.

Hassan greeted the fat man like an old friend, shaking his hand warmly and opening the passenger door. Cloying airfreshener curdled the car's over-heated interior; thrown by fast manoeuvres, the bouquet of plastic roses was wedged at the parcel-shelf's end.

'So,' said Hassan, as the fat man made himself comfortable, 'back to Vrisi, eh, my friend? You surprise me. You don't strike me as a man for such a place as Vrisi.'

'Sometimes a place like Vrisi calls my name,' said the fat

man. 'Or, more accurately in this case, someone with an interest there has called. I gather you have some drama at the moment.'

'You'd think we were the centre of the world,' said Hassan. He pulled away from the taxi stand, forcing oncoming traffic to a stop as he joined the road without regard for rights of way or legalities, and the fat man averted his eyes from the insulting gestures of an angry driver. Without indicating, Hassan made an abrupt left turn. 'You can't move for the press, photographing the cemetery and the statue. They say the TV may come, for the funeral. But the family won't like it, if they do. The family wants to be left alone. And who can blame them, when he's dragged them from embarrassment to scandal?' He turned his head to look at the fat man. 'Is the funeral why you're back amongst us, friend? You have an interest in the poet, don't you?' He looked back at the road, and finding himself too close to a bus's rear bumper, braked sharply but fell back only a metre or two, so the taxi's heater fans still sucked in the smoke of the bus's oily exhaust.

The fat man did not immediately reply; he gripped the edges of his seat, and watched with both fear and admiration as Hassan drove through the town's streets, weaving through the traffic, making use of the side streets and alleys as ingenious short cuts. Before long, the town gave way to more open suburbs, and they joined the mountain road. Far ahead, the peaks were still white; but amongst the forest trees, all the snow had melted, and the verges showed the first new growth of spring.

'In answer to your question,' he said, at last, 'the poet does interest me, it's true. He was a man with secrets, certainly, the biggest of them being that he wasn't dead. It's an unusual trick, to fake your own death, and a hard one to pull off, but I think Santos Volakis succeeded with it. And his real death now strikes me as very convenient; but the question is, convenient to whom? What have you heard about the cause of his death?'

'They say the police told Leda that he fell on his face and cracked his head. I hear he wasn't pretty to look at, and an offence to the nose as well. He was already in a state when they found him. They only knew who he was from his ID card.' Hassan changed down a gear, and accelerated to overtake a car ahead. 'I'm wondering if you might be a policeman yourself, friend. You ask questions as if you might be a policeman.'

The fat man laughed.

'I, a policeman? No. There is no police force in this land which would employ me. My employers are a higher authority, who take an interest in matters of this kind, if it's appropriate, and necessary. They consider it necessary now, and so here I am. Tell me, is Attis Danas in Vrisi? A man who might be staying in the poet's house?'

'Someone arrived this morning; maybe you mean him? He came in a town car – nothing smart, an Opel. I passed him on the road. And with the snow, Frona and Leda never left. They'll be there a while longer still, now, I assume. They made poor Leda identify the body. That's a hard task, a daughter identifying the corpse of her own father, especially when he's not in a very pretty state. They say she might not have known him, but for his papers.'

'It's a rare daughter who wouldn't know her father, even under those circumstances,' said the fat man. 'It was the police who fetched her for the job, I suppose?'

'They came from the police station at Polineri. They took the body there when they found it, and sent it from there to the city mortuary for examination, whatever it is they do.'

They were approaching the first hairpin in the mountain road; the drop down to sea level was steep and cragged.

Hassan touched the brake and slowed the car a little; the fat man looked down at his lap to avoid the view.

'Still nervous, eh?' asked Hassan. 'Relax, friend. You're in capable hands.'

'I don't doubt it,' said the fat man. 'Tell me, do you know where the body was found, exactly?'

'I do,' said Hassan. 'It was at the chapel of St Fanourios, at the roadside opposite the shrine.'

'Then, since we will be passing, when we come to the place, I wonder if you'd be good enough to stop.'

When they reached the chapel, the shrine's lamp was unlit. Hassan chose a cassette of Turkish music from his small collection, and as the fat man climbed from the car, turned the volume loud and relaxed back into his seat.

The fat man bowed his head in salutation to the skulls, then left his holdall on the damp grass at the shrine's foot and crossed the road.

The forest's edge was close to the roadside, and the first trees of the dark acres were rooted above a gentle slope which rose up from the carriageway. The fat man moved along the roadside, his eyes on the sparse plants which grew on the sandy gravel, until a short distance from the shrine, in a spot overlooked by the skulls' fourteen hollow eyes, he found the grasses flattened and crushed over an area the size of a man's body, and the ground disturbed by the marks of many men's feet.

He studied the place where the body had been discovered, considering what Hassan had said: that the poet had tripped, or slipped, and cracked his head. The fat man frowned. There were, in that spot, no rocks or other hazards; and the question remained of why anyone with the level carriageway open to him would choose to walk instead on the rough verge.

168

Above the road, the tree trunks grew close, and the canopy of their branches was dense. The fat man made his way, head down, up the slope to the first of the trees, where he stopped and looked back at the road below. Then, maintaining the line that he had followed, he walked deeper into the trees.

The carpet of rotting pine needles had been disturbed. Whereas the needles lay level to left and right, where he now stood they were mounded into ridges and swept into crescents, where someone had obliterated other marks. All the disturbed area was dimpled with the ovals of footmarks.

He went on, further into the trees, scanning for more disturbance as he went, but finding little sign that anyone had been there before him; the hollows and dips in the softness of the needles might easily have been the scrabblings of rabbits or squirrels.

But as he turned back to the road, his eye was caught by what seemed to be a pile of rags, heaped at the base of a tree a short distance away.

The fat man lifted a fold of his find with his white toecap, and let it fall back. The pile was not of rags, but of fine-meshed fishing-net, which had caught nothing in its spread but the dirt and debris of the forest floor.

He looked around, to get his bearings from the road and from the chapel; and confident he would easily find this place again, retraced his path back to the shrine at St Fanourios's.

Back on the road, Hassan left the volume of his music high. The fat man raised his voice to make himself heard.

'Are there any fishermen in Vrisi?' he asked.

'Fishermen?' Hassan laughed. 'What would they catch, here? It'd be a stupid man who took up fishing as a trade in Vrisi.'

'They have no use for nets here, then, I assume? Not to protect crops from birds, nothing like that?'

'No crops, no nets,' said Hassan. 'The Greeks learned their fishing from the Turks, did you know that?'

'So now the clan's all gathered again, when is the funeral?' asked the fat man, ignoring Hassan's last comment.

'They brought him from the mortuary this morning. The funeral's tomorrow, when the bells toll.'

'And is there a pension in Vrisi where I might stay?'

'Not in Vrisi. There's a hotel in Polineri, if you're looking for a room.'

'I expect they'd give me a room at the poet's house, but it would suit me better to stay elsewhere, for tonight at least. So drive me, if you would, directly to Polineri. Can I ask you to pick me up again tomorrow morning, in time for the funeral?'

'You can ask, and I'll be there,' said Hassan. 'And I'll come in plenty of time, since you're such a nervous traveller, so we can take the journey nice and slow.'

Though the hotel was little bigger than a pension, welcoming touches augured a comfortable stay – an arrangement of fresh-cut evergreens in an alcove, current editions of popular magazines in a rack. But Polineri was a place for passing through, and the hotel's trade was unlikely ever to be brisk. Behind the polished reception desk, the proprietress opened a ledger at a page near the front, and wrote the day's date in the first column. Behind her, eight fobbed keys waited unused in a set of pigeon-holes. By the window, three café-style tables overlooked the street, their chairs all equidistant from the tables, as if no one had sat there yet today. Outside, a young girl at a bus stop nursed a crying toddler, who time and again spat out the dummy forced between his dribbling gums.

The proprietress, though drably dressed and diffident in manner, was a woman of some attraction, on the cusp of middle age.

'Do you have your identification, *kyrie*?' she asked, hesitantly, as if her request might give offence.

'Certainly.'

The fat man took out his wallet.

'I am so very sorry,' he said, searching through its contents, 'but I don't seem to have it with me. In fact, I am wondering if I left it at the post office when I picked up my *poste restante*. How very careless of me.' He looked at his watch. 'Too late to phone them now; I shall have to call them in the morning. They would be able to provide the serial number over the phone; would that be acceptable? Would you be good enough to wait for it until then?'

With the back of her hand, she waved the question away.

'Of course,' she said. 'I'd let it go, but the regulations demand we keep records, even though they're never checked. My husband used often to forget to ask, and then he'd make up the details. They never caught him out. But I don't have his confidence with the authorities. If they did come asking questions, I should hate to be in trouble.'

'Of course you would; and there will be no trouble, believe me. In fact, you have given me an idea. If there is a police station in town, I could call in there and report the loss of my card. They might be able to get in touch with the post office concerned. If I tell them I am staying here, they would know that any omission from the records was not your fault. What do you think?'

She gave him a charming smile.

'I think that would be best,' she said. 'Could you at least give me your name and address?'

'Of course. My name is Hermes Diaktoros. As for an address, I think the Athens one would be best.'

'You're from Athens, then? You're a long way from home, in Polineri.'

'Not so far away as I often travel.' He dictated an address.

'I'll put here,' she said, her pen over the column headed 'ID', *Details awaited*. Then they'll know I've asked.'

She turned to look at the keys in the pigeon-holes and seemed anxious at the wealth of choice.

'Do you prefer to look out over the road, or would you like a rear-facing room with a mountain view? The view isn't very good, actually; the trees get in the way. I think the trees make the rooms a little dark, but some people prefer the back to the road. The road can be noisy.'

She glanced uncertainly out at the empty road. The girl with the fractious toddler still waited at the bus stop; a man was driving a donkey overladen with hay.

'I don't mind a little traffic,' said the fat man, good-naturedly, 'and I would prefer somewhere light. So perhaps a room on the front would be best.'

She chose a key from the eight behind her.

'Number three, then,' she said. 'Please, follow me.'

Though the room was chilled, there were feather-stuffed pillows and thick blankets on the bed, and the night-stand held a yellow-shaded lamp and a dish of candied almonds. There were adequate wooden coat-hangers in the small wardrobe, with an extra blanket and pillow on the shelf.

'It's not very warm,' said the proprietress. 'There's a heater downstairs, if you'd like. I have it behind the desk with me, but you're welcome to it, though you wouldn't have to leave it unattended. There's a fault in the plug, and it overheats. If it starts to smoke, you must switch it off.'

The fat man declined, but accepted her offer of an evening meal.

'Well,' she said, handing him the key. 'Since you're wanting to eat, I'd better get on. Is everything all right for you here?'

'I shall be perfectly comfortable, thank you,' he said. 'If you could direct me to the police station, I'd be grateful.'

'Out of here, and turn left,' she said. 'Then right at the junction. You can't miss it. They spared no expense when they built it. It's the smartest building we've got in Polineri.'

A bull-nosed bus arrived at the stop, its engine-cover rattling over a labouring engine. The gloss of its blue livery was weather-damaged and faded; the abundant rust on its body-work was painted over in a lighter shade of blue. Through the windows, the bus's passengers stared down on the girl with the toddler and at the fat man as he came down the hotel steps. As the fat man passed the bus's open door, the driver looked at him with open curiosity; the fat man wished him a cheerful *Kali spera*, and set off down the road.

A minute later, the bus pulled away from its stop. The fat man moved to the very edge of the narrow road, his back against the stone wall of a house as the bus passed him so close, he felt the heat of its engine and the blow of its exhaust. It disappeared around the bend, and in the quiet it left, Polineri seemed abandoned and remote; then, a motorbike tore through, one youth leaning intently over the handlebars, another grinning in the slipstream on the pillion, his hands on the back of his seat. Seeing the fat man, both young men turned their heads in his direction; but by the time the fat man had raised his hand in greeting, the boys had sped past him, and were gone.

He found the police station without difficulty. As the propri-etress had said, it was Polineri's most impressive building, recently built and modern in design; yet its fashionable archi-tecture would date quickly, and its construction – a flat roof prone to leaking, prefabricated walls with over-sized windows which would make the place expensive both to heat and to cool – was impractical.

The concrete planters at the gateway were empty except for the greenery of weeds; there were no official police vehicles in the car park, only a moped and a high-mileage Citroën saloon. A damp national flag hung limp on its pole. The fat man crossed the car park, pushed open the swing doors and entered a foyer which offered no welcoming warmth, but the chill of a badly insulated building.

Ahead of him was a reception area. A high front concealed the desk behind it, so it was unclear, from the doorway, whether or not the desk was occupied. Noiseless in his white tennis shoes, the fat man crossed a tiled floor marked with boot-prints, and leaning an elbow on the desk frontage, looked over. No one was there; the wheeled chair was empty, and the desk held no sign of recent use: no coffee cup, no ash in the ashtray, or smell of recent smoking, only a telephone, a jar of pens and pencils, a notepad with the name of an agricultural machinery company as its header and a cardboard file with blue forms showing at its edges. The telephone was connected to a simple switchboard showing several numbered extensions, with one in-use light lit.

The fat man placed his holdall between his feet, and listened. On the street, a car drove by, and a woman called out to the driver; on the wall, the hand of a clock clicked one minute on. Somewhere in the building, a man was talking, though his voice was faint; around the foyer, flies buzzed, crawling on the windows and the ceiling.

Next to a pen and holder for public use was an electric bell-push, which the fat man pressed. It rang shrilly behind a set of swing doors leading to the station's offices. He rang the bell long enough for it not to be ignored, then turned to face the view through the window of the saloon car and the moped, of the houses across the street, of the mountains that lay beyond. He waited; the extension light on the switchboard remained lit, and somewhere in the building, the man's voice talked on.

The fat man pressed the bell again, for somewhat longer. Still the engaged light on the switchboard remained lit; still there was no movement within the building, nor any indication that his request for attention had been heard. He pressed the bell once more, this time leaving his finger on the button as he counted slowly aloud, intending to stop at ten; when he reached eight, the light on the switchboard went out, and at ten, a door opened, and footsteps at last approached.

Banging back the swing door from the offices against the wall, a man strode into the foyer, his face set with the effort of controlling his annoyance. He looked across to where the fat man waited by the reception desk.

'*Oriste?*' he said, unpleasantly.

'*Kali spera sas,*' said the fat man, politely. 'I wish to consult someone on a problem with an ID card.'

'An ID card?'

The fat man smiled.

'Of course this is not my local police station, but I find myself without my card – lost, I must assume – and in this locality, with no firm date for a return home. I am hoping you can let me have the necessary forms for a replacement, and that the business can be handled from here.' He took several steps towards the policeman. 'Hermes Diaktoros, of Athens. My father is a classical scholar; the name he gave me is something of a family joke. In the same way I call these my winged sandals.'

The policeman's eyes followed the fat man's pointing finger to his white shoes. When the fat man offered his hand, the policeman shook it without enthusiasm.

'I'm Inspector Pagounis, head of this station,' he said. 'But I can't help you with your ID card. You need to speak to our desk man, Constable Takas. He isn't here at this time, as you'll have seen.'

'I noticed a lack of personnel, certainly,' said the fat man. 'That's why I rang the bell.'

'Well,' said the inspector, 'if you come back tomorrow morning, maybe he might help you, though I make no promises. I don't know the rules regarding replacement cards outside your domicile. You'll need to bring with you a certified birth certificate from your home municipality, a statement of your blood type from a registered doctor or an IKA office, four passport-sized black-and-white photographs – hair off the face, neither smiling nor frowning, and matt finish – and stamps to cover the fee. Constable Takas will no doubt see what he can do. He'll give you a statement of facts to fill in then.'

He turned to go, but the fat man stopped him.

'That is a great deal of documentation to procure in one night,' he said, 'a labour worthy of Hercules himself. Yet I have no option, do I, but to attempt the task? An ID card is so vital to our modern lives. If I were to suffer an accident on these dangerous roads, how else would you find out who I am?'

'We'll hope then that you have no accident, whilst your card is missing,' said Inspector Pagounis. '*Kali spera sas.*'

Again, he turned to go; his back was to the fat man as the fat man spoke.

'Was an identity card not vital in identifying the corpse of that poor poet, dead in Vrisi? I'm told there was some damage to the face. When a face can't be recognised, then we only have the paperwork to go on, don't we?'

The policeman turned back to face him. On the swing doors, a fly crawled.

The fat man smiled.

'Something occurred to me, about that case,' he said, 'though I wouldn't expect you to discuss it with a layman. And I'm sure there's a simple explanation; but what I found intriguing was, how could a man already dead be carrying his ID card? Anyway, I have plenty to occupy me, and so, no doubt, do you. *Yassas*.'

He reached the door; but as he put his hand on the glass, the inspector called him back.

'Just a minute,' he said. 'What do you mean?'

'Well.' The fat man smiled, again. 'Only that Santos Volakis, from what I've heard, is the very rarest of men, a man lucky – or unlucky – enough to die twice. And I couldn't help wondering, when I heard about this intriguing matter, why a dead man would be carrying the papers of a live one. Were his papers not handed in to the police, the first time he died? If not, where have they been, from that day to this? And I was wondering if the simplest explanation might be the obvious one – that the poet had been issued with two cards. In short, perhaps he applied for a replacement, as I am doing now. Perhaps he was issued with a replacement for a lost card, which was later found. To temporarily mislay an object is easily done. I myself am guilty of it, now.'

Inspector Pagounis frowned.

'That's easily checked,' he said, and went behind the desk, where he opened one of its drawers and took out a leather-bound notebook. 'We don't issue many replacements. Most people take good care of their official documents.'

The fat man ignored the intended reprimand, and the inspector turned the ruled pages of the notebook, running his finger down columns of names and dates. A fly landed on the back of his hand; the inspector brushed it away.

'You seem to be troubled with flies,' said the fat man, looking up at several on the ceiling. 'That's somewhat unusual, so early in the year. And if I am not mistaken, these are not common house flies, but carrion flies.'

'They brought the body here,' said Inspector Pagounis, still running his finger down the columns of names. 'In this warmer air, the damn things started to hatch. And venerated poet or not, he stank bad enough.'

The phone on the desk rang; the inspector seemed not to hear it.

'You'll be thinking, I am sure, of spraying them with chemicals,' said the fat man. 'But my father has an interesting way of catching flies. He uses a *drakondia*, a stink plant; he brings one into the house, and lets it draw the flies so he can catch them in a net.'

'A net?' Inspector Pagounis looked puzzled. 'Why would you want to catch flies in a net?'

'They have their uses, believe it or not. Not least of which is their role in the decomposition of bodies.'

The phone became silent. A fly landed on the back of the wheeled chair. Pagounis closed the notebook.

'No replacement was issued here, and that book goes back seven years. My guess is, since he wasn't dead, he kept his ID with him. That would be logical, wouldn't it?'

'Perhaps,' said the fat man, thoughtfully. 'If he wasn't smelling too sweet when they brought him in, he must have been dead at least a few days.'

'Long enough. They don't stink like that when they're fresh.'

'You found him under the snow, did you?'

'When it melted, yes. The old woman who found him had rather a shock.'

The fat man retraced his steps to the desk, and leaning on the high counter, reached into his pocket for his cigarettes. He held the box out to Inspector Pagounis.

'Smoke?' he said. The inspector looked at the packet with interest, and the fat man held it out for him to see. 'You don't find these everywhere these days. They're Greek manufacture, but the tobacco's good. Try one.' The inspector accepted, and the fat man lit the cigarettes with his gold lighter. 'I smoke too much,' he said. 'I keep meaning to give up. When you smoke, it makes you unhealthy. And with all these hills, if I lived around here, my poor lungs would let me down. I assume our poet wasn't a smoker, if he was walking all the way to his house. Surely no smoker would volunteer for such a trek as that?'

'For a layman, you've a lot of interest in *Kyrie* Volakis,' said Pagounis. He drew on the cigarette and studied the fat man. 'Yet you don't strike me as a journalist. Them, I can smell at twenty paces. So come on, level with me. Why all the questions?'

'To tell the truth, my interest is professional,' said the fat man. 'The poet's agent, Attis Danas, hired me to look into Volakis's disappearance from his grave. But the puzzle has evolved, now, into something different, namely his mysterious reappearance at the roadside.'

'Do you find his reappearance mysterious?'

'Don't you? Don't you think his accident might have been convenient?'

Pagounis knocked ash from the tip of his cigarette.

'What makes you think it was an accident?' he said.

'That's what I was told,' said the fat man, with an air of naivety. 'Is it not so?'

Pagounis smiled.

'*Kyrie* Diaktoros,' he said. 'Your acting will never get you a job on any stage. I think you have already deduced Volakis's death was probably no accident, and that fact will become public soon enough. So in your official capacity – if you have an official capacity – you can be told that we are treating this as a case of murder.'

'Really? On what grounds, if I may ask?'

'You may ask, and I will tell you, though this is information you should please keep to yourself. My reason for that request is simple: the family still believe the death was accidental. You'll say I should have been straight with them, and you're right, but I'm a man with a soft heart, and at the time I couldn't do it. When his daughter came to make the identification, I felt the situation she was in was grim enough, so I decided not to add to her distress by telling her that he'd died a violent death.'

'Was she distraught, then?'

'Heartbreakingly so. She's a lovely young woman, too young for such trauma as this. Plainly, she and her father were very close. To see her kiss his hand brought a tear to my own eye. The strain made her unwell whilst she was here, and I thought she should have a day or two to come to terms with the shock. So I told her he'd had a fall, a slip on the ice, or whatever. That's the story she and the old retainer took away.'

'But it wasn't true?'

Pagounis stubbed out his cigarette.

'I was born and raised in Polineri, but that doesn't make me some backward, backwater boy,' he said. 'I've served my time on city beats, and one look was enough for me. Volakis took a blow to the head. Not just one, actually, but several. And I can go one better than that, now we've had the autopsy report. There were fragments of glass in the wounds.'

'But I have just been at St Fanourios. I saw no broken glass.'

Pagounis raised his eyebrows, and smiled.

'So you really are an investigator, *Kyrie* Diaktoros. You think, in some ways at least, like a policeman. No, there's no glass there. We noticed that, too.'

'So with glass in the wounds, you might guess at the weapon?'

'I might.'

'And might you also guess at who used the weapon?'

'I might guess at that too, yes,' said Pagounis. 'I might guess at more than one name. But a guess is a long way from proof.'

'Will you be attending the funeral?'

'No, but I'll send a couple of men. The press are taking an interest, and it seems right to protect the family from their intrusiveness.'

The fat man stubbed out his cigarette in the ashtray, and picked up his holdall.

'Thank you for your time,' he said. 'If your officers are going to be absent in the morning, I'll leave it till the evening to bring in my paperwork. Though as I said, it worries me to be without identification. Look at Santos Volakis. Whoever would have thought of the body being a man four years dead, if he'd carried no identification?'

As the fat man crossed the car park, Inspector Pagounis watched him go. The phone on the desk rang out again; but the inspector let it ring as he left the foyer and pushed through the swing doors, back to his office.

Behind her desk, the proprietress was reading a magazine, a church-published *Lives of the Saints*.

The fat man took out his wallet.

'I couldn't supply you with my ID card earlier,' he said, 'but as I was going through my pockets, I came across it. Not lost after all, I'm pleased to say.' He slipped the blue card from his wallet and placed it on the desk. 'Please do take down whatever details you need. I should hate for you to get in trouble with the authorities.'

Dinner at the hotel was disappointing: fried chicken livers a little burned, chips cooked in oil a little rancid, a slice of chocolate cake which, though rich with cocoa, was a little dry. The fat man ate alone, silent and thoughtful, facing the dark street and a view of his own reflection in the glass.

At a neighbouring table sat a blind man, with green-lensed spectacles covering his eyes, and a long cane leaning against his thigh. He, too, seemed disinclined to talk. He was drinking ouzo and water, and each time he reached out, the fat man feared he would topple his glass; but infallibly, the blind man's hand closed easily on his drink.

As the fat man was eating his cake, the blind man at last spoke.

'Don't feel obliged to clear your plate,' he said. 'My daughter has many qualities, but she's never been much of a cook. She tries, God bless her, but the talent isn't there.'

The fat man laid down his fork. Behind his reflection, a woman hurried by on the dark street, clutching closed the neck of her coat.

'On the contrary,' he said, 'I've been fed very well.'

'You're probably wondering how I do it,' said the blind man.

'I beg your pardon?'

'You're wondering how I know how to find the glass, but it's simple. Once Elli has shown me where the glass stands on the table, I memorise the angle of my arm and the distance I need to extend it. Usually, I'm right. Which isn't to say we don't have accidents, from time to time. Will you have a drink with me, and keep me company? Elli!'

He called out to the proprietress, and in a moment she appeared behind the reception desk, drying her hands on a towel. From the doorway behind her came voices and music, the soundtrack of a TV cartoon.

'What is it, Papa?'

'An ouzo for the gentleman, *kori mou*. She takes good care of me,' he said to the fat man, 'and I'm not easy. Though I'm learning a little more independence, day by day.'

'Let me introduce myself,' said the fat man. 'I am Hermes Diaktoros, of Athens.'

'They call me Denes,' said the blind man, 'but I won't shake your hand. If I move my hand from its spot, my trick with the glass'll be ruined.'

'Forgive me for asking, but when did you lose your sight?'

Denes raised his left hand, and taking the spectacles from his face, looked directly at the fat man.

'There's nothing to see in them, is there?' he asked, and his eyes did, in fact, appear healthy. 'A degenerative disease, the doctors say. My problems began seven years ago, when full daylight began to look like evening, then evening gradually became night. I see a very small amount, still – movements, and large objects. And of course the human body is adaptable. My other senses have grown sharper, by way of compensation.'

Elli placed an ouzo before the fat man, and gathered up his plates. As she leaned over him, he caught a scent of mountain air in her hair.

'Thank you,' said the fat man. 'You have fed me very well.'

She smiled, grateful for the compliment. When she had left them, the blind man said, 'You came with Hassan, this afternoon.'

'I did,' said the fat man. 'How do you know?'

'I hear the traffic passing, and I know the sound of his engine. He still brings Elli customers when he can. He still thinks of her.'

'Has there been then some connection between your daughter and Hassan?'

'Hassan's my son-in-law.'

'Ah.' The fat man recalled a conversation, on the road back to the city. 'But as I understand, they're not together now?'

'They separated,' said Denes. 'There was some trouble, and he left. Hassan wasn't to blame. Any man would have done the same. But I worry about the children; it's hard on them. And I worry for my daughter. Her mother's gone, and I'm a burden. She struggles, by herself.'

Headlights lit the wet road outside, and a car passed, its fan-belt squealing. Denes took another drink of his ouzo, and the fat man did the same, finding the drink a little watery for his taste.

'I wonder, without being indelicate, if you'd tell me what happened between them?' asked the fat man. 'I like Hassan. He strikes me as being a good man, yet I feel he's harbouring some bitterness.'

'He's a man who'd do anyone a favour,' said Denes. 'He takes me to all my hospital appointments, there and back, and he won't take a single cent in payment. Sometimes he gives me money for her, on top of what he gives her for the kids. He's too proud to let her know he cares, and she's too proud to let him know she's struggling, so I say it's from my savings, and it makes it easier, all round. But you're right, there is some bitterness in his heart – the same bitterness I harbour myself towards that dog who crept in here and ruined their marriage. Elli was in the wrong; of course she was. But men know that women are weak, and it's a sin to take advantage of that weakness.

'A poet, he called himself, but I call him a snake. He wasn't well liked in Vrisi, so he used to walk over here and honour us with his company in Polineri. He'd come in here from time to time, and sit where you are now, and have a drink or two. Always when Hassan was working: I noticed that. He'd sit, and not say much. He seemed to think having no sight made me blind to what he was up to, but I was wise to him. And I told Elli what his game was, but she didn't listen. She'd bring him a drink, and he'd recite poetry. Love poems, and drama, fancy stuff. He scented an opportunity, and he took it; I wasn't always here, and Hassan's working hours are long. Then one day, he walked out of here and never came back. And that same day, Hassan packed his bags, and went.'

'I'm sorry,' said the fat man.

'I'm sorry too,' said Denes. 'I'm sorry for us all, but for my daughter, most of all. Daughters are always special to a man. Do you have children, friend?'

'Not in the conventional way, no.'

'Even so, you'll understand a father wants his children to be happy. She's a treasure of a woman, my girl, and a wonderful mother to the children. And apart from that slip – which I don't make light of, believe me – she was a sober and serious wife. But that snake robbed us all; he robbed Hassan of his honour, and wrecked my family, too. They were a good team, she and Hassan. He made her laugh, and she made him happy.

'That bastard cost us dearly. He's dead now, and though God may strike me down for saying so, I'm glad. In this family, believe me, we're all glad.'

Sixteen

Despite a window which rattled with the lightest touch of wind, the fat man slept well and woke refreshed. Overnight, mist had fallen, dank and dense; it dulled the day's light and muffled noise, muting the schoolchildren's banter as they walked by on the road below, rendering the crowing of a back-yard rooster lacklustre.

The fat man stretched – arms high, then from the waist to left and right – before touching his toes a dozen times. Lifting his elbows, he pulled them back to stretch his chest. The muscles of his limbs were well defined, and satisfied with his own suppleness, he slapped his generous belly with both hands and stepped into the lukewarm shower.

In the bathroom, he dried himself and wrapped a towel round his waist. Using a badger-hair brush, he spread shaving cream over his face, and shaved with a silver-handled razor. From a bottle of his favourite cologne (the creation of a renowned French *parfumier*: a blend of bitter-orange neroli, the honey notes of immortelle and the earthy tang of vetiver), he splashed a few drops into his palms and patted them on to his cheeks. With a fingerful of pomade from a small jar, he smoothed his damp curls, then cleaned his teeth with powder flavoured with cloves and wintergreen, ran the tip of a steel file behind his fingernails and polished each one with a chamois buffer.

From his holdall, he chose a fresh shirt in pale lavender, and put on the suit he had hung in the wardrobe. Then he sat down on the bed, and took out a bottle of shoe-whitener.

On the road below, a police car drove by at speed.

The fat man gave both of his tennis shoes a full coat of whitener, paying particular attention to the rubber toecaps and heels, holding the shoes up to the window as he worked to check no spot was missed. When he finished, the shoes had the appearance of being new out of the box. He put them on, repacked his holdall and made his way downstairs.

He took breakfast at the same table where he had dined, looking out on nothing but the mist, which obscured even the house wall opposite. Of Denes there was no sign, though on the neighbouring table, a used napkin covered a plate of bread crusts and eggshells.

Elli served him unexceptional coffee and hard rolls with factory-made preserves, which the fat man took time to enjoy as best he might; but when he had eaten, Hassan still had not arrived.

The fat man carried his holdall to the reception desk, where Elli was adding up the figures on a pile of creditors' bills.

He took out his wallet, and laid two banknotes on the desk.

'This will cover my food and lodging,' he said. 'I shall pay you now, but it is possible I shall need to return tonight. If I do, will you be able to accommodate me?'

'You'd be most welcome,' said Elli, 'especially if you'll keep Papa company again. He enjoyed talking to you last night. Would you be wanting to eat?'

The fat man remembered last night's dinner.

'Don't trouble yourself about food,' he said. 'If I need a

room, it shall be a room only; I shall take my meal elsewhere. Then you and I are not beholden to each other. Is that agreeable to you?'

She looked appreciatively at the banknotes on the counter.

'Perfectly,' she said.

'I was expecting Hassan to be here by now,' he went on. 'He was to collect me and take me to Vrisi. Do you think you could telephone, to make sure there is no problem?'

Elli hesitated.

'All right,' she said. 'I'll call.'

The previous day's edition of *Ta Nea* was in the magazine rack. The fat man took it to his table and for a few minutes browsed its most interesting stories: a lucky fisherman who'd found a rare coin in a fish's belly; an accountant who'd searched thirty years for a girl glimpsed once, on a train. The fisherman's coin had sparked a fruitless search by treasure hunters; the long-term admirer was soon to marry his dream girl, but in a photograph with his arm around his middle-aged fiancée, was struggling to raise a smile.

Ten minutes went by. The fat man glanced at his watch, and frowned as he turned the page.

In the road outside, three women met; one carried newly baked loaves from the bakery, the others were dressed for attending church. The fat man, at first, paid them no attention; but there was excitement in their gestures as they pointed up and down the road, and the volume of their voices was increasing as they strove to make themselves heard over each other.

The fat man recognised the indicators of fresh gossip. He folded the newspaper and laid it on the table, and, picking up his holdall, he made his way casually outside and stood close to the women to light a cigarette.

'Don't talk so loud,' said one. 'She'll hear you.' She moved her head to indicate Elli, inside.

'She'll find out, soon enough,' said another. 'They'll tell her themselves, no doubt.'

'Why should they tell her? They're divorced, aren't they?'

'Not divorced, no. They haven't signed the papers.'

'They'll be taking him away,' said the first. 'They'll charge him, and then it'll be prison.'

'Do you think he did it?' asked one, doubtfully.

'Of course he did it. They wouldn't have come for him if he didn't do it. They came early, so they'd catch him in his bed. They bundled him in the car and took him away. Blue lights and sirens, a real drama.'

'Don't be silly,' said the oldest. 'I saw them myself. They went in one car, and he followed in his own. There were no lights or sirens.'

'They're lucky, then, he didn't make a run for it.'

'Maybe he did. Maybe he's become a fugitive from the law.'

'Do you think we should tell her?'

They all looked through the hotel window, where Elli was still sitting at the desk.

'Better not,' said the oldest. 'It's not our job to interfere in official business.'

The fat man, too, glanced through the glass at Elli, and considered, briefly, going back inside. The women's conversation was moving on to other matters.

'Ladies, *kali mera sas*,' said the fat man politely, as he passed them, heading in the direction of the police station.

In the car park, the same moped and the Citroën saloon were parked where they had been the previous day, but alongside them now was a police car and Hassan's taxi. Through the swing doors, the foyer was somewhat warmer, and smelled of brewing coffee. Behind the desk sat a police constable in a blouson jacket, warming his hands in front of the glowing bars of an electric fire. On the switchboard, two extensions were lit.

'*Kali mera sas*,' said the fat man, as he approached the desk. The constable looked up at him, hard-eyed.

'I wonder if I might speak to Inspector Pagounis,' said the fat man. 'I have some information which I think will interest him.'

The constable glanced at the switchboard.

'He's on the phone,' he said.

'I'm afraid I can't wait,' said the fat man. 'I'm on my way to the funeral in Vrisi. Perhaps you're one of the officers who'll be attending? The information I have relates to the poet's death. Maybe you could interrupt the inspector's call?'

'He doesn't like to be interrupted when he's on the phone.'

The fat man smiled.

'I gathered as much, yesterday. Please tell him Hermes Diaktoros is here. If he doesn't recall the name, you might remind him he and I spoke of ID cards.'

Unwillingly, the constable left his chair, and went through the double doors to the station's offices. The fat man looked up at the ceiling and around the walls; the carrion flies no longer crawled there, though several were dead in a spider's web at the corner of the ceiling. Five minutes went by, and the constable did not return; then there came quick footsteps from the corridor, and Inspector Pagounis burst through double doors.

As the inspector approached, the fat man held out his hand, and Pagounis briefly shook it. The pouched skin below his eyes seemed more swollen, as if he'd passed another sleepless night.

'*Kyrie* Diaktoros,' he said. 'You're back again. Have you brought the paperwork for your ID card?'

'I'm pleased to report,' said the fat man, 'that in fact I found my ID card. It was in my wallet all the time.'

Pagounis's eyebrows lifted slightly.

'How fortunate,' he said. 'Somehow, I'm not surprised. So, how can I help you this morning?'

'I've been thinking about Santos Volakis's death,' said the fat man, 'and I wanted your opinion on whether my conclusions are correct. By the way, I see a taxi outside. Is the driver here with you, by any chance? I had booked him as my transport to the funeral.'

'What conclusions?' asked Pagounis.

'You're a busy man, of course, and I should get to the point,' said the fat man. 'So I'll be as brief as I am able. There are two aspects of the case which concern me. Firstly, the flies. Which you have managed to exterminate, I see.'

'We used a spray,' said Pagounis. 'What about the flies?'

'When the snowfall began, I myself left Vrisi ahead of the storm, via the chapel. I will happily swear a statement that there was no body there then, so the corpse must have arrived after I left. From that time to this seems a very short time for carrion flies to hatch, given the low temperatures. And it occurred to me also, that your remark about how the poor man stank suggests decomposition was advanced. Which seems impossible, again given the cold temperatures, if he died here.'

'What are you suggesting?'

'I'm only an amateur, of course,' said the fat man. 'But it seems to me that only one explanation fits the facts. Namely, that the body was already decomposing before it arrived in Vrisi. And so, by implication, the poet could not have arrived here under his own steam, because when he arrived here, he had already been dead some little time.'

Pagounis sniffed.

'Coupled with the fact there is no broken glass up at St Fanourios,' went on the fat man, 'it seems highly likely to me Santos was killed somewhere away from Vrisi. Which might broaden the range of suspects quite considerably.'

'Go on,' said Pagounis.

'What I can't figure out, is this. Why bring the corpse to Vrisi? Left a few more days where it was first hidden – wherever that was, it hadn't come to anyone's attention – it might have decayed beyond any recognition, and indeed might even never have been found. With no corpse, there's no murder investigation, and the murderer goes free. But here Santos is, laid out in full view – except for the chance snowfall – by a public road. Better yet, in case anyone should have doubts, the corpse has effectively been labelled with identification. Now, in my experience, and as you will know, most killers attempt to baffle the law by removing identifying marks. Some go to the extreme lengths of removing hands to prevent fingerprinting, or even of decapitating their victims. But in this case, we have the opposite. Someone wanted the poet found quickly, and identified. Does that not strike you as odd?'

'You would indeed have made a good policeman,' said Pagounis, drily. '*Kyrie* Diaktoros, our conclusions are the same. But thank you for taking the trouble to come and speak with me. Now, if there's nothing else . . .'

'The taxi driver,' said the fat man. 'Hassan. Bearing in mind, based on our logic, that the killer is likely to be an outsider who brought the body into Vrisi, doesn't it make sense to let him go?'

Pagounis laughed.

'Let me guess,' he said. 'The rumour is, Hassan is under arrest. What crime are they saying he's charged with? *Kyrie* Diaktoros, you surprise me. You don't strike me as a man to act on gossip.'

'Hassan isn't under arrest?'

'Hassan isn't under arrest. He's merely here as a potential witness, in case he can recall any strange vehicles on the road around that time. He's drinking coffee with my boys in the back. If you like, I'll tell him you're waiting to go to the funeral.'

'I would appreciate that,' said the fat man.

Pagounis turned to leave him, but then stopped.

'*Kyrie* Diaktoros,' he said. 'I'm not ungrateful for your interest in this case. Plainly, you've thought about it a great deal, and the conclusions you've reached are sound, in my opinion. The fact is, we have very little to go on, and so far no hard evidence which might give us a clear lead. In short, I have no obvious suspect; so – although I couldn't say this officially, of course – if you were prepared to lend us more of your brain-power, I would appreciate it.'

The fat man bowed his head.

'And I appreciate the compliment,' he said. 'Of course, I will do my best to help, if I am able.'

'Then let me give you what little more information I can. The post-mortem revealed the presence of opiates in Volakis's blood.'

'He'd been drugged?'

'So it seems, with a high dose. Enough to kill him, potentially. Almost certainly enough to put him in a coma.'

'So what about the blows to the head? Why attack him so viciously, if he was already unconscious, or semi-conscious at least?'

'An excellent question. If we put our heads together, perhaps we can find out. There's just one other thing. Your taxi driver through there.' He jerked his thumb towards the offices. 'You're not really a man to come running in here, thinking we'd charge a man with murder without evidence. Do you know something I don't? Should he, in fact, be on my list of suspects?'

The fat man assumed an expression of innocence, and shook his head.

'Not as far as I am aware,' he said. 'But if I find out to the contrary, I'll let you know.'

Seventeen

'They're not so bad, those boys,' said Hassan, as he and the fat man walked to the taxi. 'They wanted to know if I'd seen any unfamiliar vehicles on the local roads, before the snowfall. I told them I couldn't help them. I don't remember seeing anyone I didn't know.'

He climbed into the driver's seat. The fat man got in beside him, and Hassan put on one of his cassettes: pipes and drums, and a woman's nasal voice; an irregular beat, and an upbeat melody. He didn't switch on his headlights in the mist, nor did he slow the car to allow for reduced visibility, or the fat man's nerves, as he had promised. As the music went on, he didn't speak; only when the song came to an end did he lean forward to reduce the volume.

'She looked after you all right over there, did she?' he asked.

'I slept well, thank you,' said the fat man.

Hassan nodded.

'I understand,' he said. 'Ready for something good to eat, maybe? If you are, I have a suggestion. You go to your funeral, do what you have to do. I'll stop at the *kafenion* later on, and let Eustis know we'll be coming for *mezedes*. You can meet me there when you're finished at the cemetery.'

'That sounds a good idea,' agreed the fat man.

'You can tell me all about the funeral,' said Hassan. 'Who came to see him properly buried, and who didn't.'

They passed the first of Vrisi's houses. A woman with a hoe walked down the centre of the road, and stepped smartly out of the way to let them pass; an old man with a bag of loaves rested on a bench by the spring. Through the mist, the church bell tolled.

At the far end of the village, Hassan turned up a side road, and rounding a bend, pulled up at the cemetery gate. When the fat man offered him money, he declined.

'Later,' he said.

Like Vrisi's houses, the cemetery was laid out in terraces, the graves distributed amongst the different levels. The stone chapel and the ossuary stood on the broadest terrace, level with the road; stone stairways with their cementing painted white linked the upper terraces to the lower. The wall around the perimeter was high, and made a barrier to the density of forest pines behind; both trees and mist enclosed the place in gloom, lit in places, above and below, by the comforting glow of candles in memorial lamps.

The fat man climbed to the uppermost terrace and walked from the steps to the outer wall, where trees overhung the graves. On a terrace below, the sexton was making tidy Santos Volakis's waiting grave, shaving the edges straight with a shovel, treading the heaped-up earth with his boot-soles to stop its trickle into the grave. Against the wall leaned the marble headstone and borders, so recently removed from the grave.

The fat man wanted a vantage point where he would not himself be seen, and he chose a tomb of white marble, close to the wall. The headstone's photograph showed a handsome young man, dressed in a suit and tie, though the inscription made the deceased over seventy years old when he died. The grave's unlit lamp had been toppled by the wind, and the fat man stood it upright; he brushed fallen pine needles from the slab covering the tomb, and took a seat there.

'Forgive the liberty, Michaelis,' he said, patting the cold stone, 'but you have the best view in this place of what I want to see. Your relatives seem to have neglected you for a while, so perhaps you'll allow me to keep you company instead.'

He placed his holdall at his feet, and lighting a cigarette, crossed one foot over the other to wait. As he finished a second cigarette – he stubbed the butts out carefully, and buried them in the gravel – on the road below a procession came into view. A yellow pick-up truck drove very slowly, carrying a coffin, whilst a small group of mourners kept pace behind; behind them followed a police car, and, at a distance, a battered red Fiat.

The truck drove through the cemetery gateway, and the mourners gathered round, close enough now so the fat man could hear the sound of their voices. The coffin was unloaded on to the shoulders of four men, one of whom was Attis Danas. Father Tomas was helped down from the truck; he straightened his robes and replaced his hat, then asked amongst the men to borrow matches to relight his censer. When the coffin bearers were comfortable with their burden, Father Tomas led the way to the chapel, where the elderly custodian caused some delay as he struggled to turn the iron key in the lock.

The red Fiat pulled up beyond the cemetery gates, and two men got out; one – dressed in slacks and a sheepskin jacket – carried a notebook, the other had a professional's camera slung round his neck. The man in sheepskin seemed keen to follow the mourners, but the photographer pointed out the police car and held him back to wait in the road.

Ten minutes went by. The cortège emerged from the chapel, and moved slowly to the waiting grave. As the coffin was lowered into the ground and handfuls of earth were thrown on to the lid, the photographer took pictures through a tele-photo lens – of Leda and Frona, of Attis and Maria. No one else stepped forward from the small gathering; there were no laments, and no weeping. Father Tomas said the last necessary words, and wiped the dirt from his hands.

The mourners walked away; only Leda and Frona stayed at the graveside. Attis paid Father Tomas his fee, and went to meet the men from the press, greeting them cordially and clapping the photographer on the back. As he spoke, the jour-nalist began to write.

By way of farewell, the fat man patted the tomb on which he had sat and brushed a few pine needles from the back of his coat. Carrying his holdall, he made his way down the terraces; he avoided the paths and stairways, and picking his way instead between the tombs close to the cemetery walls, descended in a direct line towards the open grave where Leda and Frona still stood.

The sexton leaned on his spade, the pipe in his mouth producing clouds of fragrant smoke. He watched the fat man's approach with an interest which caught Frona's eye, and she looked up from the coffin at the grave's bottom. There were no tears on her face; she seemed more tired than afflicted by grief. With the fat man's intention to address them apparent, she touched Leda's arm.

'Time to go,' said Frona.

Her contemplation interrupted, Leda too looked up from the grave.

'Let's go,' urged Frona, and without another glance at the fat man – who was now drawing very close – she walked away, towards Attis and the journalists.

But Leda didn't follow. She gave a last look at the coffin, and nodded to the sexton, who dug his shovel into the banked earth and dropped the first spadeful into the grave. Stones and dirt spattered the coffin lid.

At the grave-foot, the fat man rooted in his pocket and brought out a coin the size of a 500-drachma piece, though highly polished and more gold than bronze in colour. He tossed the coin into the grave. Intrigued by the glint of the metal, the sexton peered after it and looked over at the fat man, who gestured to the sexton to continue.

'He must pay the ferryman, and I am happy to provide his fare,' said the fat man. A shovelful of dirt covered the coin. 'We've met before, I think,' he said, to Leda.

Leda's face was wan, and dark circles beneath her eyes showed lack of sleep; but like Frona, her cheeks were dry of tears.

'Have we?' she asked.

'At the chapel of St Fanourios. You have other matters on your mind, so let me remind you. I had an interest in the shrine with seven skulls, and you, I think, were making a request for the return of some lost property. So tell me: has the saint answered your prayer?'

Her eyes went to the slowly filling grave.

'Yes,' she said. 'Yes, he has.'

'I should formally introduce myself. I am Hermes Diaktoros, of Athens. Attis Danas may have mentioned me to you. We fell into conversation when I was last here, and he asked me to look into the circumstances regarding what was, as we thought at that time, the disappearance of your father's mortal remains. That mystery seems sadly solved, though the solving of it has generated others, perhaps more serious. May I ask your name?'

'They call me Leda.'

'Leda. That's right: Attis told me. Such a pretty name. May I walk with you, as far as the gates? Attis and the woman who was with you . . .'

'My aunt, Frona. My father's sister.'

'Your aunt, of course. They are waiting for you, I think, so I won't keep you long, but I'm afraid I must ask you some questions, if we are to untangle the circumstances of your father's death.'

They began to walk towards the gates, where Attis, with Frona at his side, was still talking to the press.

'Why?' Leda seemed weary; her head hung down as they walked. 'Why must there be questions? Questions won't bring him back. Nothing will. Attis is only worried about the money. That's why he hired you.'

'Do you not want your money, then?' asked the fat man. 'You may face another four years now, before you get your legacy.'

She pressed a fingertip into her eye, as if to stem a tear.

'I don't expect you to understand,' she said. 'I don't expect anyone to understand. But my father's legacy, as far as I'm concerned, has nothing to do with money. His legacy is his work and his standing as a poet, as a national treasure. I'm the proudest woman in Greece, to be his daughter. And that is much more valuable than money.'

'Is it easy, then, to be proud here, where the people must know a great deal of your business?' The fat man indicated the sexton, who was leaning on his shovel, watching them. 'How common is the knowledge of the conditions put on your legacy? I know how small communities can be, and my guess is, they assume here that the conditions were put in place as some kind of punishment. Is that what they think?'

'I've no idea what they think, nor do I care. I live in the city now, where people don't know our business. I haven't lived in Vrisi for years. Let them gossip all they like. Their opinions are of no interest to me.'

'There's just you and your aunt, is there? No other relatives?'

'There's just us, yes. Frona's been like a mother to me. I owe her so much.'

'And your birth mother? I'm sorry to press you, but I need to understand the background to this affair.'

'My mother lives abroad. She and my father are divorced. I never see her.'

'Do you know the reason for their divorce?'

'I was very young. Why is it relevant, anyway?'

'When a man has died in the way your father has, sometimes it's necessary to dig deep into the past. I have known people harbour grudges for years, and wait decades for revenge.'

Leda stopped walking. The fat man went on several paces, and turned back to her.

'My father's death was an accident,' she said. 'You talk as if it was – something else.'

The fat man walked back to stand close to her.

'You're an intelligent woman, Leda,' he said. 'I don't think you ever believed Inspector Pagounis's story about a fall, did you?'

She put her hands up to her face, and spoke through the screen of her fingers.

'I wanted to believe him,' she said. 'I really, really wanted to believe him. But there were cuts, and gashes . . . Why do that to him? Why hurt him in that way?' She lowered her hands, and looked at him, seeming older than her years. 'And I loved him so much; I worshipped him like a hero!' She began to cry. 'I'm sorry. It's been such a strain.'

'Of course it has,' said the fat man. 'But I must ask you this, difficult though it is. Your father loved you, of that I am sure.

Yet – forgive me if this seems harsh – it now appears he disappeared for four years and was somewhere alive through all that time, but left you effectively an orphan, with no inheritance except his reputation; and whilst I agree that reputation is something to be proud of, it doesn't put bread on the table. He let you believe he was dead; in effect, he abandoned you. That seems to me the act of a cruel man, a hard man; yet, having read his work, I didn't get the impression that your father was hard in any way, rather that he was a man with a heart which knew how to love, and a soul which knew great passion.'

She gave no reply. Ahead of them, Attis and Frona were moving through the gates.

'Why would a loving father leave his child?' went on the fat man. 'Were there financial difficulties, Leda? Is that what he ran away from – not you, but financial disaster? Is that why his assets have remained frozen, to protect them for you, to shield them from someone else?' He thought again. 'Someone you know, perhaps?' He glanced at Attis. 'Or someone you don't know, someone like the tax man? Was he not abandoning you, but protecting you in the long term, I wonder? What do you think?'

'I can't say,' she said.

'Do you mean you can't say, or you won't say?'

Again, she was silent.

'Did he have enemies that you knew of, Leda? Someone who would kill to prevent his return from the dead?'

'I don't know.'

'If there's someone you're protecting, I advise you not to do so any longer,' he said, in a sterner tone. 'It would be madness to protect anyone when a violent crime has been committed. Not only because the killer must be caught, but to protect the innocent. Inspector Pagounis has a job to do, and without clear leads he will likely start questioning anyone with a connection to your father. Now, I don't know what kind of policeman he is, but many are very orderly, and loose ends are an abomination to them. I have known a number of cases, over the years, where innocent people have been jailed, just to close a case and let the paperwork be neatly filed away. Think too, of people's reputations. You don't live here now, so maybe you don't care, but in these small places, mud sticks. Hassan the taxi driver was questioned this morning, and already they have him serving twenty years. So if you know anything, you must tell me. Or tell the inspector. But please, don't think you have any loyalty to a killer.'

She looked at him. There was nothing to be read in her expression.

'I tell you, hand on heart,' she said, after a moment, and like a patriot she placed her hand on her chest, 'I swear, by God and all the saints, I would never do anything to protect my father's killer.'

The pledge was sincere.

'I'm sorry, I must go,' she said, and walked away.

'Did you find any sign of my ring, by the way?' he called after her; but she was apparently already out of earshot, and didn't reply.

The fat man didn't follow her from the cemetery but wandered back instead in the direction of the sexton, who was holding a lighted match to the bowl of his pipe, sheltering the flame with a cupped hand, puffing on the pipe stem in phuts and spits to encourage the tobacco to burn. Though not a young man, he was lean and fit; despite the early season of the year, he wore twill shorts which showed well-muscled legs, thick socks up to his knees and a builder's boots.

The fat man gave him a smile.

'Please, don't let me interrupt your work,' he said. 'I am a visitor here, making a pilgrimage to the burial place of this great man.'

'You'll not interrupt me; I've time to spare,' said the sexton. He shook out the match and dropped it into the grave. 'And great man or not, this one's a troublemaker. Let me tell you something.' He pointed at the fat man with the stem of his pipe, prodding at the air. 'This is a big day for me, a memorable day. This is the first time in thirty years I've had to bury the same man twice.' He gave a laugh. 'Died twice, buried twice. Doesn't happen very often, does it?'

'Rarely,' agreed the fat man. 'You're right, it happens very rarely. But is it truly the case, even here? I gather what you buried on the first occasion was, in fact, the carcass of a pig.'

The sexton puffed on his pipe.

'Damn that beast, yes. All that work, just for some animal we'd have been better off butchering and roasting, though I should say this one'll be finding things much hotter than he'd like.' He pointed hell-wards with his pipe-stem. 'He racked up a few sins when I knew him; who knows what he got up to whilst he was gone, and our priest's not happy, not happy at all. He's complaining about a pig in hallowed ground, and so he should complain; the man's been made a fool of, saying the rites over a few pork chops! So that's another sin on the poet's account outstanding. Still, he found his way home, at least. He got here in the end.'

'And now he is here, he must be treated with the respect due all the dead.' The fat man took out his wallet, and handed over two large banknotes. 'Bury him well, and make the grave tidy. And when the ground has settled, make a good job of putting in the borders and the trimmings; there is unlikely to be family here to make sure you do the job right. As for the headstone, leave that for the time being where it stands. When the time comes to put the headstone to this grave, I shall personally come and help you.'

'You, *kyrie*?' asked the sexton. 'Are you family, then?'

'A friend of the family,' said the fat man, 'as I am friend to any family who is friend to me. Mark what I say. Wait until I return before you re-erect that headstone.'

He left the sexton, but went only as far as the chapel, and sat down on a bench at the foot of a cypress tree where pigeons fluttered in the branches. With the mourners gone, and still no rattle of soil and stones from the sexton's spade, the place was peaceful.

From his holdall, he took out the volume of Volakis's poems and turned the pages, choosing poems to read. Some were verses of only a few lines, others covered a page or even two, but all were beautifully constructed, showing both extraordinary mastery of the language and a rare and deep understanding of the human condition. All mankind's emotions were explored and exposed: joy and pain, love and loss; some were apparently memories, summer days by seashores and winter nights by firelight; some were light and humorous, others dark and filled with grief.

At the front of the book was a short essay the poet had written; its title was, 'Love and Death'.

There is in every love – regardless of how flawed, or ill-advised, or futile – perfection at its heart, the purest, whitest light, celestial and clean, unblemished and incorruptible, like the brilliance in a perfectly cut diamond; and it is Death's gift to reveal to us this other-worldly beauty. Like a carapace, repression shields this marvellous kernel; but, like warm sun on snow, the shade of Death melts away obstructions and our ignorance, and reveals this purest love in blazing glory.

Death takes away self-consciousness, and offers open land-scapes, where between two human souls is nothing but the empty space of love, where all truths may be said, with no fear of retraction or regret. No holds are barred, for what's the point? In Death's presence, mouths may speak what might – if there were a future, and an ego to be guarded – remain unsaid. Like soldiers in a battle lost, our souls may meet, clasp hands and hold each other. At our road's end is where the gilded moments lie, and our secret can come forth, that we are all the world to each other.

The pity is, that it is Death's gift to birth our nobility. We are not warriors in our daily lives; we lack the courage to open our hearts, before our ending comes. But this glori-ous, God-given love is our soft tissue, our guts and our glory, and yet we are too vulnerable, in our hard world, to bring it forth. But when it shines, it is the gift of angels. A few moments of its brilliance may make a wasted life worthwhile.

The fat man read this passage twice, and sat on for a while, alone and silent, until the sexton picked up his shovel and began to fill the open grave; then the fat man replaced the book in his holdall, and walked away through the cemetery gates.

Eighteen

When the fat man arrived at the *kafenion*, Hassan was waiting at a table in front of the counter. The place was busy. The old men following rituals of coffee and socialising had lingered over their uninformed debate, and had been joined by those who'd done a morning's work, calling in for a shot of something to take the mist's damp off their lungs. The fat man made his way between the men, who stank of goats, and cement dust, and the sweat of labour; they sat in their outdoor jackets and dirt-clogged boots, caps on their chair-backs and the lines of outdoor life deep in their faces.

By the window, a woodsman rubbed a hole in the condensation and looked out across the *kafenion*'s empty terrace, at a woman leading a small child by the hand.

'Head down, Vasso,' he said to one of his companions. 'That's your sister-in-law, going towards your house.'

'I'm a dead man if she spots me,' said Vasso, shielding his face with his hand. 'I said I'd drive her and the wife over to town. If they know I've been drinking, they'll have both my balls on a plate.'

The men at his table laughed and jeered.

'Balls? What balls?' asked one. 'She had your balls the day

you married her, you pussy! If she wants a ride to town, tell her to call a taxi. Isn't that right, Hassan? She can call a taxi!'

But the fat man's approach distracted Hassan from responding.

'Sit, friend, sit,' he said, pulling out the chair beside him. 'We've got the best seats in the house. What'll you have?'

Hassan himself was drinking lemonade.

'You'll forgive me if I don't follow your lead,' said the fat man, 'but the hour, to me, calls for a splash of ouzo. Especially if we are going to be eating *mezedes*.'

'He's ready for us,' said Hassan, turning to the counter where Eustis, the patron, was making notes on a pad of paper, writing with the pencil he kept behind his ear. He acknowledged Hassan with no more than a flicker in his eyes. 'And an ouzo!' Hassan called after him, as Eustis tucked away his pencil and headed for the little kitchen behind the counter. 'So, tell me; did you find anything to interest you at the cemetery?'

'The proceedings were far from being as harrowing as some. Under the extraordinary circumstances, I suppose the mourners came to terms with their loss some time ago. Their grief today was restrained, for which I, at least, was grateful.'

'Maybe they had no grief to show. Some men no one misses. Was there a good crowd?'

'The gathering was small; I suspect the family preferred it so. The sister was there, and the daughter – who, it turned out, I had met before. The poet's agent, Attis Danas, of course, and a few others. But no one to sing laments. I wondered why that was.'

'Bad feeling,' said Hassan, leaning closer to the fat man like a subversive. 'Many wouldn't go. They went last time, they say, and wasted their laments and their sympathy on a pig. They say they won't be fooled a second time, with the casket closed again and no proof of who's in there. If they can't see the corpse with their own eyes, they prefer to stay away. The women who went, did you notice who they were?'

'A few widows. Apart from those I've named, I didn't know them.'

'Any from Polineri?'

The fat man looked closely at Hassan.

'Not that I knew,' he said. 'Certainly none that I had met before.'

The patron carried out a battered tin tray whose painted view of an island harbour was scratched and fading. He placed a glass of clear ouzo and a small jug of water before the fat man, and at the centre of the table laid three dishes: small pieces of flour-dusted liver fried with onions; thickly sliced, toasted bread, drizzled with green olive oil; boiled chickpeas with a squeeze of lemon juice. He laid two forks beside the dishes, and wished Hassan and the fat man *kali orexi*.

The food was warm, its smell appetising. The noses of the other men twitched.

'Hey, Hassan!' called out a forestry warden – a man of self-importance, who wore his uniform whether he was on his shift or off it. 'What have you got there? What's he brought you?'

'Liver,' said Hassan, picking up a fork and spearing a piece, putting it in his mouth and chewing. 'Goat's liver. Very fresh. Very tasty.'

The forestry warden stood, and straightening the jacket of his uniform, pushed his way between the tables to the counter.

'*Elá*, Eustis!' he called. 'Bring us some *mezedes*!'

'How many for?' shouted the patron.

'All of us!' replied the forestry warden, waving his arm over the company.

'*Amessos*,' called the patron, and only a moment later appeared with more dishes of the same, distributing them to each of the five remaining tables.

The men's faces showed their pleasure.

'He knows us too well,' they said. 'Eustis, bring us some salt!'

'All breaking the Lent fast,' called Hassan to the other tables. 'Your God will take offence.'

'Don't you eat anything, Dinos,' said Eustis, touching one man on the shoulder as he passed with a salt-shaker. 'Your wife's forbidden me to feed you. If you don't eat what she's cooked when you get home, she'll come in here after me, and it won't be only Vasso with no balls.'

'The hell with her,' said Dinos, a man with no hair on his head, except for his moustache. 'If she'd learn to cook like you do, I'd be glad to eat her food. Her mother's a lousy cook, too; burning and boiling dry is in their blood. Bring us another round of drinks here, Eustis; another round for us all.'

The fat man tasted the liver; it was, as Hassan had said, a fresh, well-flavoured mouthful: a touch of pink at the centre, the onions soft and flavoursome, the whole made interesting with a scattering of thyme.

'Excellent,' he said, pouring water into his ouzo to make it cloudy, and taking a drink. He bit into a piece of the crisp bread, which had the smokiness of flame-toasting, and the strength of the garlic Eustis had rubbed it with before it went on the grill. 'You were right, our patron here knows his food. So, I want to talk to you about the poet, this twice-dead poet who's now buried again. His story is certainly interesting – remarkable enough to draw the gentlemen of the press.'

'Did the family send them away?'

'No,' said the fat man, 'they did not. In fact, I rather wondered whether they might have been there by invitation. The poet's agent seemed keen to help them with their story.'

'Publicity,' said Hassan. 'And what do they say – there's no such thing as bad publicity?'

The fat man laughed, and speared three chickpeas on the tines of his fork.

'That's a common misconception amongst the fame-hungry,' he said, putting the chickpeas in his mouth. They were soft to the palate, their musty flavour sharpened with the lemon. 'Publicity and notoriety are first cousins, and often go hand in hand. Like the faces of Janus, one will favour you, the other will bite you in the backside; one will raise you to the stars, the other will drag you to the gutter, and the first can easily metamorphose into the second. A wise man is always cautious in courting publicity.'

'I suppose it's the agent's job to work for his client,' said Hassan. 'It's his job to sell as many books as he can.'

'I suppose so,' said the fat man, taking more liver. 'But who is his client, now? In whose interests is he working?'

'The family's, and his own, surely?'

'Maybe. But what if those two interests were conflicting?'

'Why should they be?'

'Now that,' said the fat man, 'I do not know.'

The fat man finished his toast, and brushed crumbs from his lapels.

'I've been rereading Santos's work,' said the fat man. 'I know you prefer the work of your national poets, but Santos's work is really very fine. He was a man who delighted in our landscapes, clearly a patriot who had a gift for eulogising this great country. But his work reveals other aspects of the man. There was tragedy in his life, I think. It is life's tragedies which produce our greatest art, and he is a fine example of that. But what is the human story, Hassan? Who was the woman who caused him such heartbreak when he lost her? He blamed himself, I think, for whatever happened; there's a quality in the poems beyond straightforward grief. I sense regret, and guilt. I'm sure you know the story; tell me.'

The patron leaned over the table, and removing the empty plates, replaced them with three more.

'Pigeon breast,' he said, 'stewed in red wine. A little potato frittata, and some of my home-pickled vegetables.'

The fat man tried the pigeon, and found the flavour excellent, the sanguineous taste of the game, the garlic and the herbs all married perfectly with dark-red wine.

Hassan took a small square of frittata; the omelette's colour was bright with the yolks of the eggs, in contrast to the pale lemon of the carefully fried potatoes.

'So,' he said, 'you want to know the family secrets?'

'Does the family have secrets?' asked the fat man.

'If you're an investigator, then you know all families have secrets,' said Hassan. 'Just some conceal them better than others.'

The fat man laughed, and took a drink of his ouzo.

'You're right, of course,' he said. 'And I should be honest with you. Yes, I am very interested in the family's secrets. They have become an interesting family, with their Lazarus poet. Tell me his story.'

'What can I tell you?' asked Hassan, taking another piece of frittata. 'I didn't know the man.'

'I assume that what you mean is, you didn't know him well. But you knew him, of course; you told me so, last time I was here. And I don't ask you as an intimate acquaintance. I ask so I can understand the background to his life.'

'All I can tell you is what anyone else would say. He lived in that big house up there, which he somehow inherited. Of course it should have gone down the female line to his sister, but she's not a country-lover. She left to work in the city – she studied accountancy, I think – and married a man there, who kept her until he found a younger model and left her – not destitute, but not very well off either. But our poet claimed to love this place; he said it was in his blood, his soul, and that's the reason he gave for staying in that old house that had been his parents' and his grandparents'. Frona, of course, wants to see it sold, but until the terms of the will are met, it isn't hers to sell. So she's stuck with paying old Maria to look after it as it slowly falls down round her ears.'

'So what about his wife? What happened to her?'

Hassan picked out a creamy bloom of pickled cauliflower and bit down on it. The fat man tried the frittata, and waited for him to go on, pouring a drop more water into his glass.

'A good question, my friend,' said Hassan at last, taking a piece of pickled carrot. 'Eat, eat. I can have Eustis's delicacies again tomorrow; you may have to wait a while longer.' The fat man chose another piece of pigeon. 'When Santos was nobody . . .' Hassan gave an unkind laugh. 'The fact is, to many here in Vrisi, Santos was never anybody except a village boy. When they put up that memorial, there were objections at the waste of public money and complaints that Venizelos would have made a handsomer statue. But when he was nobody to anybody, the people used to ridicule him and take the piss. You've only to look around you to see a poet doesn't count for much in Vrisi. Time was, there wasn't a woman here would look at him. What was there to look at, after all? And he was a loner; he spent too much time by himself, shut away writing his poems.'

'It is the nature of the work to be solitary, I suppose,' said the fat man, as Eustis placed another dish on the table: cubes of aubergine, dipped in batter and deep fried, liberally sprinkled with salt. 'Another ouzo, if you please, patron, and – Hassan, will you join me?'

'Another lemonade will do me fine, thank you,' said Hassan, giving his empty bottle to Eustis as he left. 'But when Santos's book was published, it was as if he'd been coated in golden honey. Oh, life was very different for that dog, then.

'Listen, friend, the fault around his wife was Santos's own. Every man alive knows how weak women are; their urges are strong, and they've no self-control to deny them, without a man to hold them in check. You've seen it a thousand times; they take the step so easily, from respectability to tramp. Now Santos's wife wasn't beautiful, but she wasn't the worst you've seen, either. And she was clever; she had some kind of university degree, so she was never going to settle easily, here in Vrisi. He left her too much to her own devices, whilst he was attending to the needs of the local ladies who'd decided the touch of fame made even him a worthwhile prospect. Well, he made up for lost time, all right, for all those years when even a port whore wouldn't touch him; and he left his own wife bored at home, with only old Maria and a crying baby for company. So what can you expect? She got herself a boyfriend.'

'And who was this boyfriend?'

Hassan helped himself to the aubergines.

'A so-called friend of Santos's, an American-Greek, who also called himself a poet. But he was having no success at all, so he came to stay in Vrisi because he'd nowhere else to go. Santos had him in the house as a favour, as a guest. His friend was in need of a roof over his head, and Santos offered his hospitality. Crumbs to the beggar, and not doors; but it was a grave mistake on his part to let that wolf into the fold. Two months later, this so-called friend was gone, and Santos's wife went with him.'

'Where did they go?'

Hassan shrugged.

'America. But America's a big place. Who knows?'

'And the baby?'

'Little Leda went nowhere. Maria looked after her, for a while. Then Frona got divorced, and came to look after both her niece and her brother. Which wasn't, I imagine, what she'd planned out of life, though being childless herself, she took to Leda as her own. With his wife gone, Santos became the stone that never smiled. That house, I suspect, was less than cheerful.'

The fat man offered the last of the aubergine to Hassan, who waved it away, so the fat man ate it.

'And our poet never tried to fetch her back?'

'I don't know. To look at him, moping round in cuckold's horns suited him quite well.'

'You had a low opinion of him.'

'Is that a crime?'

'And Leda? Does she never see her mother?'

'Not as far as I know. She and her father were very close, and she grew attached to Frona. She's no need of a woman who abandoned her for some man she hardly knew.'

Eustis brought Hassan's lemonade and replaced the fat man's empty glass with another tumbler of ouzo.

'She's not the only one who abandoned poor Leda, though, is she?' said the fat man, when Eustis returned to the kitchen. 'Now she has to come to terms with the fact that her father's been alive, somewhere, these past four years, and left her and his sister to grieve. What kind of father would do that?'

'A poor one,' said Hassan. 'A very poor one indeed.'

'I agree,' said the fat man, thoughtfully. 'And now he is back in Vrisi, but this time, properly dead. What has been going on, Hassan? Where was he, these past four years? And when he came back here for the last time, how did he get here, and where from?'

'Who knows? If you had the answer to that, it'd kill a lot of gossip.'

The fat man took out his cigarettes and offered them to Hassan, who shook his head.

'What are they saying?' asked the fat man, lighting a cigarette.

'They're saying plenty. That he was coming back here secretly to take something hidden in the house. That sounds possible, to me. Why else would he be walking up the road? But he didn't walk all the way here; it would have taken him hours, and he'd have been seen by someone passing. No: he had transport of some kind. He didn't come by bus, so the bus driver says. So I presume he got here by car.'

'But where is that car?' asked the fat man.

'Maybe someone else was driving,' said Hassan. 'Parked up and left him to walk up the hill unseen, and waited for him elsewhere. When he didn't come back, they left him to it. With snow coming, no one would want to wait. Once it snows, without the right vehicle and the right driver, you're stuck. And anyone who wanted to avoid being seen wouldn't want to get stuck. Or maybe that person knew the poet had come to grief, and let things take their course. A slip on the ice, down he went, and that was it.'

'Maybe,' said the fat man. He drew on his cigarette, and exhaled a stream of smoke. 'But don't you think that, if it were an accident, most people, under any circumstances, would call for help?'

'You don't agree with me,' said Hassan.

'In part I do. You're right, we must assume someone brought Santos to Vrisi. But he didn't walk – he couldn't have done. The crucial factor you didn't mention is the condition he was in when he was brought here.'

'What do you mean?'

'His body was covered in snow. Snow is cold, and flies and maggots don't like cold. It slows down their life-cycle. Yet as soon as Santos's body was taken into the police station – as soon, almost, as it was brought into the warmth – carrion flies hatched. And his body stank; that's what the police told me. Bodies kept in ice from the moment of death don't stink.

Which means only one thing. Santos had already been dead some time, before he ever returned to Vrisi.'

'But it was an accident! Surely he tripped and fell?'

'An accident? Impossible. No, there was no accident here, my friend. There was no accident at all.'

They finished, between them, what was left on the plates. As the fat man drank the last of his second ouzo, Dinos – who had eaten his share of *mezedes*, despite Eustis's plea – called across to their table.

'Hey, Hassan!' he said. 'Take me home in style! I'm not in the mood for walking up that hillside, and I'm in trouble already for eating an edible meal. A few drachmas spent on your fare will make no difference; I might as well make the tongue-lashing worthwhile!'

His companions laughed and called him names; smiling and good-humoured, Dinos pulled on his dirty cap, and put on his jacket over clothes which carried the stink of sheep.

Hassan raised his hand in acknowledgement.

'One minute,' he said, 'and I'm at your service.'

He turned to the fat man, reaching into his pocket for cash, but the fat man stopped him.

'It's on me,' he said. 'I owe you for my fare this morning, and for finding me a decent lunch.'

'Thank you,' said Hassan, 'and I'm sorry to leave you in a hurry.'

'You have your work to do,' said the fat man. 'And whilst you're doing it, you might do me a favour. If any of the people we have spoken about today – any of Santos's family, or anyone connected with them – calls on your services, be good enough to let me know.'

The fat man glanced around to make sure he wasn't watched, and pressed four 5,000-drachma notes into Hassan's hand.

'Take this money,' he said, 'and use it, if necessary, on my behalf. Whoever calls on your services, do your very best to find out where they are headed. If you need to grease a few palms, please do so, but bring me back what information you can.'

Hassan held out his hand to give the money back.

'I can't take this,' he said. 'I'm not the one to help you, friend.'

'On the contrary,' said the fat man, closing Hassan's fingers over the cash. 'You are uniquely placed to do so, and your help may be invaluable. But remember, Hassan: keep this to yourself. Your discretion is vital to my investigation. Tell no one at all what I have asked of you.'

When Hassan had left, the fat man asked for his bill, and when told the amount owing by the patron, left money to cover it on the table, along with a generous tip.

'Your pride in your talent is quite justified,' he said, as Eustis picked up his payment, 'and it is good to see your skills appreciated. Have you never thought of expanding your business, and tackling a bigger market?'

Eustis shook his head.

'That's not for me,' he said. 'My pleasure in the cooking would soon evaporate, if I were to do it every day, at the beck and call of customers, to their order. Here, the menu's down to me. If I want to try something different, I do so; if I fancy something my grandmother used to cook, that's what we have. They know me here, and they know it's all pot-luck. And as long as they appreciate what I give them, that's enough.'

The fat man laughed.

'You'll never make a million, serving these few tables,' he said.

'If you mean there'll never be a big balance in my bank, then you're quite right,' said Eustis. 'But I have my family and my health, and above all I have the freedom to live my life as I wish. I regard myself as a very wealthy man.'

The fat man patted his shoulder.

'Well said. And you may add profound wisdom to your list of attributes. If more of the world would share your philosophy, we'd all be happier.'

At the payphone on the wall, he took out the notebook where he had the publisher's number, and deposited enough coins in the slot for a long-distance call. When he heard the phone ring out, he turned his back on the assembled company.

Yorgas Sarris answered promptly.

'*Nai?*'

'*Kyrie* Sarris, this is Hermes Diaktoros.'

'Ah, yes,' said the publisher. 'My Athenian friend. What can I do for you?'

'I was simply wondering,' said the fat man, 'how was your dinner at Georgio's?'

There was a smile in the publisher's voice.

'Excellent indeed,' he said. 'I had the *kleftiko*, and the lamb was soft as butter. And we had a very good retsina, from the barrel.'

'We are birds of a feather, you and I,' said the fat man. 'The food always comes first. But my secondary interest is in Attis Danas and his poems. Did you learn anything of interest?'

There was a silence.

'I'm considering whether I should tell you this, or not,' said the publisher, at last. 'But I think I should, because I've been asking myself whether what I agreed with Attis was either wise or legal. I poured plenty of wine for him, to get him to talk; but I matched him glass for glass, and that might have clouded my judgement.'

'And what did you agree?'

'I made him an offer for the poems.'

'A good offer?'

'The best offer I've ever made anyone. But that's not what it'll look like, on paper. On paper, it'll look as if I've bought the work for almost nothing.' Yorgas sighed. 'I may have been unwise. Still. Nothing is signed or sealed.'

'May I ask you for a summary of your agreement?'

'We drank too much retsina,' said Yorgas, ruefully. 'He's dropped the price, but on condition I go along with the way he wants to structure the deal. I pay a nominal sum for the poems, with the balance as an ex gratia payment to him. He suggested it might go through our books as publicity, or hospitality. How we would handle that doesn't matter. The point is, he wanted a personal cheque.'

'What reason did he give you for that?'

'He said he would pass the money on to Frona and Leda, as soon as the cheque cleared. If we did the deal as it should be done, with the full amount paid to Santos's estate, they'd be waiting another four years before they saw a cent. I could see his point, last night. And I can see it now. The difference is, I can see the danger in it, too.'

'And what is the work's provenance? Did you ask him that?'

'Of course. New poems from a dead man's hand are not a common finding.'

'And what did he say?'

'He claimed he'd come across them by luck, that he'd found them whilst going through some papers.'

'In short, he claimed he was acting in the family's interests?'

'Yes.'

'And if it turned out he wasn't, what then?'

'That's my concern. I would have made him a large payment, to which Santos's heirs would have no legal rights whatever. And yet what he proposes seems sensible, under the rather unusual circumstances.'

'Why do you not speak to Santos's sister and ask her view? If she trusts Attis and gives the proposal her blessing, it would not be your fault if the deal went sour.'

'*Kyrie* Diaktoros, listen to me. I'm a man of business, and my business is to make money. For that reason, I want to acquire those poems. But as I said to you before, this house has old origins and a sterling reputation I don't wish to tarnish. By speaking to Frona and agreeing to this deal, my conscience tells me I'm colluding in something shabby, which might, at worst, be illegal. That concerns me. And I'm concerned, too, that Attis specifically asked me not to speak to Frona. He wants to surprise her, he says. He has romantic ideas in that direction.'

'You think his interest in the lady is romantic, rather than monetary? I have no wish to be ungallant; but in four years from now, Frona will be quite a wealthy lady.'

'You're right. But who can know for certain what's in a man's heart, and whether his words are honest?'

'Who, indeed?'

'So what would you advise, *Kyrie* Diaktoros? Should I trust Attis, and go along with his proposal, or is it an arrangement I would come to regret?'

The fat man considered.

'I would stall, if I were you, another day or two,' he said. 'I shall be on my way to find Attis, very shortly. He and I are due another chat; and after we have spoken, I shall give you my opinion on whether you are safe to proceed, or not.'

Nineteen

In the orchard, the sparse-leaved branches of the almond trees were showing their first blossom. Frona carried a three-legged stool and Maria's milk bucket to where Tina, the old nanny-goat, was tethered in the grass. Tina raised her head, and watched Frona's approach with baleful eyes. The goat's udder was baggy rather than full, and she was years beyond any useful productivity; but Maria had raised the animal from a kid and kept her out of sentiment beyond Frona's understanding. In the bottom of the bucket, Maria had sent her pet a bowl of table-scraps – breadcrusts and potato peelings, the cores of the tart apples she had used in a pie. Frona let Tina snatch a crust of bread from her hand, then tucked the scrap-bowl into the branches of the nearest tree, out of Tina's reach, until they were done.

The goat bleated. Frona placed her stool close to the tethering peg, and lowered herself on to the stool. She grabbed Tina's hind leg to pull her close, and the goat, accustomed to the routine, backed up to Frona, her back legs splayed. Frona grasped both teats in her fists, and began competently to squeeze milk from the udder. At first, a steady stream ran frothy and steaming into the bucket; but the udder was soon flaccid and the teats dry.

Frona slapped the goat's rump, and Tina moved away to strain at a patch of dandelions beyond her reach. Frona stood, and reaching up for the bowl, tossed the food scraps into the grass.

She looked into the bucket.

'There's not much there, Tina *mou*,' she said, sympathetically. 'No more than a couple of glassfuls. Drier and drier, with every season. We're neither of us getting any younger. You'll have to do better, or . . .'

She ran a finger across her neck, to illustrate the animal's possible fate; but as she did so, a man's voice spoke, coming, as it seemed, from nowhere.

'That would seem an unkind end for an animal who's doing her best.'

Startled, Frona turned. The fat man stood close behind her.

'*Mori!*' she said. 'You scared me half to death! What on earth are you doing, sneaking up on a woman like that?'

'Forgive me,' said the fat man. 'It was not my intention to frighten you. I was taking the liberty of having a look around the property before I called at the house, when I heard your voice, and followed it.'

'And who gave you the right to take liberties? This is private property. If you have business here, use the front door, like a respectable person.'

The fat man laughed. He held out his hand to the goat and made soft noises to attract her attention; but Tina had her nose in the potato peelings and ignored him.

'Whether I am respectable or not is open to debate,' he said, turning back to Frona, 'but my inquisitive nature is undeniable, and my curiosity led me to want to see the outside of this place before I entered it. Curiosity is essential, in my profession.'

'And what profession is that, that it needs someone to be

curious? And what makes you think you'll be entering my house?'

She picked up the stool, the bucket and the bowl, and set off through the orchard towards the house, following a path worn down to bare earth. The fat man's less direct route was drawn in a trail of flattened grass, winding through the trees.

'I am an investigator,' he said, to her back.

She stopped, and faced him. There were white hairs from the goat's rump on her black sweater; the lipstick she had applied for her brother's funeral remained only at the outer edges of her lips, and without the colour to brighten her complexion, she seemed closer to old age than to her middle years.

'So you're Attis's investigator,' she said. 'You're the one who's to find out what happened to Santos. Is that why you were at the funeral? Doing your investigating?'

'Forgive me,' said the fat man. 'I should introduce myself. Hermes Diaktoros, of Athens.'

He offered a hand, but she looked down at her own full hands, and shrugged.

'Frona Kalaki,' she said. 'Santos was my brother. *Chairo poli.*'

'*Chairo poli.* But I already know who you are. Having seen you at the funeral, I drew my own conclusions. I have come to see Attis. I thought I might find him here.'

'He's in the house. Let me show you the way.'

She led him to the walled edge of the orchard, where a narrow gate of wooden staves led into a garden overgrown by weeds and unchecked shrubs. Chickens scratched amongst the roots; a skinny cockerel jerked his head to watch them pass, setting his ruby comb and wattle trembling. Close to the house, a strip of land had been cleared for cultivation; here, the last of the winter's tall artichokes and hardy spinach grew, and shoots of new crops showed green against the stony earth.

'Are you the gardener?' asked the fat man, as they passed.

'Not me,' said Frona. 'I'm never here. Maria does what she can, but she's getting too old to manage very much.'

'Is it your intention to sell the house?'

'That might be my intention,' said Frona, 'but my intention won't find a buyer. I'm not hopeful of getting a sale. The value of the place is in the land. Someone might take the land off our hands, knock down the house and build something civilised people could live in.'

They reached the open back door, and the fat man followed Frona into an old-fashioned kitchen, where polished copper pans hung on flaking lime-plaster walls, and the embers of a wood fire smoked in a raised fireplace. Frona placed the milking stool on the bare floorboards and pushed it under the pine table with her foot; she took an enamel jug from the dresser and poured in the goat's milk from the bucket. The milk only half-filled the jug. She put the bucket on the stool, under the table.

'Not worth the trouble,' she said, holding up the jug. 'Poor Tina belongs in a *stifado*. Can I offer you coffee? Though you'd have to put up with my brew. Maria's gone home. She has to take care of her mother.'

'Maria has a lot of work,' said the fat man, 'for someone you describe as elderly.'

'Not really,' said Frona. 'She airs the house and uses the garden as she wishes. She's cooking for us whilst we're here, but in a day or two, we'll all be gone.'

'Do you know what I would prefer to coffee?' said the fat man, placing his holdall by his feet. 'A glass of that goat's milk. Though I see it's not a plentiful commodity. Would you mind?'

'Not at all.'

She filled a glass from the jug and handed it to the fat man, who tasted it, and smiled.

'Still warm,' he said, 'and full of the flavour of the orchard. Your brother, I believe, loved this house; his poetry shines with the affection he felt for it. Yet you – forgive me for rushing to conclusions – seem not to share his sentiment. Is that true?'

She pointed to a chair and asked him to sit, taking a seat herself as he did so.

'Let me tell you a little about my brother,' she said. 'Whether it will help you or not, I don't know. I shouldn't speak ill of the dead, of course; but anyone but a saint would be angry with him for what he's done to us.'

'Are you angry with him, then, Frona?'

She laid a hand across her forehead and closed her eyes.

'He was my brother, and I loved him,' she said. 'But for this disgrace, and this deception, if he walked alive into this kitchen at this moment, I would kill him with my own hands.' She opened her eyes, took her hand from her face and looked earnestly at the fat man. 'Try and understand how it has been. I hate this house and this village, with its small minds. I came back here after my divorce, when Santos was alone too, to take care of him and Leda. I've cared for Leda as my daughter since she was a baby. That was my duty, and I fulfilled it. Not uncomplainingly, to tell the truth; but my conscience is clear. God sees all, and God knows I did what was right. When Santos died – when he led us to believe he had died . . .' She stopped, and shook her head. 'You have to get to the bottom of this for us, *Kyrie*. If I never understand what's been going on, I shall lose my mind, I swear. When we thought he was dead, I took Leda with me back to the city and we made our lives there. I make a little money, though not much. I do accounts for some small businesses, help out with their taxes – only a few hours a week, but I've a settlement from my husband, too. But it's been hard. Leda wanted to go to college;

she wants to be an actress, and I've done my best for her. But why my brother tied up her – and my – inheritance has lost me many nights' sleep. Bills that couldn't be paid, and his money mouldering in some bank. I cursed him; I cursed my own brother his stupid, dramatic gesture! Because that's what I assume it was: the same old Santos, always with the drama! No wonder his daughter wants to be an actress! She's inherited nothing from him, thus far, but his love of theatrics.'

She fell silent.

'You have no idea, then,' asked the fat man, 'where your brother was, or what he was doing, these past four years?'

Vehemently, she shook her head.

'If I'd known he was anywhere but in his grave, would I have left him there and struggled to feed his daughter, *his* flesh and blood, *his* responsibility? I would not! I would have tracked him to the ends of the earth, and fetched him home! But this, this – what can I call it but a farce? He was always secretive, withdrawn. Always one to keep things to himself. Being the only one of us to know where he was – that would have amused him, I'm sure. Amused him, at our expense! That kind of cruelty, I wouldn't have expected of him.'

'Tell me about him,' said the fat man, quietly. 'What kind of man was he?'

She became pensive; her face took on a look of sadness.

'He wasn't a bad man,' she said, 'which only makes this odd affair more troubling. He loved this house, you're right; he loved its peace and quiet. He had good memories of it, from childhood, and there was a large part of Santos which never really grew up. He wasn't a good father; he was too absorbed in his own world, his words and poems. Words were his world, and there wasn't room for Leda, or a wife. Leda was noisy and disturbed him, and he liked everything calm and undisturbed. He never cleaned his study, and he wouldn't let Maria clean it either. He used to say he liked dust; he said it absorbed noise and made the room quieter. Isn't that ridiculous?' She looked at the fat man; there were tears in her eyes. 'His study was such a mess, all books and papers, and things he used to pick up on his walks. Hours and hours he'd walk, alone and in all weathers, and he'd bring things home with him, like a child – pine cones, flowers, pebbles, all kinds of rubbish. He was a magpie; he collected things that interested him, and that was most things. He was interested in people, too. He used to eavesdrop on others' conversations. He was quite shameless about it; if he found a conversation really interesting, he would join in.'

The fat man smiled, and she smiled back, though sadly.

'He never liked electricity,' she said. 'He preferred the natural light of fire and flames. He used to burn church candles, three or four together, in preference to any electric light. He used to say, "Fire begets fire"; I suppose he meant his own imagination and ideas. He never drew the curtains at the windows. When it got too dark to read what he was reading or writing, he used to stop and lie down on that old sofa, and sleep a while. And with his candles, he used to say they gave him better dreams, that dreams flourished in their warmth. He said sleeping by candlelight evoked his best work. All he had in the study was one electric lamp. He even took the bulbs out of the overhead fitting. He said if the light was only dim, Maria wouldn't see the dust, and try to come in and clean.'

Again, she fell silent.

'He sounds a remarkable man,' said the fat man.

Frona wiped tears away from under her eyes, and the anger came back to her face.

'Oh, he was remarkable, all right,' she said. 'Only a remarkable man would abandon his own family, and leave them as good as penniless, and go and hide himself away for four years, just to make fools of them.' She stood up from the table. 'You wanted to see Attis. I'll go and find him.'

'I'm pleased to find him still here,' said the fat man. 'I thought a man as busy as he is would be rushing back to the office.'

Frona blushed.

'Attis wants to stay a couple of days, and I agreed,' she said. 'He's been very good to me. He thought it would be helpful to me, if he was around.'

The fat man's eyebrows lifted.

'Really?' he asked. 'That is most kind of him. And does Leda appreciate his offer of help, too?'

'Leda? Leda's already left. She said she wanted to get away, get out of Vrisi. She hasn't been easy, these past days. I was glad to let her go.'

The fat man frowned.

'And where has she gone?'

'To see some college friends, in Patras.'

'When did she leave?'

'A couple of hours ago. Hassan's driven her to the port. I'll go and call Attis for you. Come with me, and you can talk to him in Santos's study.'

When Attis entered the study, the fat man was by the bookshelves, a cloth-bound book in his hand.

'Ah, Attis,' he said, 'I'm pleased to see you again.'

He turned the book to hold it by its spine, and with the page edges towards the floor, shook it, hard.

'What on earth are you doing?' asked Attis. 'That book may be valuable!'

'My thought exactly.' The fat man replaced the book on the shelf, and selected another, at random, from the shelves above. 'I'm conducting a search,' he said, shaking the book he had chosen in the same way as the last, 'but I am finding very little. It is a time-consuming business; but I am told that our poet was a secretive man. I think there may be undiscovered poems hidden here, but the question is, with all these works to choose from, where might they be? What do you think? If you were hiding poems, which shelf would you choose?'

He stood back, appearing to consider all the rows of books which lined the wall.

'I really don't think you should do that,' objected Attis. 'I don't think it's your place . . .'

Swiftly, the fat man turned.

'You don't think it's my place to do what?'

Startled, Attis took a step away.

'To search Santos's study. I don't think Frona would want you to do that.'

'But you invited me here to help you solve the mystery surrounding Santos,' said the fat man, reasonably. 'Who knows but that the answer lies in one of these volumes? You expect me to be methodical, I am sure, in my investigation, and the methodical approach is to take down these books, one at a time, and search them in sequence.'

'But I don't see what you would gain.'

'Why? Because you have already looked? Or has there not been enough time for you to do so, and you'd like to be the one to get there first?'

'Really, I object . . .'

But the fat man held up a hand to silence him.

'A moment,' he said. 'I have a feeling about . . .' He stepped up to the shelves, and from a high shelf on the far left chose a black-bound book whose title was embossed on the spine in gold. '*Explorations in Classical Drama*. Now here's a promising work, since it is in a drama we find ourselves here.' He opened the book at its centre, and allowed the first half of the pages to flutter through his fingers, then the second half. Towards the back of the book, folded into four and tucked away, was a sheet of paper. 'Well, a lucky strike indeed,' he said. He replaced the book on the shelf, and carefully unfolded the paper, which was discoloured with age and dog-eared, and bore the round mark of some cup or glass; but the fading handwriting was clear. 'Behold, a poem! *Sea Nymphs*. Did Santos ever write a poem called *Sea Nymphs*, that you know of?' Attis shook his head, and intrigued, moved forward to take a look, and the fat man held it out to him. 'Here, see what you make of it.'

Attis read through the verses, and sighed.

'It's an early version of one of his best-known poems,' he said. 'But he didn't call it *Sea Nymphs*. It became *View from the Rocks*. This is inferior to the final version, of course; but it's fascinating to see the thinking behind its development. I'll keep this; it must be preserved.'

'By you?' asked the fat man. 'Are you, then, custodian of Santos's work?'

'I suppose I must be. Who else?'

'Santos's daughter, perhaps? Or his sister?'

Attis refolded the paper and slipped it into his pocket.

'I'll show this to Frona, of course,' he said. 'But is it wise to be looking for poems when you might be looking for answers?'

'Do you think I am wasting time, then? It is my view that Santos's poems are at the root of this difficult situation, as you describe it. And I include, with those poems, the works you have recently acquired. I have spoken with your publisher friend, who is anxious to prove their provenance or be clear about their lack of it. But I don't think you are trying to deceive him, are you, Attis? I believe you think – maybe you even know – you have the genuine article in your hands. But

I'm wondering why you're so keen to sell them quietly, outside the terms of Santos's will. And I have a suspicious mind, especially when it comes to conveniences like this one. How come these poems have suddenly appeared? Where exactly did you find them?'

Attis gestured at the far side of the room.

'Here,' he said, 'in the desk.'

'So you have been searching Santos's room. No wonder you wish to stop me. Finders, keepers: is that what you're thinking?'

'On the contrary, I have no intention of keeping anything. Nor did I come sneaking in here motivated by self-interest, and you have read me wrong if you think so. I came looking because I was prompted to do so.'

'Prompted by what?'

'About six months ago, I had a letter. Not even a letter, really – an anonymous note, just a few words, suggesting Santos had left publishable work here. I dismissed it at first; there was nothing I could do about it, anyway. I had no reason to come to Vrisi, gain access to the house and start hunting in Santos's desk. I took it as some kind of joke. But when I was here for the exhumation, I thought I might as well take a look, and there they were.'

'How very convenient. Providential, in fact. There's no doubt in your mind that it's Santos's work?'

'None whatever. There're more than twenty poems, in a collection he called *Odes to Nemesis*. The work is wonderful, and unmistakably his. Listen, *Kyrie* Diaktoros. I haven't told Frona I have these poems.' The fat man's eyebrows raised. 'I want to present her with a piece of good news, with a sale already made in such a way as she will immediately benefit, not with another untouchable asset. It's been hard for me to see her in financial difficulties whilst I've reaped

231

some of the benefits, at least, of Santos's improved fortunes. I've offered to help her, of course; but she's a proud woman, and reluctant to accept what she calls "loans". It's my intention to structure this deal such that she'll have her money now, and not in another four years. But to do that, we'll have to be unorthodox.'

'So what is your intention, exactly?'

'That I should sell these new poems for a pittance, nominally. The meat of the advance would come to me, personally, and I shall give it to Frona, for her and Leda.'

'You'll forgive me for pointing out that such an arrangement appears highly dubious, to an outsider like me.'

'It will only appear dubious until the cash appears in Frona's account.'

The fat man regarded him.

'Has it occurred to you that perhaps, in some way, you are being set up?'

'Set up? What do you mean?'

'That you might be the victim of some fraud?'

Attis shook his head.

'Impossible. I know Santos's work. His quality has not been matched in a generation. The poems are his work.'

'You recognise, of course, that you are taking a huge risk in selling this work without declaring it to Santos's lawyers? They will certainly find out what you have done, before too long. And, though I have great sympathy with Frona's position in regards to the legacy, you are going against the wishes a man took the trouble to stipulate in his will. You and his family do not understand why Santos laid out those conditions as he did, and so you take them to be punitive, and unfair. Yet might there not be factors involved here of which you know nothing? You are playing with fire, Attis, by taking this matter into your own hands, and I advise you to proceed with extreme caution. The truth still has a long way to come to light in this case; in fact, even the barest of facts are still concealed. So be careful you are not deceived into taking action which will reflect badly on you. You might see yourself as coming to the rescue of a distressed damsel; but many a man has come to grief over a damsel who turned out to be a black widow.'

'Frona's a decent woman,' said Attis. 'She deserves an easier life, and I wish to help her towards that.'

Outside, a car drew up, its wheels scattering the gravel as the driver braked and sounded a blast on the horn.

Attis crossed to the window, and looked out.

'It's a taxi,' he said. 'Did you order a taxi?'

The fat man smiled.

'Perhaps,' he said. 'I shall go and enquire. Be cautious whom you trust, Attis. I'll be in touch, once everything becomes clear.'

He held out his hand, and Attis took it. Outside, the taxi's horn blew again.

'It seems I am in a hurry,' said the fat man, picking up his holdall. 'But I have one more question, before I go.' He reached into his pocket, and took out the diary Attis had removed from Santos's desk. 'Tell me, where did Santos die, the first time?'

'In Nafplio.'

'And why did he go there?'

'Well,' said Attis, 'there's a sad story, there. He was booked to do a reading at the university, but at the last minute, it was cancelled. I tried and tried to phone him before he left, to save him a wasted journey. I tried right up to midnight, but no one answered the phone. Probably it was out of order, or he hadn't paid the bill. But the fact was, he didn't need to go. They'd written to him, I gather, and told him not to come; I assume, in this backwater, the faculty's letter didn't reach him. The man who'd organised the visit was heartbroken, and blamed himself; he thought if he had given Santos more notice, he'd never have gone there, and he wouldn't have died.'

'But he didn't die there, did he?' asked the fat man. 'And I think it would be a kindness if you telephoned that gentleman, and told him to blame himself no longer. I think Santos did get his letter, and went there anyway. Look.'

He opened the diary at the date of Santos's death, where the word 'Nafplio' was written in the poet's hand, in ink; the word had been struck through, with a pencil.

In puzzlement, Attis looked at the fat man.

'But that's absurd,' he said. 'Why would he have made that long journey, if he knew he didn't have to go?'

'That's an excellent question,' said the fat man, 'and one I intend to have an answer to, very soon now.'

Hassan waited at the wheel of his taxi, riffling through his collection of music cassettes. When he saw the fat man, he wound down his window to speak to him.

'I thought I would find you here, my friend,' he said, 'though you move through Vrisi like a snake in the grass.'

'I hope I am no snake,' said the fat man, 'and yet a snake's slyness may sometimes be emulated to advantage. Why did you want me?'

'I'm bringing you information,' said Hassan. 'I've been your eyes and ears, as you asked. I've taken a young lady on the beginning of a journey.'

'And do you know where she has gone?'

'I certainly do,' he said. 'Get in, and I'll tell you whilst we travel.'

But the fat man hesitated.

'The bird has already flown,' he said, 'and if you know where she has gone, it will do no harm to let her get a head start, and think she is not followed. There remains something here in Vrisi I must take care of. Can you pick me up at the *kafenion* later on? Let us say eight o'clock. That should give me long enough to do what needs to be done.'

'Eight o'clock it is,' said Hassan.

'In the meantime,' said the fat man, 'I'd appreciate a ride down to the village.'

Early evening, and Maria was visiting the neighbours, talking over the gossip the day had brought: the low attendance at the funeral; Leda's departure for Patras, and the dangers of travel to unescorted women; the dangers to Frona's reputation, being alone in the house with Attis Danas.

'She's lonely,' the neighbour was saying, as she shelled beans. 'Lonely women fall so easily into sin.'

'He's a predator,' said Maria, sipping tea. 'He's preying on her. Like a wolf, he's waiting to take advantage.'

But the neighbour's husband laughed.

'There's only one predator, up there,' he said. 'A fine specimen of the most dangerous predator there is: a middle-aged woman with no man.'

The first stars glittered in the darkening sky. Close by Roula's truckle bed, Maria had left an oil lamp burning on the dresser; the glass was missing from the lamp's door, and the flame danced in the draughts, throwing changing shadows across the room. A cold wind blew off the hills, and Maria had spread overcoats on top of the blankets to keep her mother warm; and Roula was warm enough, if her hands stayed under the blankets, though the cold had reddened her nose, and the blanket's rough wool scratched her chin.

Outside, a dog barked an alarm, then gave a troubled whine, and was quiet.

Roula fell into a doze, a twilight sleep where memories seemed real. She travelled to a night when she, as a young girl with a friend, had come across a youth stripped naked, bathing away the midday heat in a mountain pool; she remembered how they had hidden, and watched. Smiling as she dozed, or dreamed, she didn't hear the door open, or notice the oil lamp flicker as it did so; but she sensed someone was there, and opened her eyes to find Hermes at her side.

He crouched down at the bedside, offering his hand. She took her own hands from the blankets and grasped his, and in the lamp's light it seemed her hands were no old woman's, but delicate and unblemished, as they had once been; and the blankets no longer scratched her chin, but were soft and warm as cashmere.

'Hermes,' she said, returning his smile. 'I thought you'd gone without saying goodbye.'

'Never,' he said. 'But goodbye is why I am here.'

She looked into his unreadable eyes, and saw her own reflection in their depths.

'Where are you going?' she asked.

'I am going to find the truth about Santos's death,' he said, 'and the answer to the puzzle isn't here.'

'I'm glad you're here,' she said. 'I have a feeling I am going away, too.'

'I think perhaps you are.'

'I want to go, but I worry about Maria. It's her I don't want to leave.' She was silent for a while, looking away from him and at the lamp's flame. 'All lights burn out in time,' she said, at last. 'Will you stay with me?'

'Of course, my precious one,' he said. 'I shall be here. Now sleep.'

He bent down to her, and touched his warm lips to her cheek. In the coop, the chickens were restless; in his kennel, the dog began to whine. Roula touched Hermes's face and squeezed his hand, and, keeping it in her own, she closed her eyes to sleep.

The clocks struck eight. In the *kafenion*, the card-players ordered up another round and the cards were dealt again, as their eyes were fixed on the pot of money growing before one man. Eustis rose from his stool and poured more drinks, a cigarette clenched at the corner of his mouth. At a table by the payphone, the fat man sipped his beer and picked at a bowl of salted peanuts.

Outside, a car pulled up, its yellow headlamps lighting up the road, the sign on its roof showing 'For Hire'.

The fat man left a banknote on the table, and shook Eustis's hand on his way out. Wishing the card-players *Kali nichta*, he pulled the *kafenion* door closed, and climbed into the taxi to follow Leda.

Twenty

'I did as you asked,' said Hassan, taking a bend in the road too fast. Even on full beam, the headlamps illuminated too little of the road ahead to settle the fat man's anxiety, but Hassan knew the road so well, he drove by a series of guideposts: a junction marked a straight where he could pick up speed; a chapel meant a series of tight bends and a narrowing of the road. There was little oncoming traffic: only a labouring truck, overladen with straw bales, and a motorbike or two. From time to time, the headlamps caught night creatures: rabbits, and red reflections from the pinpoint eyes of rodents.

The fat man gripped his seat as they sped round a bend he couldn't see.

'First tell me about you and Santos,' he said.

In the dark, Hassan's shoulders tensed.

'Me and Santos? I barely knew him. There's nothing to say.'

'You may have barely known him; but am I right in thinking your wife knew him quite well?'

Hassan was silent.

'When Santos left Vrisi four years ago – when he set out on his needless journey to Nafplio – how did he travel?'

Hassan shrugged, and touched the brake to take a bend.

'I drove him. I drove him to the station, same as I drove you. What of it?'

'You must have found that hard, sitting there next to him, knowing as you did about him and your wife.'

Hassan laughed; but even in the dark, the fat man could see he wasn't smiling.

'Not hard at all,' he said. 'I let him think I was the fool he took me for. I played along, as if I'd no idea at all of what he'd done. I let him think it, until we reached a stretch by Profitis Ilias, where there's the devil of a drop into a chasm. And I pulled up right at the chasm's edge, with the headlights shining into nothing, and I told him I'd drive both of us over, if I thought he might ever go near my wife again. And he cried and snivelled like a baby, and begged me not to do it; and I gave my word, on condition he never came back again to Vrisi.'

'And he gave his word?'

'Easily. I didn't believe him, of course; when you've a man's balls in a vice, he'll promise anything. But evidently he took me seriously. He's never been seen in Vrisi since then.'

'Not alive, at least. And what was your plan, Hassan, if he did come back?'

'I was going to shoot him. I kept my shotgun loaded for the purpose. Or I might have cut his throat, or brought him back up here and pushed him over that edge.'

'Then you would have gone to prison.'

'Obviously,' said Hassan. 'But he took away my honour, and my marriage. There was no way I could have lived in Vrisi, with that dog, that scum, tucked away up there in his house, thinking he'd got away with it. I was ready for him, whenever he came back. But if you're thinking that I killed him, friend, you'd be wrong. I didn't need to kill him because someone beat me to it. And I don't know who that was, but in my eyes, that someone did me a favour, and spared me jail.'

'Yet you agreed to help me in tracking that person down.'

'Agreeing to a thing and doing a thing, are not the same. You might have found me less willing to help, in other circumstances. But to tip you off that Leda was gone – no harm in that. No daughter kills a father. So I made enquiries on your behalf. It didn't cost you much; I brought you change, in there.' He pointed to the glove box. 'The clerk in the ferry ticket office was happy enough to talk to anyone prepared to listen. She bought a ticket to the end of the line. But the crewman on the boat she sailed on, he wanted cash – ten thousand, to watch where she went after they docked.'

They reached the crest of a hill, and began to descend the mountain foothills. The night was clear, and the view from the road – of the coastal flatlands, and the splendid, vast sea – was lit by a grey half-moon. To the south glowed the lights of the city; in a few miles, the road would widen and be lit with streetlights.

'How will I find this crewman?' asked the fat man.

'The ferry is the *Poseidon*,' said Hassan, 'and it makes its journey daily. Nufris, they call the crewman, and he's always on the boat; dark-skinned and out of Kos, or somewhere south. You'll know him easily enough; he wears a red bandanna. He's not a bad-looking man, with it on his head, and in his job he probably has a bit of luck with the women. But I saw him once without the bandanna, and he's near enough completely bald, so no doubt the ladies get a shock when they find out what he looks like underneath.'

'I'll find him,' said the fat man. 'You've done a good job in putting strings on her, and I shall catch up with her, before long. A delay in my arrival – wherever she has gone – may anyway be beneficial. It will do no harm to let her settle in and let down her guard. I shall travel as fast as I can, and if that's not fast, then I can use the time for thinking.'

When they reached the port, Hassan parked the taxi on the harbour-front. The fat man bent down to unzip the holdall at his feet.

'Now, your fare for this journey,' he said. 'I can pay you in cash, of course, and I'll be leaving what's in the glove-box as a tip; but I wish to offer you an alternative payment.'

Reaching into his bag, he drew out a porcelain swan wrapped in bridal netting. The swan sat easily on the palm of his hand; its hollow back was filled with mauve-coloured fondants, shaped into sugar-dipped flowers.

'A gift for you, to give to your wife,' he said. 'I think you should consider reconciliation. The swan is a symbol of life-long fidelity, which you and she can enjoy together, if you can find it in yourselves to make a fresh start. The sweets are made by a relative of mine, who refuses to divulge the recipe, though she swears by their ability to smooth the creases in cases where a couple are foundering, as you are. Take my advice, Hassan, and don't be the servant of your pride. Your wife made a grave mistake, but I don't think she loved the poet. You quizzed me, to know if she went to his burial, and I tell you, she wasn't there. Take heart from that; she carries no candle for him, but might still have a spark for you. If the approach is never made, you'll never know. So, which will it be, my friend – the money, or the swan?'

'Your swan is very pretty,' said the taxi driver, 'but I put my faith in cash. From Vrisi to the port, six thousand drachma.'

The fat man placed the porcelain swan on the dashboard, and smiled as he reached for his wallet.

'You are a stubborn man, my friend,' he said. 'Happily, I am feeling generous. Take both.'

The fat man took a room at a small pension close to the port, and dined in a waterfront taverna. He chose whitebait caught only hours previously, dredged in flour and fried crisp, served salted, with lemon on the side, and a plate of okra, stewed to melting with garlic and tomatoes. To drink, he ordered a bottle of Kefalonian wine, a blend of Robola and Tsaoussi grapes; and finding its chilled fruit and honey flavours very much to his taste, he sat on amongst the other diners after he had eaten, and drank the lion's share of the bottle.

The wine brought on a pleasant drowsiness; and, though his bedroom was cold from the sea, and roaring motorbikes passed close under his window, he fell asleep with no difficulty at all.

When the first daylight came to Vrisi, Maria went downstairs to put her mother on the commode. But Roula couldn't be woken; and Maria shattered the morning's stillness with the first wails of her grief.

The fat man frittered away the morning at the harbour-side, where seagulls cried over the returning fishing boats, and the outbound and inbound ferries kept the port lively. From a travel office, he bought a ticket to the end of *Poseidon*'s route, then passed the time in writing postcards bought from a *periptero*, in breakfasting on croissants and sticky pastries, and sipping coffee amongst the travellers and sailors.

As the time of his departure grew close, the fat man walked the line of moored boats and yachts, of cargo ships and forlorn cruisers abandoned for the winter, to the dock where the *Poseidon* was preparing for her journey, and made his way up the ramp amongst the other embarking passengers. Merchants shouted instructions to the indifferent crew on where to offload their cargoes; nervous women lingered on the quay, anxious to spend as little time as possible afloat.

The fat man held out his ticket for inspection by a crewman blowing bubbles from a piece of tired, pink gum, who ripped the piece of paper almost in half.

'Thank you,' said the fat man, politely. 'I'm looking for one of your colleagues, a man they call Nufris.'

The crewman was dealing with the next passenger, snatching a ticket from the hand of a young man with a shorn head and a soldier's pack.

'Up,' he said, jerking his head back to signal the direction, as if the fat man couldn't distinguish it for himself.

Carrying his holdall, the fat man followed an iron staircase to the upper deck, where rows of orange-painted benches faced the stern and a view of the port, and lifeboats hung suspended from pulleys rendered non-functional by multiple coats of paint. A second crewman leaned on the deck rail, a red bandanna on his head, the last inch of a burning cigarette in his mouth as he watched the comings and goings on the quayside. The stubble on his chin grew grey in the heavy folds of his face, and one of his canines was missing; the stitching of his quilted jacket was going into threads, and the dirt and stains on its fabric were obvious, in spite of its dark-blue colour.

The fat man's tennis shoes were silent on the deck, and when he spoke – 'Yassas' – the crewman turned, startled.

'For God's sake!' he said. 'You frightened me half to death!'

'Forgive me,' said the fat man. 'It was unintentional. Do they call you Nufris?'

The crewman looked at him with suspicion.

'Who's asking?'

'I believe a friend of mine asked a favour of you, yesterday. It concerned a young lady passenger.'

The crewman smiled an ugly smile. Flicking the stub of his cigarette over the side so it flew in an arc into the water below, he leaned back on the deck rail.

'I remember,' he said. He looked expectantly at the fat man's pocket, then down at his own extended hand, which he seemed surprised to find empty.

'Did my friend not pay you for your trouble?' asked the fat man.

'He gave me something,' said the crewman. 'But small sums pay for small favours. I took my work seriously, friend. I stuck with your young lady when she left this boat. All the way to the end of the line she went, and then I made it my business to stick by her a while.' With a broken-nailed and oily finger, he pointed to the outer corner of his eye. 'I made observations, you know, on your behalf. I did more than you might have expected, and if you wanted, I could tell you what she did when she left our boat.' He raised his eyebrows, and gave a devilish smile.

The fat man hesitated; then he took two banknotes from the folds of his wallet.

'I shall give you one of these,' he said, 'and if your knowledge warrants it, you shall have the other, too. What did she do?'

'She took another boat,' said the crewman, slipping the note into his pocket. 'She asked around until she found the one she wanted, and she boarded another ferry.'

'What ferry?' asked the fat man. 'Do you know where it was going?'

'Oh yes, I know where it was going. I'm tight with the lads who work the other lines. Like brothers to me, they are, and I know their routes as well as I know my own. Soon as I saw which boat she was on, I knew where she was going. Only one destination, that boat. Only goes one place.' He folded his arms over his chest, waiting.

The fat man held out the second banknote.

'Tell me, then,' he said. 'Where has she gone?'

The crewman pocketed the note in no hurry, and turned to spit into the water below. On the quayside, a truck laden with boxes of cabbages was backing up to the ramp. The crewman watched frowning for a moment, and called down to his colleagues below.

'Take the cash from him first, Harris! He owes us already for three trips. And stack 'em at the back, and stack 'em high! We've no room to spare down there today.'

He left the railing, and moved past the fat man as if about to leave him standing there, without delivering the debt of information he still owed.

But as he crossed the deck to the staircase, he looked back over his shoulder.

'Seftos,' he called out, as he descended the stairs. 'Your lady-friend took a boat to the island of Seftos.'

Twenty-one

As the ferry drew into Seftos's port, the fat man's view through the *salone* window was of the island's unremarkable landscape, of its commonplace architecture and its uninteresting geography, and of the medlar orchards behind the town, rose-tinted and flourishing on the low-rising slopes.

He let the other passengers disembark, keeping his seat until most of the small cargo was unloaded, waiting until the last crates and boxes were carried away, before picking up his holdall and making his way off the boat.

In the swell, the ramp between ferry and quayside shifted under his feet. The crew were already heading home. Two had mounted a moped inadequate to carry them both, the pillion passenger clutching with one arm the waist of the teenage driver. In the pillion rider's other hand was a bag of purple-shelled oysters, which he held, like the goddess Themis with her scales, at arm's length, to avoid the oysters' watery juices dripping on to his trousers. The driver started the engine and moved the moped incompetently forward in jerks and stops, his passenger laughing and calling him *malaka*; but the young driver then picked up speed, and his nervous passenger called to him to slow down, his feet dangling over the road in preparation for a fall. Amused, the fat man watched them go, until the moped and its passengers disappeared down the back-streets, its underpowered engine echoing off the house walls.

The ferry had docked at the harbour's northernmost point, where the wide bay's waters were at their deepest. Between the dock and the town's first houses, no other boats were moored, and as the fat man walked along the harbour-side, from time to time he looked down into the shallow waters, where small fish swam over rocks spotted with spiny urchins.

In the wake of the ferry's arrival, the place was quiet. Two boys in jeans and sweaters prodded sticks into the harbour wall, to extricate soft-shell crabs hiding in the crannies; their hats lay upturned on the quayside, ready to hold their catch. At a little distance, a man with the gentle features of a half-wit – he was perhaps as young as thirty, but the close-shaved stubble on his head was entirely grey – crouched on an upturned bucket, an unbaited fishing line dropped in the sea at his feet, and watched the two boys covertly from the corner of his eye.

With no shelter in the harbour, the wind was cold across the open sea, and the house doors were all closed. Ahead of the fat man, an old woman dressed in black walked slowly in the direction he was heading, using a pink umbrella as a cane; with frivolous nylon frills around its edges, the accessory was unsuited to its owner, and yet the widow carried it with pride, though the frills were fraying in places, and the grubbiness of the fabric told of use through many seasons.

The fat man soon caught up with her, and as he drew level, slowed his pace.

'*Kali spera sas, kyria,*' he said.

She stopped, and peered at him through black-framed glasses. Even in this early season, her lined face was tanned from outdoor life.

'*Kali spera sas,*' she said.

She might have let the fat man pass by, and go on; but as

she looked at him, her interest grew, and she stopped in her promenade, and leaned panting on the umbrella, breathless even from such slow walking.

The fat man gave her an affable smile.

'I'm a stranger here,' he said, 'as you will no doubt have observed.'

'*Kalos erthaite*,' she said, in a traditional welcome.

Her eyes moved to the half-wit fishing, who was no longer watching the end of his own line, but the activities of the two boys, who had caught a small green crab, and were shrieking as it scuttled over their four hands in its desperation to return to the sea.

'Manolis!' The woman called to the half-wit, and the boys looked across at her, and at him, and quickly dropped the crab into one of their caps, folding it in half to make the crab their prisoner. They glowered with hostility at the half-wit, who, like a shamed dog, dropped his head, and sadly gave his attention back to his empty line.

'Forgive me,' said the fat man to the woman, 'but Manolis there won't be catching many fish if he has no bait.'

'He's no bait because whatever bait he has, he eats,' she said. 'Stale bread, or fish guts, it makes no difference. God gave him a good heart, but no sense.'

Manolis seemed to sink under her words. The two boys picked up their sticks and their caps, and keeping their captive secure inside, moved away along the quay, to what seemed to them a safer distance from Manolis.

'You seem to take an interest in his supervision,' said the fat man.

'I've no choice but to take an interest,' said the woman. 'He's my sister's son, and she's a fly-by-night; she abandoned his care to me some years ago. But the Lord sees all. I do my duty, and God provides, as he sees fit.'

'A dutiful woman is to be admired,' said the fat man, 'but the man must be frustrated, fishing without bait or hook. Surely a little bread would do no harm?'

'He spears his fingers with the hooks,' said the woman. 'I used to spend hours pulling them from his thumbs and fingers. He's fine as he is. I thank you for your interest.'

The fat man bowed his head, in apparent deference to her point of view.

'Do you live close by?' he asked.

'My house is there.' She pointed to a house along the road, where the front step was swept and whitewashed, and geraniums were planted in gallon cans which had once held Kalamata olives.

'I imagine the care of him keeps you close to home, does it not?'

'I'm a church-woman, *kyrie*. I attend the services I should.'

'But the rest of the time, you are not far away, I assume?' persisted the fat man. 'For instance, when the ferry docks, are you usually there to see?'

'I see it often enough, if the weather's fit. If the boat comes in, I see it; I see it come, and I see it go.'

'And I expect an intelligent woman like yourself sees who travels with it, too: who comes, and who goes.'

'I know most folk who take the ferry. It's good manners to greet them, wouldn't you say?' Her eyes were on Manolis and his line.

'I would indeed say so,' said the fat man. 'And it's good manners to greet strangers, like myself. A welcome from the locals warms a stranger's heart. But I suppose there aren't many strangers on your ferry?'

'Rarely,' she said, frowning in Manolis's direction as if ready to reprimand him again. 'More rarely still, this time of year. We keep to ourselves, in Seftos. We're not people to encourage visitors. Manolis, stop throwing stones!'

'Which makes it perhaps the more surprising, then,' said the fat man, looking with sympathy at Manolis, 'for two strangers to arrive within twenty-four hours?'

'I suppose it does.'

'The young lady who arrived yesterday, did you speak to her?'

'I had no call to. She offered me no greeting, and I offered none to her.'

'But she went by here?'

Behind the lenses of her glasses, the woman's eyes grew sharp.

'What's your interest in young girls, *kyrie*? If I might ask?'

The fat man smiled, and wagged a finger at her.

'You are protective,' he said. 'You have a mother's instincts, no doubt from taking such excellent care of your nephew. But my interests in the girl are nothing sinister. On the contrary. I bring her news of a legacy, and have tracked her down – with some difficulty, and at my personal expense – to Seftos. If you can tell me where I might find her, I would be grateful.'

'She was collected from a spot just down the quay there,' she said. 'I saw him waiting for her when the boat came in. He took her off with him, over there.' She waved her hand across the bay.

'Who took her?'

'The man living on the little island,' she said. 'The man they call the hermit.'

At the general store, the shopkeeper sat on his stool behind the counter, a fresh cup of coffee at his elbow, a tumbler with a shot of Metaxa to one side. On a paper napkin were the crumbs from a slice of cake, and the vanilla scent of baking mixed with the smells of salami and onions, of soap powder and brine-soaked olives. The aisle from door to counter was again obstructed with sacks of rice and lentils; the shop was still dimmed by the boxes of stock stacked up over the window. The cheese fridge hummed; the linnet in its cage pecked at its bars, and chirped for attention.

'You're back,' said the shopkeeper, to the fat man. '*Kalos tou, kalos tou*. But you're still too early for medlars, friend. You've a long wait, if you've come back for the medlars.'

'Life takes extraordinary turns, does it not?' said the fat man. 'A chance visit to Seftos only a short while ago, and now I find myself here on official business.'

'Official, are you?' The shopkeeper looked the fat man up and down. 'Well, you certainly look the part. On whose behalf are you official?'

'My business is likely to be brief,' said the fat man. 'But I need to find someone with a boat to take me where I'm going. I'll pay well, for someone to carry me.'

'Pay well, will you?' asked the grocer, taking a slug of his Metaxa. 'And where will you pay to be carried to?'

'I'm heading for the house of a man you mentioned to me, when I was last here. My business is with the man you call the hermit.'

'Not such a hermit at this moment, I gather,' said the shopkeeper. 'I hear he has a visitor with him. A young lady, who arrived on the boat before you. He whisked her away before anyone got a look at her. He's a dark horse, is our hermit. She looked too young for him; but if you can get them young, why not? My wife was sixteen years my junior when I married her, and I never had any regrets.'

'I don't believe they are married,' said the fat man, choosing a packet of cheese-flavoured snacks from a shelf.

'Don't let old Father Nikos know, then,' laughed the shopkeeper. 'He's a stickler for morality, in certain areas. If you're looking for a ride over there, maybe I'll take you myself. I'll get the wife to mind the store.'

'I shall want taking, and bringing away,' said the fat man. 'As I say, my business is not likely to take long.'

'If you want me to, I'll wait,' said the shopkeeper. 'For a consideration.'

'I'm sure we can agree on a fair price.'

'Give me half an hour, then,' said the shopkeeper, 'and we'll go.'

Twenty-two

The shopkeeper's boat was broad and well-balanced, and cut comfortably through the swell, raising only light spray at the prow, though the cold engine billowed dark smoke at the stern.

'She'll go through anything, this one,' said the shopkeeper, as they motored away from the harbour. 'My grandfather made her with his own hands. In the war, he used her to smuggle provisions, right under the Germans' noses. She was passed down to my father, and now she's come to me. She's no oil painting, but she's reliable. A good rule to choose a woman by, that is. That's how I picked my wife. You'd be a fool to marry a pretty wife, wouldn't you say?'

The fat man gave no answer. Seated on a bench spanning the boat's hull, he held his holdall on his knees, and rested his feet on the plastic tablecloth which had wrapped the engine. The boat was not clean; the bilge-water threw up the stink of diesel and dead fish. Noticing a smear of oil on one of his shoes, the fat man frowned.

The shopkeeper sat at the stern, his arm on the tiller, steering a course to an unlit beacon which marked the island's most southerly point. Beyond the beacon, the distance they travelled was short, to a tiny island which appeared, at first, to be no more than uninhabited scrub and rock; but as they drew closer, the fat man picked out a short stretch of beach he remembered, and a jetty where an open boat was moored. Behind the beach, on levelled ground, was a roughly built shack, and beside it, a garden fenced to keep out goats.

The wind might have covered the sound of the engine until they drew closer; but when they were still at a distance, the hermit's hound rose up from beside the shack and ran barking to the jetty they were approaching, where he snarled and barked to ward off the intruders.

The shopkeeper gripped the side of the moored boat, and pulled his own in close, holding it steady as the fat man stood.

'What about the dog?' asked the shopkeeper, apprehensively. He called out to the animal, reminding him they had recently been companions, but the dog seemed to have no memory of their acquaintance.

The fat man seemed unperturbed.

'He is protecting his territory, nothing more,' he said. 'Will you wait for me here? I expect to be an hour at most, no longer.'

'That's long enough to try for a bite or two,' said the shopkeeper. 'Though our hermit may not be very pleased if he thinks I'm taking his fish.'

'Your hermit will have more than fish to think about, when he and I are finished.'

The shopkeeper looked concerned.

'Won't he welcome your visit?' he asked. 'He's a good customer of mine. If you're bringing bad news, he might blame me and shoot the messenger.'

'You are in no danger whatever of being shot,' said the fat man. 'I give you my word on that.'

He stepped on to the moored boat, and from there on to the jetty, and as his foot touched land, the dog stopped barking, lowered his head and, wagging his tail uncertainly, came forward to lick the fat man's hand.

The fat man touched the dog's head and set off along the beach towards the shack, whilst the dog followed at a short distance behind, his head still down, his tail low.

But the animal had done his job, and roused his master. As the fat man approached, the hermit opened the door of his home and looked down towards the jetty. He waved at the shopkeeper.

'Did I leave something behind?' he shouted, with both hands cupped to his mouth for amplification. 'Or have you only come for my fish?'

The shopkeeper shouted some reply, but the wind carried his words away. He pointed at the fat man, and the hermit, following his gesture, looked along the beach, where the fat man walked towards him with the hermit's dog meekly following him as if he were the fat man's own.

The hermit frowned, puzzled both by the dog's behaviour and by the stranger's unusually smart dress.

'*Chairete*,' said the fat man, in the most formal of greetings, as he grew close. He stopped in front of the hermit, laid his holdall on the ground and looked him somewhat rudely up and down, taking in his shabby clothes, his uncombed hair and half-grown beard, and scrutinising his face. 'So you are Seftos's infamous hermit?'

'What do you want?' asked the hermit. 'This is private property.'

The fat man unzipped his holdall, and took from it a paperback book, which he laid on top of the bag.

'Hermes Diaktoros, of Athens,' he said. 'Forgive my intrusion, but I am looking, in the first instance, for an acquaintance of mine, a young lady named Leda. Is she, by any chance, here with you?'

'I am.' Leda stepped out from behind the door, and stood at the hermit's shoulder. Over her own clothes, she wore a man's pullover, and her arms were wrapped around herself, against the cold; her eyes were red and swollen from recent crying.

'What are you doing here?' she asked.

'I have to admit,' said the fat man, 'that I followed you from Vrisi.'

'How could you have done? I would have seen you.'

'You might easily have seen me, had I travelled on the same vessels as you; and if I am being pedantic, I should say I did, in fact, travel on those same vessels, but not at the same time. It is a sad fact, *kori mou*, that many things can be bought for money. It was a simple matter to buy the route of your journey from one of the sailors who crewed the boats.'

'But why?' she asked. 'Why on earth would you follow me?'

'For your own sake. But the wind is cold out here, and you are not dressed for it. Is there a fire lit inside? Perhaps we should talk in there.'

The hermit held up his hand.

'Forgive me, *kyrie*,' he said, 'but I don't know you, and I'm not in the habit of welcoming strangers into my home. So state your business, and let's be done. Our grocer has a shop to run, and no matter how well you've paid him to be your taxi, I'm sure he's anxious to get home.'

'You do not speak like an islander, my friend,' said the fat man. 'Are you not a local man?'

'I'm as local as the next man, these days. Now, what do you want?'

'He's the investigator Attis Danas asked to look into my father's death,' said Leda, touching the sleeve of the hermit's dirty jacket. 'Aren't you?'

'I am indeed,' said the fat man. 'Though as it turns out, that is not the mystery to hand. When we first met, Leda, I think we were both looking for something we had lost. What you had lost was never clear, but I had lost a ring, a gold ring. I asked you to look out for it on the road. Do you remember?'

Leda was silent.

'I'm hoping that you do,' he went on, 'because I have come, in part, to ask if you might have been lucky, and if you were, if you might return my property to me.'

From neck to brow, Leda blushed.

'Speak up,' said the fat man, not unkindly. 'Did you find it, or not? The ring is very precious to me, and I would like to have it back.'

'I gave it away,' she said. 'I didn't expect to see you again.'

'Did you not?' asked the fat man, in apparent surprise. 'But you knew how to find me; through Attis, it would have been a simple matter to return it. To whom, may I ask, did you give my property?'

The hermit glanced at Leda.

'I think,' he said, 'she gave it to me.' He held out his left hand. On the third finger was an antique ring, a band of old gold set with an unusual coin, stamped with a rising sun on one side, and a young man in profile on the other. 'Is this it?'

The fat man smiled, broadly.

'It is indeed,' he said. 'If you would be so good as to return it, I would be grateful.'

The hermit grasped the ring and tugged at it; but it seemed tight on his finger, and wouldn't move over his knuckle.

'It's stuck,' he said. 'I don't know why; it was loose when I put it on.'

'That is a puzzle,' said the fat man. 'Your fingers, I am sure, are thinner than mine. Please, try again.'

The hermit tugged at the ring, until his finger reddened and began to swell.

'Oil,' said Leda. 'I'll get some oil, to grease it.'

She went inside the shack. The hermit continued to tug at the ring, but the fat man's interest had moved elsewhere.

'You two seem an unlikely couple,' he said. 'Princess and peasant, almost. What is your relationship, exactly?' Intent on his swelling finger, the hermit didn't answer. 'I'm sure you weren't expecting that question in this remote location, but, as you're about to discover, your island isn't remote enough. No matter how far you go, it's hard to cover your tracks when those tracks lead to a man's death.'

Leda reappeared, holding a bottle of olive oil.

'Death?' she asked. 'What death?'

'An untimely death by another's hand,' said the fat man, 'more simply called, in the common tongue, murder. I'm talking of that recent death in Vrisi. The death you have perhaps been persuaded was no more than a convenience.'

'How dare you call my father's death convenient!' She handed the oil to the hermit. 'Here,' she said. 'Take off the damned ring, and let him go!'

'You shouldn't need more than a drop,' said the fat man to the hermit. 'I can see by its colour it is good oil, and it would be a shame to waste it. Leda, your commitment to your role is most impressive; that act of indignation would easily fool a more gullible man. As for your father's death, rarely have I heard of one more convenient than your father's first demise. And I'm sure you played your part in that very well, too: the grieving daughter, a figure of tragedy. A difficult role, for certain, even for an actress as talented as you; sustaining the part through a period of years must have been a terrible strain. You got through it all right, though you made one or two small errors. The neglected grave, and the uncared for statue in Vrisi, raised questions in my mind; they seemed at odds with the character of a devoted daughter. Of course you had no interest in either, because you knew your father was not in that grave, nor did he need any stone memorial. Even so, the role was beautifully played; but how did it feel to be asked for an encore? Are you sure you wouldn't like to talk inside? You're shivering, out here.'

The hermit poured a dribble of oil on his finger, and placed the oil bottle at his feet. He twisted the ring; it left his finger easily.

'Here,' he said, wiping the ring on his jacket and holding it out to the fat man. 'Take this, and go.'

With a bow of his head, the fat man accepted the ring, and slipped it on to his own, fatter, finger.

'How strange,' he said, admiring it. 'It fits me better than you. I shall leave you, soon enough. But it is your father's second death that interests me, Leda. That death was trickier, wasn't it, involving as it did an actual body. You must have found that difficult, to look upon a very unpleasant corpse, with the eyes of the police watching your reaction. That's a great deal for a man to ask of his own child; to face a stranger's corpse, and lie to the authorities.'

'I lied to no one!' objected Leda.

'Oh, but you did,' smiled the fat man. 'You lied as you'd been told to by this man here. You misidentified the body as that of your father, Santos Volakis, but it wasn't him, was it? How could it be, when Santos Volakis stands here with us, as large as life? I know you, Santos; hide though you may, you cannot ever be far enough away from me. I shall show you the proof of it. Look.' He picked up the paperback book from the holdall, and held up the author photograph on its back cover: a dark-haired man, clean shaven, with intense, grey eyes.

'You're mad,' said Leda.

The hermit laughed.

'You think that's me?' he asked, stabbing a finger at the book. 'She's right, you're mad! Santos Volakis was a world-renowned poet, and a handsome man. Perhaps I should be flattered that you see his face in mine.'

'But I do,' said the fat man. 'You are he; I know it. But if you continue to deny it, I shall leave you and contact the police instead.'

'To what end? What do you have to say to the police that could possibly concern me?'

The fat man took a step closer to the hermit.

'Don't take me for a fool,' he said. 'I tracked your daughter here with no difficulty at all, and you'll find me very skilled at tracking down whatever I want to find. I might want to find the place you killed your victim, and the vehicle you used to carry him to Vrisi. You'd be surprised what people remember, when their memories are prodded: a car on an empty road, a late-night traveller who thinks himself unseen. Without a doubt, you've left a trail, which I shall find, if necessary. But if you put me to that work, it'll go the worse for you. Tell me the truth now, and perhaps some unpleasantness can be avoided. You might yet avoid seeing Leda punished for her part in this ugly business. You chose a good hiding place, but by letting her in, you have let the world in, too. I am the world; I represent it. Tell me the truth of what you've done, and give me reasons; tell me who he was, and let me assess the damage that you've done.'

'Who are you?' asked the hermit. 'On whose authority do you question me?'

'On the highest possible authority,' said the fat man. 'On behalf of those who will not tolerate crimes unpunished. For you have committed a crime, have you not? Tell me – and tell your daughter, if you have not already done so – exactly what you did.'

A smile spread to the hermit's lips, and he spread his arms wide in the air, and threw back his head.

'Behold!' he shouted, so loud the shopkeeper in his boat looked up from the lead weight he was tying on his line. 'Behold before you Santos Volakis, the twice-dead poet, this century's greatest talent of Greek literature!'

Abruptly, his features became earnest, almost desperate.

'Have you told my secret, stranger?' he asked, grabbing the fat man's arm. 'Is the cat out of the bag?'

'The bag is still knotted at the neck,' said the fat man, looking steadily at the poet, 'but do not be getting ideas about silencing me. I am a difficult man to silence, even more so when offered force. But persuade me of the merits of your case, and we might yet come to some arrangement.'

The poet looked down towards the jetty, where the shopkeeper was now showing some interest in what was being said.

'Walk with me,' he said, 'a short way to the island's end and back, and we'll talk. I suppose I must talk to you, since you have found me; I suppose you are determined to extort money from me for silence, or sell my story to the gutter press.'

'On the contrary,' said the fat man. 'I am a man of independent means. I have no use for your money.'

'What, then? Leda, wait inside.'

Leda left them, and the poet and the fat man set off along the beach, where ragged fragments of fishing nets lay bleached amongst the stones, and the incoming waves brought lustre to the shingle and the many-coloured pebbles. They came across a woman's slipper, waterlogged and sandy, washed up by the sea, and the poet picked it up, and tossed it further up the beach, away from the water's reach.

'I've been here some time now, and yet the detritus that washes up here still surprises me,' he said. 'Every day, I clean the beach, and every day, some new object brings its story to my door. Where might that slipper's pair be, do you think?

Did it slip off some woman's foot, or was it thrown by a naughty child, or an angry husband? Is it from someone drowned? Is its mate still on a rotting foot, on the seabed?'

'You have a vivid imagination, and a somewhat morbid one.'

'Ah, but my imagination is what makes me remarkable,' said the poet, with some arrogance. 'That, and my mastery of language.'

'And has your imagination become more morbid recently, Santos?'

The poet looked away from the fat man, across the sea.

'Why do you ask?'

'Because in my experience,' said the fat man, 'those who have stepped across certain lines become prey to their imaginings. Are you seeing shadows at your shoulder? Are you hearing noises in the night? Such things may be the products of a guilty conscience. If you want your conscience cleared, unburden yourself to me. Believe me, it will help.'

The poet veered away from the fat man, and took a few paces towards the water. He bent to pick up a flat stone, and threw it with some skill on to the water, so it skipped several times across the surface before it sank and disappeared. As he bent to choose another stone, the fat man came and stood close to his shoulder.

'Why have you come to disturb me?' asked the poet, as he set another stone skimming on the waves. 'Are you not a lover of the arts?'

'On the contrary. I both practise and patronise the arts.'

'Have you read anything of mine?'

'I have.' The fat man said no more. The poet glanced in his direction, and seeing him patting his pockets as though hunting for something mislaid, frowned.

The fat man smiled.

'You are waiting for my compliments and my praise, the stroking of your ego,' he said. 'That is what you have come to expect. Your work is good, Santos. There, I have said it. Does it make you happy?'

The poet gave a shrug of apparent indifference; but in his face there was a hint of his displeasure.

'Now you are annoyed at my lack of respect,' said the fat man. 'How dare I not fall at your feet! Have you missed that adulation, Santos – your celebrity, your disciples hanging on your every word? You must have missed it, because you fished for it so early in our acquaintance. But this is not a place for your adorers. It's the kind of place a man might go quietly mad. Did they not say as much to you, when you first came here?'

'I'm not mad,' objected the poet; but the expression on his face showed a lack of certainty.

'I think we should go back,' said the fat man. 'I think you should tell me your story, and then I can decide what happens next.'

The fat man sat on the only chair, at the cabin's table; Leda sat beside her father on the poet's single bed, stroking the dog's head as it rested on her knee. The fat man reached into his pocket, and took out his cigarettes and a matchbox; he shook the matchbox, but hearing no answering rattle from within, placed it in front of him on the table, and took out his gold lighter.

'You don't mind if I smoke?' he asked, and the poet shook his head.

Leda stood, and handed the fat man a saucer from the shelf to use as an ashtray. The fat man took a cigarette from the box, and lit it, inhaling deeply, blowing the smoke towards the fireplace, where a fire of rough logs gave off little heat.

'Where shall we begin?' he asked, and looked expectantly at the poet; but the poet offered no suggestion, and so the fat man reached again into his pocket, and brought out the little diary Attis had given him.

'Let us then start with this,' he said, and laying his cigarette on the saucer, opened the diary at the page where the word 'Nafplio' was written and struck through. 'The date, here, of your first death; an engagement to read poetry that you apparently knew was cancelled. But you went there, anyway. Why?'

The poet smiled.

'Obviously, I went to die,' he said. 'The idea came to me after I had the letter from the university, telling me not to go. It was another disappointment, I suppose; and I had been toying with the idea of dying for some time. It seemed an ideal opportunity; a distant town, where no one knew me. I talked it over with Leda, and she agreed.'

'Did you agree, Leda?'

Leda looked at the fat man; her tear-swollen eyes made her seem both young and vulnerable.

'I saw no reason not to,' she said. 'I thought the plan was clever. At the time.'

'And Frona? What about your aunt?'

'My daughter's an intelligent girl,' put in the poet. 'She could see we would all benefit, in the end. As for Frona, what could we do?' He spread his hands. 'I knew she wouldn't play along; and she lacked the imagination to play a part, and pull it off. I thought it better if she knew as little as possible.'

'Did you not think it cruel, Leda, to let her think your father dead?' asked the fat man.

'We both knew it was cruel,' said Leda. 'But I was younger and more foolish when I made the commitment. I didn't understand that grief doesn't last days or weeks, but months and years. I hadn't thought how she would struggle to support me. I put my father's talent above everything. And when I began to understand the wrong we'd done, I couldn't find the courage to tell the truth.' In despair, she shook her head. 'How will she ever forgive us?'

'I've told you,' said the poet to Leda. 'There's no reason for her ever to know.'

Leda looked away from him, to the wall, her jaw tight from the effort of suppressing more tears.

'So why did you do it, Santos?' asked the fat man, flicking ash from the end of his cigarette. 'What has been behind all this theatre? I hope you're going to tell me it wasn't just for money.'

'In part it was for money,' he said. 'But there was more to it than that. I wanted to prove a point, about how little art is valued. Every day, I saw no-talent artistes – actors, singers, novelists – make millions from their work, whereas I – a true artist, a unique talent, the best in a generation, the critics say – earned nothing but a golden reputation. Poets make no money till they're dead; so I decided I would die, and improve my lot.'

'And then, like Lazarus, you'd rise up from the dead, collect your royalties – which you had prevented, through your will, from being distributed to your heirs – and once again claim the crown as prince of the literary establishment. Have I understood correctly?'

'It was a simple plan.'

'Simple to imagine, but very hard to execute, surely. How, exactly, did you do it?'

'In Nafplio, I bribed an undertaker. He was a clever man, though without soul. He'd never read a poem in his life, and my name meant nothing to him. I told him that the tax man was after me, and a wife who wanted to keep me from a pretty mistress; I told him I was heading for Australia on forged papers. I paid him, more than I could afford, but he provided the necessary forms, and packed a pig in a casket to pass as me. Of course there had been no death, so he took on the role of policeman and made the "official" calls. The plan was simple and, actually, full of flaws. If Frona had asked questions – about post-mortems or locations, or anything at all – the truth might easily have come out. But she asked no questions, and nor, of course, did Leda. No one asked questions – why should they have done, when they had been officially informed and all the paperwork was supplied? – and so I was, officially, dead. And I became another man, with another life. Only Leda knew where to find me. I told her to expect me at my exhumation, and to look surprised.'

He spread his arms, as if to invite applause.

'But she was surprised,' said the fat man, taking a final draw on his cigarette and stubbing it out in the saucer. 'You didn't appear.'

'I never planned to stay dead,' said the poet. 'But something happened here, in my isolation, something only an artist could understand. Of course I could have hidden more easily in a city, but my work led me to choose this place. I chose this place for the purity of my art, and I struggled, at first, as does a monk when he takes his vows. But when I was free from the need for anyone's approval, or critical acclaim – in short, when I had no readers, and could let my work run in whatever direction it chose, and develop in a natural, untainted way – it was a revelation to me! I have written poetry which soars, which stretches boundaries and reaches depths of my own soul I could not have dreamed of, outside this place!'

'How gratifying,' said the fat man. 'I'm glad your work has gone so well. But I can only imagine how frustrating it must be to have written this great work of yours, and have no avenue to sell it. Dead men don't write poetry, after all.'

'Yet I wanted that persona – the old Santos – to stay dead.

I didn't want to go back to my old life. All I need is here. I have my writing, and my books.' He indicated a trunk, pushed up against the wall; on its lid were dozens of volumes, new editions and vintage, the works of both Greek and the most renowned of international authors. 'My life here is dedicated to my art, and that is purifying.'

'Is there nothing that you miss? The company of women, maybe? Or are you playing your old games, and preying on the wives of other men?'

The poet glanced uncomfortably at Leda.

'My muse flourishes in my celibacy,' he said. 'She rewards my self-denial with inspiration.'

The fat man raised his eyebrows.

'Really?' he asked. 'If that is true – and I somehow doubt it – I suspect it's only because you're a less attractive prospect to the fairer sex without the mantle of fame draped round your shoulders. And if this life you have crafted is so perfect, why not simply stay here, where you're hidden?'

'Because of what I had written in the will.'

'Because of what you had written to protect your own interests? I assume the clause regarding your bones and the light of day was to ensure that, when you returned from the dead, you'd come back as a man of means?'

'Yes, in truth,' said the poet. 'But I understood that, even if I was thriving in this place, on next to nothing, it wasn't fair on Frona, or on Leda. It was time, I thought, for them to reap some of the benefits of the success I had enjoyed, following my untimely death.'

'So it wasn't that you were, yourself, running short of cash?'

'There was only a little left of what I'd brought with me, it's true. Though I make enough for my modest day-to-day expenses. Honest work amongst labouring men refreshes a weary intellect.'

'But your honest labour wouldn't by any means cover Frona's day-to-day expenses in trying to educate your daughter. Did that not prick your conscience?'

'What Frona will ultimately gain from my estate will pay her back a hundred times. Anyway, I have taken steps to ease her financial burden.'

'The poems Attis found in your desk?'

'The *Odes to Nemesis* – the finest work I've done. I sent them to Leda, to hide there, and she wrote anonymously to Attis, telling him to search for them. Attis has a creative mind in business, and I knew he'd find a way to get cash for them, outside the terms of the will. Leda and I wrote to each other, from time to time. I phoned her occasionally, if I knew Frona wasn't there.'

The dog grew tired of having his head stroked, and with a yawn lay down at Leda's feet.

'So you decided, in the interests of your art, to die a second time?'

'Shall we have a drink?' said the poet, suddenly. He stood up from his bed and reached up to the shelves above it for a bottle, a glass and a coffee cup, then strode across to the table, and filled glass and cup with a measure of *tsipouro*. 'This is the result of one of my new skills; I learned the sacred arts of distillation. It's much in demand by the locals. Leda, our grocer will be getting cold, down there by the water. Take the bottle, *agapi mou*, and a cup, and give the man a drink. Tell him we won't keep him very much longer; our visitor will be leaving very shortly. Isn't that right, friend?'

'I shall be leaving when the time is right,' said the fat man, 'but you may tell the grocer, Leda, that I shall keep him no longer than is needful.'

She rose from the bed.

'When you leave, may I go with you?' she asked.

'Leda,' said the poet, trying to grasp her hand. 'Stay. There's no need . . .'

'I shall go,' she said, 'if the gentleman will take me.'

She left them. The poet picked up a poker, and hid his face from the fat man by prodding at the smoking logs on the fire.

'She's angry with you,' observed the fat man. 'Why?'

The poet took his cup, and seated himself back on the bed.

'Young women,' he said. 'They have moods.'

'Or has she found out more than you wanted her to know?' The fat man sipped at the rough spirit. 'Did you consult with her, when you decided on your second death? Did you tell her what your new plan entailed? Of course, what you tell her – and what you don't – is up to you, but if she asks me direct questions, I shall answer her. If you want our discussion done before she returns, make it quick; the walk to the jetty and back is but a short one. Who is the man who is buried in your place, and where did you acquire his body?'

The poet drank from his cup of *tsipouro*.

'You know,' he said, 'whilst I was first dead, I had great freedom. I moved like a ghost in places I had never dared go before. When I was fettered to a name and a reputation, I had no freedom at all, though I didn't realise it. But dead men walk free from any ties or expectations. That's what I've discovered: there's no freer man than a dead man. I bought myself a new identity; it was easily done, in the port bars where a certain class do business. I chose a new name; two days later, I was officially a different man, with papers to prove it.'

'And the identity card found on our mystery man's body – the card proving him to be none other than yourself – how did you come by that? I presume your own identity card was given to the police when you died, as is required by law?'

'You presume, then, incorrectly. I kept my card; I knew I would need it for my resurrection. When the Nafplio police

269

called the police in Polineri to let them know I was dead, they confirmed that my ID card had been given to them. The undertaker played the policeman's role, of course.'

'And did your undertaker, by any chance, provide you with your body?'

The poet laughed, and took another drink.

'I can see why you would think that. And I had thought of him; I would have gone there. But in my dead man's shoes – and looking the part, as I now do – I went back to those port bars I had discovered in the early days of my decease. Life's underside is there, and depiction of that underside adds seasoning to my art. In one of those places – as tawdry a bar-room as you could wish to find – an opportunity presented itself which seemed God-given. I simply took that opportunity.'

The fat man frowned.

'What opportunity?'

'A wretched man, beyond help. His liver was destroyed by drinking.'

'What happened between you?'

The poet drained his cup, and gave the fat man an unpleasant smile.

'I see no reason to share those secrets with you.'

'Tell me the truth,' said the fat man, quietly, 'or I will take you away from here this afternoon, and see your name disgraced. There are police on Seftos, aren't there?'

'What pass as policemen. They wear the uniforms, at least.'

'They'd serve my purpose; and they'd be glad to have the interesting job of jailing you, no doubt.'

'Jailing me? What for?'

'Tell me what happened, and tell me fast; your daughter will be here at any moment.'

The poet stood again, and fetched down from the shelf a

fresh bottle of *tsipouro*, and filled his cup. The fat man's glass was still half-full, and he declined.

The poet drank.

'He was close to death,' he said, 'so close as made no difference. He suited what I needed: about my age, about my height, with something of the look of me, if I had taken no care of myself, for twenty years. So I took him from the bar – it was an act of mercy, really – and took him with me to my hotel room, and stayed with him, until his time was done.'

'What did you do, then, for this dying man? Listened to his confession, and held his hand? Gave him comfort, and sang him songs of home?'

'I talked to him.'

'Who was he then, this unfortunate? Where was his home, where was he from?'

'I don't know.'

'His name, then.'

'I don't know that, either.'

'A man dying before you, and you didn't ask his name? How is that possible, in a decent human being?'

'I didn't want to know. He gave me a paper with a number on it, his daughter's phone number. He wanted her to come and say goodbye. I would have called, but how could I? The complications were obvious.'

'Can this be true, that our nation's great poet, who writes so eloquently of love and death, when faced with the real thing, lacked all compassion? Are you a man or a monster? Where is this paper?'

'I threw it away.'

'So you had a man not yet dead, and a date you were due to appear at your own exhumation. Is that right?'

'I was already late for the exhumation. Leda will tell you, I am not good at keeping commitments in that way. But it troubled me that questions would already have been asked. They would be calling me a fraud, or worse. Something had to be done.'

'So what did you do?'

'He was in pain. In agony. I helped him.'

'You helped him how?'

'He craved a drink. I gave him one. And he had medication for his pain. I helped him take it.'

'You gave alcohol to a man dying of liver disease.'

The poet closed his eyes, and rubbed his face with his hands.

'That was a mistake,' he said. 'He began to vomit blood. I hadn't expected anything so . . .' He shuddered at the memory. 'He was in a great deal of pain, so I persuaded him to take more of his tablets. It was a miracle he kept them down.'

'You gave him an overdose.'

'It made no difference. He was close to the end.'

'How close?'

'How should I know? Close enough.'

'Hours, days, weeks – what?'

'Not weeks.'

'But days, potentially?'

'I should say that was very unlikely.'

'Hours, though?'

'Yes, hours; most probably a few hours.'

The poet took another drink.

'And are the hours of a man's life yours to dictate?' asked the fat man. 'May you choose how many remain to a man, and when his time is up?'

'His life was over. What could I have done?'

'You might have made his last hours, good hours. You might have phoned his daughter, and let him spend a little time with her. You might have been a friend to a friendless man, and called him a doctor so he could leave this earth properly sedated and pain-free, instead of hurrying him off so you could make use of his body. And why, tell me, did you think his mortal remains were yours to claim?'

'I needed them. They were no more use to him.'

'And his family?'

The poet was silent. The dog rose, and yawned, and went to the door.

'What did you do next? Your daughter's on her way back. Answer me, quickly.'

'I had to wait for the right time to move him. My hotel was in a busy part of town; I tried to get him out several times, and was interrupted.'

'So there was a delay,' said the fat man. 'Enough for the beginning of decay. How did you transport him to Vrisi?'

'In the car that I'd rented. It was hard to move him at all, by myself; for a man so thin, he was heavy. In the end I had the idea of wrapping him in a net, so I could drag him.'

'You sat him beside you, in the car?'

'I laid him on the back seat, and covered him with a blanket.'

'And the weather was cold?'

'Bitter. I was worried about keeping ahead of the coming snowstorm.'

'So you turned on the car's heater, and further hastened the life-cycle of the flies,' said the fat man.

'Probably so. In Vrisi, it was a simple matter to unravel the net and roll him into place at the roadside.'

'But why did you take him all the way to the village? If you'd left him where he was and called the police anonymously, with your identification on him, the result would have been the same.'

The door opened, and Leda entered the cabin, without the bottle of *tsipouro*.

'I left him the bottle,' she said. 'He asks when you'll be ready to leave.'

'Sit down, just for a while,' said the fat man, and Leda did so. 'Your father was just telling me why he saw it necessary to drive the body to Vrisi, rather than let it be found where it lay.'

The poet shrugged.

'It seemed important to me to deliver myself personally,' he said. 'And I wanted to get a look at the old place.'

'And did you?'

'I drove around a little, yes. I walked up the driveway, and had a look at the house.'

'You were homesick, then.'

'A little.'

'Do you miss your old life, Santos?'

The poet lifted his chin.

'The work I'm doing now makes my old attachments irrelevant. The muse is here with me, and I have everything I need, for her service.' He drank more *tsipouro*. 'What ties us to the earth, friend? Only gravity, the gravity of forces, and the gravity of our natures, our focus on the dull and fundamentals, on our comfort and the needs which we assume. But I've discovered how few our needs are: food to eat, water to drink, warmth against the cold, a place to rest in sufficient comfort to sleep well of a night. I take my dog as my role model. I try to be like him, and live on my wits and instincts.'

The fat man laughed. The poet looked annoyed.

'Forgive me,' said the fat man. 'Your little homily amused me. Do you take me for a complete and utter fool? I see the plan too clearly, my friend, and I see – as I think your daughter does – what a hypocrite you are! I know why you drove that poor corpse over to Vrisi; nothing to do with homesickness at all, but a piece of carefully staged publicity! Your body found dramatically by a roadside, close to your home, is a much, much better story than Santos the once-great poet found dead of alcoholic poisoning in some cheap hotel. Always the drama with you, Santos! Leaving the body at the chapel so near your old home was guaranteed to provoke more interest in you, and your work. More interest, more sales! And with a new batch of poems discovered by Attis . . . It was a publicity stunt, pure and simple! You were creating a spike in sales! You sell yourself as the dedicated artist, my friend, and perhaps you are; but there is nothing noble or poetic about your lust for money. You put your imagination to excellent use in creating mystery, and therefore interest. You faked your own death once, and then you staged it a second time – yet here you are, still with us! What is your ultimate plan, Santos? Is Leda to channel you money, and see you comfortable? What is the betting this shack might evolve, over time, and become a comfortable house? Then you would really be sitting pretty, wouldn't you? A house on your own private island, your daughter with you when she chooses to be. Will there be electricity here soon, a television? A better boat? All paid for by the nameless man in your grave.'

'If he wasn't in my grave, he'd be in a pauper's grave somewhere.' The poet drank again.

'Maybe so. But if that were the case, someone, somewhere, would have gone to the trouble of naming him. What else does a man have, when he is gone, but his name?'

'I shall have my work. It will live on, beyond my death.'

'You are right, Santos; you will be remembered. That is important to you, but you have not considered that to be remembered might also have been important to him. You have cut short his life – by how long, you do not know – and deprived him of the right to a memorial. And there is one very significant detail we haven't yet got to the bottom of.' The fat man took another sip from his glass. 'You took a big risk, Santos, having your body – your second body, that is – found in Vrisi, because it was likely – more than likely – to be found by someone who knew you. Someone, in other words, who would know that the corpse wasn't you at all. How did you make sure the wrong identification wouldn't be made?'

Santos shrugged.

'It was a chance I had to take. I'd been gone for years. He wore a beard, and that disguised a lot. Still, it was a risk, but I took it.'

But the fat man shook his head, and smiled.

'You are far too clever a man to take a risk like that. Leda, I turn to you for my answer. Did your father take a risk? Could anyone have said the body wasn't him?'

Leda recalled the room at the police station – the covered, stinking corpse, the flies, the horror of the stranger's battered face – and shuddered.

'He didn't look much like anybody,' she said, faintly. 'No one could have said for certain who he was.'

'So even if it had been your father, you wouldn't have known?'

'No.'

The fat man frowned.

'So what made this unfortunate so hard to recognise, Leda?'

The poet drained his glass.

'You should go,' he said. 'You have your ring, and the grocer grows impatient.'

'Leda?' prompted the fat man, as if he hadn't spoken. 'What made it difficult?'

'It was the swelling, and the bruising,' said Leda. 'His face looked as if it had been beaten.'

'He fell,' interrupted the poet. 'I dropped him. He fell facedownwards on the floor. I was sorry, but I couldn't help it.'

'You know,' said the fat man, 'I don't think I believe you. You say you dropped him on his face; your daughter says he was bruised and swollen, as you needed him to be, to avoid proper identification. I think the dropping of him – if that's what caused his injuries – was deliberate. What do you think, *kori mou*? Is your admirable father the kind of man who would drop a dead man on his face?'

She looked into the fire.

'Tell him the truth, Papa,' she said. 'You tell him, or I will.'

'Your daughter advises you well,' said the fat man. 'Your version of events, Santos, does not have the ring of truth. I have warned you once already, that if you do not tell me the truth, I shall make my way to the police station and tell them there what you have already told me; and then I shall call my friends in the press, and suggest they might find a newsworthy story in Seftos. Your disgrace, then, will be complete. You didn't drop him, because there was no need. Tell me what you did.'

The poet drank more spirit.

'I hit him in the face,' he said. 'He didn't look enough like me to fool anyone who knew me.'

'With what did you hit him?' asked the fat man.

'With what came to hand. An empty bottle.'

'You broke his face with an empty bottle,' said the fat man, 'for your publicity stunt. How many blows?'

'Two, or three. What difference does it make? He was already dead.'

'If his face was swollen and bruised, as Leda says, the chances are he was not already dead,' said the fat man. 'But if he was, so much the worse for you.' He pointed a finger at the poet. 'You are guilty of a very serious crime, and of the greatest sin, according to the ancient Greeks. Hubris: arrogance and pride, a belief that your gifts, your talents, set you above the laws of other men. But no man is above the laws of decency, Santos, and mutilation of a corpse is, in my view, as low as any man can stoop. You reached for the stars, and have ended in the sewers of immorality. Why did you think you had the right to mutilate that poor man's body? Have you succumbed to madness in this place? Without the moderating effects of the world – of other people, all of whom see themselves at the centre of the universe – has your ego grown to monstrous proportions? You seem to have become convinced that nothing has more value than your talent and your poetry, and that makes you, in my eyes, a very misguided man. Poetry is poetry, Santos – words on a page, no more. But a man is a man, with a name, and a soul, and a right to dignity; and whoever it was whose corpse you stole, and dishonoured, deserved much better.'

He turned to Leda.

'And you, *kori mou* – what do you make now of your heroic father? Rarely have I known a man make such selfish use of his own child! You agreed to be his accomplice when you thought the game was harmless. Relatively harmless, we should say; we must not forget poor Frona. But he changed the rules, and demanded you still play along, and lie to the police, and keep silent about his theft of another man's identity, and his life. He has treated you badly, *kori mou*. But I think you already know that, don't you?'

Leda stood up.

'I'm ready to go now,' she said. 'I'm going home, to confess to Frona.'

The poet jumped to his feet.

'Leda! Please, stay, and we'll talk.'

He grasped his daughter by the shoulders, but firmly and calmly, she removed his hands.

'I'll come with you, then!' he said. 'I'll come with you, and we'll talk to Frona together!'

'You will not,' said the fat man. 'You will remain here, alone, and reflect for what time remains to you on what you have done. Stay here, write your poems, develop your genius; no one will either know, or care. Slip slowly into obscurity, poet; become a name fading within literature's dusty pages. The world's indifference, and the loss of your daughter's love and respect, is the greatest punishment I can conceive for you. Your sister is unlikely ever to forgive you, and you may reflect on that, too. And there is another matter.' From his inside jacket pocket, he produced a folded document – several pages, held together with a lawyer's seal – and a silver-cased ballpoint pen. 'This is your new will. You will find it identical in every way to the original, except that it post-dates the version Attis supplied to me, and your clever clause denying your heirs immediate access to their inheritance has been removed. And, in a departure from the usual protocol, you will find your signature has already been witnessed – by three good friends of mine – in your absence. So, in your daughter's and your sister's interests, please, sign.'

He turned to the will's final page, where three signatures stood alongside the empty place for Santos's own, and held out both document and pen.

The poet seemed ready to object.

'You'll sign voluntarily, of course,' said the fat man. 'For your daughter's sake.'

Angrily, the poet scrawled his name. The fat man took back the will and his pen, and returned them to the security of his pocket.

'The great poet's final autograph,' he said. 'This young lady and your sister will now rightly benefit from your published work, and from Nemesis's odes, and after the way you have used them, it is right they should do so. As for you, your claim to enjoy life at its most basic level will now be tested.

There'll be none of the comforts of wealth for you, Santos. Seftos will be your prison, and if you attempt to leave, it will only be for a smaller jail, and disgrace. If you set a foot beyond the island's boundaries, I shall make sure that you are arrested and charged with the murder of the man who lies in your grave, and you will see all the esteem and honour you have earned vanish, and the stain of scandal will leech all value from your precious verses. It remains to me now to do all I can to identify your victim, and let his family know where he can be found.'

He rose, and picked up his cigarettes and the matchbox, which he tossed to the poet, so it landed in his lap.

'A parting gift,' he said. 'Open it.'

Cautiously, the poet pushed out the matchbox tray with his fingertip. A horde of black flies flew up into his face, and scattered through the cabin. The poet dropped the matchbox to the floor, and swatted at the flies, which buzzed and settled through the room.

'Carrion flies,' said the fat man. 'Hatched from maggots which feed on the flesh of the dead. They are there at the end for all of us, no matter who we have been in life. The flies do not distinguish between poets, and paupers. Leda, *kori mou* – shall we go?'

'He went too far,' said Leda, as she and the fat man walked towards the jetty. 'I knew it as soon as I saw that poor man's body. I felt so sad for him, and so sorry for what I'd agreed to do. I kissed his hand, and said a prayer for him, but it didn't help. What my father did is unforgivable. Yet Papa just doesn't see it.'

The shopkeeper had seen them coming, and fired the boat's engine.

'Your father's pride in his gift has swollen beyond all

rationality,' said the fat man. 'It's a trap many have fallen into before him.'

'Can things be made right for the man in his grave?'

'I hope so.'

'And what about Inspector Pagounis?' she asked. 'I'm worried he might arrest an innocent man.'

'I'll talk to him, without giving too much away. We'll tell him you have doubts about the identification you made. He may ask you more questions, but the part you'll have to play in handling him will be nothing to a woman of your talents. In the interests of literature, I aim to protect your father's reputation, so I will do what I can to make matters right without the whole truth coming out.'

'I thought we'd be a family again,' she said, wistfully. 'When the four years were over, I thought he'd just come home. Except there would be money, and he'd be happy.'

As the boat motored back to Seftos's harbour, the day was drawing to its end; on the hillsides behind the town, the first flushes of the sunset enhanced the medlar blossom's pink.

Leda sat alone at the prow.

'They call the young lady Leda,' said the fat man to the shopkeeper.

'Is that right?' asked the shopkeeper. 'Is she some relative of his, then?'

'I believe so,' said the fat man. 'In some versions of the myths, Leda and Nemesis are one and the same. Perhaps they are, and perhaps they aren't. Nemesis is the bringer of retribution, and it was Leda who led me to this place. What should we make of that?'

The shopkeeper seemed uninterested. He offered the bottle of *tsipouro* to the fat man. Little of the spirit remained.

'No, thank you,' said the fat man, shaking his head.

The wind was cold. The shopkeeper put the bottle to his lips, and drank.

Along the quay, Manolis was still sitting on his bucket, though his line was no longer in the water but coiled around a wood offcut at his side. The fat man stood behind him and looked across the bay, in the direction of the poet's island.

'There are so many big fish swimming in that ocean,' he said.

Manolis turned to look at him with interest.

'You strike me as a man who has a fisherman's most important quality,' said the fat man, 'that of patience. If we wait long enough, we all get our dues, whether our dues are big fish or no catch at all. But I think you're overdue a decent catch, don't you?'

With a theatrical flourish, the fat man first showed an empty hand, then reached up to Manolis's ear and seemed to pull something from inside it. Between three fingers, he held up an object to show Manolis; it was a glass bead, in mottled colours of blue and yellow.

Manolis's eyes opened wide.

'You must promise me, if I give you this bead, you will keep it safe,' said the fat man, and Manolis gave a slow nod. 'This bead is special. Tie it on your line, and wait and see what comes to you. With a bead like this, you need neither hook nor bait; the fish will love the colours, and you wait and see, Manolis! When you come out here fishing tomorrow morning, those fish will jump from the water into your lap. What do you think?'

He placed the bead in Manolis's hand.

'I'll come and see how you're getting on, before I leave,' said the fat man. 'And if you've caught anything over a kilo,

I want you to keep it for me. I shall give you a fair price for it, of course. Do we have a deal? Excellent.'

Towards evening, a benevolent breeze cleared away the clouds to leave a starlit sky.

Denes sat at a window table, a glass of ouzo to hand. In a chair beside him, Elli was mending a rip in a pair of boy's trousers.

On the road outside, a car pulled up; a man climbed the steps to the hotel door.

'Father-in-law, *kali spera*.'

'Hassan, *agori mou*! How are you, son, how are you?'

'I'm well, father-in-law.'

Unsure of his welcome, Hassan looked at his wife.

'*Yassou*, Elli.'

'Hassan.'

'I brought you something.'

He took a single step forward; then, finding resolve, he approached her.

He held out the porcelain swan, and Elli smiled.

In Frona's city apartment, the phone rang.

She turned down the volume on the television.

'*Oriste?*'

'Frona, is that you? It's me, Attis. I was just phoning to ask if you were busy.'

Frona glanced at the TV screen, where a man in a lamé jacket was shaking the hand of a talent-show contestant.

'Not really,' she said.

'I was wondering, then,' said Attis. 'It was just a thought, in case you might . . . Would you have dinner with me?'

'When?'

'Now. I hope you'll say yes. I've booked a table, and I could pick you up in, say . . . Well, now. I'm outside, Frona. I'm in a taxi outside.'

Frona looked out of the window, where a grey Mercedes waited, engine running, at the kerb.

She ran a hand uncertainly through her hair.

'What if I say no?' she asked.

'Then I shall have to eat an excellent dinner alone. Please , do come.'

'I'd love to,' she said. 'Give me five minutes, and I'll be down.'

In Memoriam

Epilogue

Some months later, on the island of Kerkyra, the fat man knocked at the door of a village house. A young boy ran to open it.

'*Yassou, mikre*,' said the fat man. 'Is your Mama here?'

His mother joined him at the door.

'Can I help you?' she said. 'Myles, go inside.'

'I think, perhaps, I can help you,' said the fat man. 'Are you the daughter of Myles Antonakos?'

The woman grew pale.

'I am,' she said. 'Do you have news of Papa?'

'I do,' said the fat man, 'though I must tell you that the news is not good.'

Tears came to the woman's eyes.

'I expected no good news, after all this time. What's happened to him? Where is he?'

'He's in a village called Vrisi, in the northern mountains,' said the fat man. 'If I might come in, I have a difficult story to tell.'

Late summer, and in Vrisi's cemetery, the dried-out weeds and grasses were burnt pale by the August sun. The sexton wore a straw hat against its heat; his water bottle lay almost empty in the oak tree's shade. Sheltering the flame with a cupped hand, he held a lighted match to the bowl of his pipe, and puffed on the stem in phuts and spits to encourage the tobacco to burn.

At the grave where Santos Volakis had never lain, a new headstone had been erected. The fat man looked down at the carved white marble, and read out the inscription.

'Myles Antonakos, born in Kerkyra,' he said. 'His name is there, now, as it should be. His resting place is marked.'

'You never solved our mystery, then, did you?' asked the sexton, speaking with his pipe still in his mouth. 'You never tracked down our poet. Where the devil he got to, we shall never know, shall we?'

'You may never know, no,' said the fat man. A lemon-winged butterfly fluttered around the posy in his hands: roses and gerberas, bound with a ribbon. 'Incidentally, I saw as I passed through the village that you have swans again, at the spring.'

'Only one,' said the sexton. 'A cob, without a mate, only recently arrived. He's lonely by himself, no doubt. He ought to find himself a female.'

'Maybe he will, in time,' said the fat man. 'Did you know that swans are supposed to carry the souls of great poets, when they die?'

'I didn't know that, no,' said the sexton. 'Are you done here? Aren't you leaving your flowers?'

'My flowers are not for him,' said the fat man, 'they're for Roula, if you'll show me where she lies.'

'Old Roula,' said the sexton, with some surprise. 'You knew her, did you? They say she was a great beauty, in her prime. Time's a cruel master, wouldn't you say? Come on, and I'll show you to her grave.'

THE MESSENGER OF ATHENS

Shortlisted for the ITV 3 Crime Thriller Awards

When the battered body of a young woman is discovered on a remote Greek island, the local police are quick to dismiss her death as an accident. Then a stranger arrives, uninvited, from Athens, announcing his intention to investigate further. His name is Hermes Diaktoros, his methods are unorthodox, and he brings his own mystery into the web of dark secrets and lies. Who has sent him, on whose authority is he acting, and how does he know of dramas played out decades ago?

'Powerfully atmospheric . . . Zouroudi proves a natural at the dark arts of writing Euro-crime'
INDEPENDENT

THE TAINT OF MIDAS

For over half a century the beautiful Temple of Apollo has been in the care of the old beekeeper Gabrilis. But when the value of the land soars he is forced to sign away his interests – and hours later he meets a violent, lonely death. When Hermes Diaktoros finds his friend's battered body by a dusty roadside, the police quickly make him the prime suspect. But with rapacious developers threatening Arcadia's most ancient sites, there are many who stand to gain from Gabrilis's death. Hermes resolves to avenge his old friend and find the true culprit, but his investigative methods are, as ever, unorthodox . . .

'More transported Agatha Christie here ... Hermes is a delight. Half Poirot, half deus ex machina, but far more earth-bound than his first name suggests ... A cracking plot, colourful local characters and descriptions of the hot, dry countryside so strong that you can almost see the heat haze and hear the cicadas – the perfect read to curl up with'
GUARDIAN

THE DOCTOR OF THESSALY

A jilted bride weeps on an empty beach, a local doctor is attacked in an isolated churchyard – trouble has come at a bad time to Morfi, just as the backwater village is making headlines with a visit from a government minister. Fortunately, where there's trouble there's Hermes Diaktoros, the mysterious fat man whose tennis shoes are always pristine and whose methods are always unorthodox. Hermes must solve a brutal crime, thwart the petty machinations of the town's ex-mayor and pour oil on the troubled waters of a sisters' relationship – but how can he solve a mystery that not even the victim wants to be solved?

'If you don't find yourself in Greece this summer, then Zouroudi's latest mystery brings the Hellenic vibe tantalisingly close . . . Once again Hermes Diaktoros – a reassuringly earthbound investigator – finds himself dealing with a chorus of colourful locals'
INDEPENDENT

THE LADY OF SORROWS

A painter is found dead at sea off the coast of a remote Greek island. For our enigmatic detective Hermes Diaktoros, the plot can only thicken: the painter's work, an icon of the Virgin long famed for its miraculous powers, has just been uncovered as a fake. But has the painter died of natural causes or by a wrathful hand? What secret is a dishonest gypsy keeping? And what haunts the ancient catacombs beneath the bishop's house?

'Anne Zouroudi writes beautifully – her books have all the sparkle and light of the island landscapes in which she sets them. *The Lady of Sorrows*, her latest, is a gorgeous treat' Alexander McCall Smith

BLOOMSBURY

THE BULL OF MITHROS

It is summer, and as tourists, drawn by the legend of a priceless missing artifact, disembark on the sun-drenched quay of Mithros, the languid calm of the island is broken by the unorthodox arrival of a stranger who has been thrown overboard in the bay. Lacking money or identification, he is forced for a while to remain on Mithros. But is he truly a stranger? To some, his face seems familiar.

The arrival of the investigator Hermes Diaktoros, intrigued himself by the island's fabled bull, coincides with a violent and mysterious death. This violence has an echo in Mithros's recent past: in a brutal unsolved crime committed several years before, which, although apparently forgotten may not yet have been forgiven.

As Hermes sets about solving the complex puzzle of who is guilty and who is innocent, he discovers a web of secrets and unspoken loyalties, and it soon becomes clear that the bull of Mithros may only be the least of the island's shadowy mysteries.

ORDER BY PHONE: +44 (0)1256 302 699; BY EMAIL: DIRECT@MACMILLAN.CO.UK
DELIVERY IS USUALLY 3–5 WORKING DAYS. POSTAGE AND PACKAGING WILL BE CHARGED.
ONLINE: WWW.BLOOMSBURY.COM/BOOKSHOP
FREE POSTAGE AND PACKAGING FOR ORDERS OVER £20.
PRICES AND AVAILABILITY SUBJECT TO CHANGE WITHOUT NOTICE.

WWW.BLOOMSBURY.COM/ANNEZOUROUDI

B L O O M S B U R Y